Agent 00

Agent 00

Volume I

Ramona

Lee Soo-Jun

Action Lee

Paperback ISBN: 978-1-7392786-3-2

Book cover art by Paul Harrison
Edited by Jason Cheung

ramonaleesoojun.com
Action Lee

"A layered insight into the world of old-school Hong Kong cinema. A great read." *Cynthia Rothrock (Martial Artist and Actress)*

"An entertaining story with heroes you can't help but cheer for." *Andy Cheng (Action Director & Jackie Chan Stunt Team member)*

"An exhilarating journey to different realms." *Diana C. Weng (Actor and Dialogue Coach for Jackie Chan on films from "Rush Hour" to "The Foreigner")*

"Interesting layers and suspension, with a vivid and energetic writing style." *Ron Smoorenburg (Martial Artist and Actor; "Who am I?" 1998)*

"Immersive and thrilling action." *Mark Stas (Martial Artist, Actor & Founder of Wing Flow System)*

"Introducing new action heroes who should jump from the printed page to the big screen." *Mike Leeder (Casting Director & Producer)*

DEDICATION

This trilogy is a heartfelt homage to the incredible career of *Jackie Chan.*

Jackie's unique blend of storytelling through movement has left an indelible mark on my soul, inspiring me to embark on my own writing journey and shaping the person I am today. Every emotion his movies have ever stirred within me has been poured into the pages of this series.

I'd also like to dedicate this to *Michelle Yeoh*, an absolute powerhouse and a role model for women in action. She has shown us that we too can conquer multiverses and kick some serious butt.

Back in 2015, when I was seventeen, I proudly published this book for the first time in Romanian. It marked a milestone as Romania's very first martial arts action novel. And now, in 2023, I'm thrilled to finally bring it to the English-speaking audience. Please forgive any hiccups in the translation—I'm learning and growing every step of the way.

Big thanks to the incredibly talented illustrator, Paul Harrison, for his amazing work on the book cover. A special shoutout to my partner Jason for keeping my Ramonglish in check and giving me a loving kick when needed. And last but definitely not least, I owe a massive thank you to my mum, who ignited my love for action cinema. None of this would've been possible without her support.

This "Agent 00" series holds a special place in my heart and I truly hope it brings you as much joy as it has brought me.

— the author

PART ONE

Chapter I

Dragon Dynasty, 215 AD

The Dragon Emperor, hailed as the final scion of the Dragon Dynasty, was a visionary ruler who fostered the growth of technology, literature and martial arts. He surrounded himself with devoted taxpayers who shared his passion for progress and innovation. Above all, he strove to bring peace and prosperity to his realm, tirelessly crafting new theses and strategies to achieve this goal. To protect his people, he created an Imperial Guard of thousands of soldiers and legendary martial arts masters, unmatched by any dynasty in history. These warriors devoted their entire lives to the welfare of their empire, serving as the staunch defenders of their beloved sovereign.

The Imperial Bureau of Aesthetics safeguarded the empire's artists, whose poetry and paintings embellished the land and enriched its treasury. Meanwhile, the Court's administration was divided into seven essential ministries, each tasked with a unique role: Finance, Culture, Aid for the Poor, Assassinations, Ancestral Worship, Ecology, and of course, The Royal and Not-So-Secret Concubines. The Ministry of Foreign Affairs, the Ministry of Internal Affairs, and the Imperial Administration were as indispensable to the emperor as his preferred tea served in a cherished cup. Each ministry upheld the sovereign's vision for the realm, ensuring its stability, prosperity, and longevity.

The Dragon Dynasty fell apart in 215 AD following a rebellion.

The Last Spring of the Dragon Dynasty

The sun crept over the mountaintops, casting a gentle glow upon the world below. The sky adorned itself with a sprinkling of clouds and the balmy morning breeze coaxed a flurry of cherry blossoms from their boughs. The soft babble of a nearby spring harmonised with the rustling of fresh blades of grass, swaying gracefully with every gentle gust. In the Dragon Dynasty, the essence of nature was felt deep within the soul.

As spring unfurled its vibrant tableau, the valley lay nestled beneath the embrace of majestic mountains, their peaks veiled in wisps of ethereal mist. Nature brushed the landscape with hues of emerald. Fields stretched across the land, a verdant quilt woven with delicate wildflowers and swaying grasses. Sprightly streams meandered through the countryside, their crystal-clear waters mirroring the cerulean expanse of the sky above.

A symphony of scents pervaded the air, as the fragrance of cherry blossoms gently wafted on the breeze. These ephemeral blossoms adorned the slender branches of ancient trees, like delicate pink clouds in a sea of green. The valley resonated with the melodies of nature—the chorus of chirping birds and the soft rustle of leaves as the wind whispered through the forest.

Above, the sun cast its golden radiance, illuminating the landscape with a warm and gentle glow. In that tranquil haven, General Ma Lai Ji slumbered peacefully, cocooned in a realm of undisturbed tranquillity. Stirring from his power nap, he emerged from the depths of slumber, garbed in plain garments, his hair hastily bundled up in a haphazard bun. Alone amidst the captivating embrace of nature's majestic splendour, he luxuriated in the profound serenity that enveloped him, basking in its ethereal embrace.

Unbeknownst to all, the sun would soon set on the Dragon Dynasty, marking the end of an era.

Lai Ji had recently passed his imperial exams and belonged to a new generation of imperial guards. Often, he wandered incognito through remote and uncharted territories, disguised as a humble villager.

This was his method of ensnaring malefactors—he was the so-called: undercover general.

A single gust of wind seized Lai Ji's attention, as the sound of hurried footsteps grew louder. With lightning-fast reflexes, he seized the moving silhouette, who had been preparing to attack, and locked them in an arm hold. A sense of accomplishment flooded Lai Ji, as he gazed upon the subdued thief with a grin. However, his satisfaction was short-lived, as he suddenly found himself facing the rest of the band of thieves, led by their imposing leader. Lai Ji's expression shifted from one of triumph to one of concern, as he observed the leader's confident stance and wicked grin. But then, to the surprise of his opponents, Lai Ji burst into laughter.

"I urge you to line up in an orderly fashion so that we can overcome this situation sooner rather than later."

He shoved the thief back towards his cohorts, his eyes widening as he continued to laugh uncontrollably. The leader furrowed his brow, trying to make sense of this odd display. Lai Ji's laughter only intensified, his gaze seeking validation from the rest of the group. Despite their best efforts to maintain their composure, the three other thieves couldn't help but crack a smile. Lai Ji's laughter grew more and more boisterous as if he were a madman without a cause. The thieves soon joined in, chuckling along with him, while the leader ground his teeth in frustration. Tears streamed down Lai Ji's cheeks, as he urged his companions to keep the laughter flowing. Before long, everyone was howling with laughter, clutching their sides in exhaustion. A vein throbbed on the leader's forehead, as his face turned a deep shade of red.

“Everyone, shut the hell up!”

Silence. Lai Ji's countenance grew serious. In a swift motion, he produced a rope and coiled it tightly around his wrist. Without a moment's hesitation, he lunged towards the crowd. The thieves jostled one another in a frantic attempt to evade the attack and defend themselves simultaneously.

Lai Ji seized the first brigand within reach and looped the rope around his neck. As the other assailants charged at him, he thrust the choking thief towards them, bowling them over.

"Get the hell off me," was the final outcry of the leader, trapped at the bottom of the pile.

Minutes later, the gang of thieves were knelt in an orderly line before Lai Ji, with their limbs bound and their faces bruised.

"I've been waiting for you," Lai Ji said, taking out his imperial mandate.

The leader's focus shifted downwards, consumed with horror and bitterness. Lai Ji's snickering caught the attention of the others, their muted grins morphing into unrestrained laughter. The leader wriggled and writhed in vain, desperate to break free from the tight grip of the rope.

"Stop laughing, you fools!"

Silence.

"A thousand times! I promised myself a thousand times that I'd get the hell out of having these morons as my responsibility! But no, I chose to live my whole life in idiocy! With clowns like you! Ha Ha! Hu Hu," he continued shouting, ready to slap each and every one of them if the opportunity arose.

"But what happened, Boss?" one of them dared to ask, meekly. "We can't read."

"Ha Ha! Hu hu!" The leader fooled around, mad with spite. "It's General Ma Lai Ji!"

"General Ma Lai Ji?!" they all exclaimed in unison, shocked and amazed at the same time.

"Yes, my idiots, yes! It's General Ma Lai Ji!"

Another moment of silence. One of the thieves pulled his snot back into his nostrils.

"And what does that mean?"

The leader threw himself in front of Lai Ji's feet and looked up at him in despair.

"Please... Please, General! Anywhere! I can stay locked in the coldest jail without food! I'd go anywhere! But please, lock me away from these idiots!" Lai Ji shook the dust off his clothes and turned towards the nearby food market. He smiled to himself in satisfaction. Tying his messy black hair back into a simple bun, he blinked a few times, as he stopped dead in his tracks.

"Ju...?"

Lai Ji looked towards the silk shop.

In fact, the silk shop held no interest to him at all. His eyes ran from the silk shop towards the tavern and then from the tavern to the courtesan's house. In front of the silk shop, leaning against the wall, was Ju. Slumped over, hungover and still muttering something to himself. Lai Ji sighed, touching his bun once more before proceeding to summon his friend away from the ground.

"Lai Ji, ugly chap, what are you doing here?" Ju shouted as soon as he noticed his friend approaching him.

"That's what I should be asking you," Lai Ji mumbled as he helped his friend up.

Ju. Also known as The-Left-Hander-With-The-Right-Fist. Lai Ji's childhood friend and also a member of the imperial rank, despite coming from a poor family. Ju's devotion and special fighting technique had brought him great success, although he had not yet been able to explain his technique to anyone, not even to himself. Ju still dreamed of finding the perfect bride, but oftentimes lost his temper and woke up in strange places.

"Lai Ji, my friend, life is a sin," Ju began to shout agitatedly, drawing curious glances from passersby. "A life lived to the fullest is a sin! A life lived in torment leads to sin! Life is an enemy, life is a friend that stabs you in the back! Lai Ji, my friend—"

"Leave life for now and hurry up," Lai Ji whispered, embarrassed by the situation and eager to leave.

"Leave this life," Ju muttered, pausing for a moment to think about the meaning of these words. "Leave life, that's right!" he roared, raising his fist as if raising a goblet. "Let's hurry up and leave this sinful life! Lai Ji, my friend, let's die together!" he yelped while shaking his head.

Noticing the looks on the villagers' faces, Lai Ji mimed a friendly smile as he covered Ju's mouth with his right palm, and passersby went on with their business.

"Lai Ji, my friend," Ju started again as if ready to continue.

So Lai Ji struck him across the face with the same right hand. Ju shook his head, starting to wake up. Noticing that his action had a reaction, Lai Ji scrunched his lips.

"Hm."

By slapping him again, Lai Ji brought him back to reality. Ju frowned, holding his jaw. Confused, he touched his coat. Suddenly desperate, he patted himself all over his body.

"I lost my coins!" he concluded, looking at Lai Ji's face.

Lai Ji shrugged.

Just then, a young woman darted past them, jostling Lai Ji's shoulder in her haste. He instinctively swivelled his head to catch a fleeting glimpse of her. At that moment, Ju noticed her eyes peeking out from behind the strands of hair that had momentarily obscured her face.

"It's that piece of shit! It's that thief!" Ju shouted, pointing at her.

The young woman clenched her fists and quickened her pace. Still pointing his index finger at her, Ju watched her run away.

"She had me drinking all night. She robbed me!" he yelled with his last word before chasing after her. "Stand still and give me back my coins, you little—"

Lai Ji sighed and reached for his bun. He sniffled the air around him.

"I think I need a bath," he said, straightening his back and proceeding to run after the two.

The capital's fair was one of the busiest places in the empire, where aristocracy met peasantry, and young generals sometimes shared a kind word with less privileged kids. The emperor's greatest wish for his land had always been a harmonious cohabitation between social classes. This peace and friendship had been preserved since the early days of the Dragon Dynasty.

“Give me back my coins, you piece of shit!” Ju’s roar spread throughout the surroundings.

Demonstrating considerable agility, the young woman threaded her way through the crowd. Her hairpin fell to the ground as her hair came down, floating in the breeze. Ju ran past the accessory, panting hard as he felt like he was losing all of his remaining energy by shouting and accusing the culprit. He didn't leave her out of sight, not even for a moment. Lai Ji stopped to pick up the hairpin, while the young thief spillt some of the fresh fish she ran past and Ju waded straight through the remains.

“You dirty brats!” A saleswoman jumped from behind her bench.

“We’re deeply sorry,” Lai Ji shouted while running past, his words lingering in the air like a wave of noise disappearing in the same instant.

The salespeople looked around in confusion, not knowing if a magic spell had just run past them or if the noise had only been a draft of cold air.

"Stop right there!" Ju shouted for the last time when he realised that the young thief had almost slipped from his grasp.

Leaving the market, the girl took a turn towards a deserted road. Checking behind her, she noticed that the two had lost track of her. The young thief smiled to herself. While slowing her pace, she took a deep breath and made her way into the forest.

She laughed as she pulled the bag of coins out of her boyish coat and tossed it in the air just to catch it again. But then, raising her head, she felt the weight of Lai Ji's focus. Her enthusiasm faded as Lai Ji greeted her with a friendly but determined smile, holding out his hand to ask for the coins. Terrified, she took a few steps back.

The moment Lai Ji tried to approach her, she took a knife out of her sleeve and waved it around. She then blinked a few times, waiting for a reaction. Lai Ji snorted and pulled out his own knife, jokingly threatening her in the same way. After he stabbed the air a few times, he noticed the fear on her young face. He decided to make peace, so he dropped the knife onto the grass and lifted both his hands. She sceptically watched every movement. Lai Ji then beckoned her to attack.

She didn't hesitate and stepped forward, chin up and knife pointed at him. She mimed an expression of firmness and stabbed her way forward with a straight back. With a battle cry, she prepared to dig into Lai Ji's flesh. He smiled as he forcibly grabbed her wrist–the handle fell from her limp fingers. His solid grip brought their faces together. Only a single breath separated their lips. She stared into his eyes, unable to even try to defend herself. She was captive in his charm.

"I got you, you bastard!" Ju then exclaimed, appearing at last. "I got you, stay put!" he added, barely able to speak, leaning with both palms on his knees, squinting his eyes with fatigue.

Taking a deep breath and standing up straight, he approached her like a street urchin, with both his hands on his hips.

"You thought you were getting away with this, huh?"

The corners of her mouth dropped, and she looked at him with disgust.

"You hold her, I'm getting the coins," Ju ordered his friend, taking the lead as it should have been from the beginning.

General Lai Ji gripped her shoulders with just enough strength that wouldn't hurt her. Ju shook his head, showing his clear disapproval of thievery.

"You're lucky we're not locking you up, although that's precisely what you deserve!" Ju said while kneeling to pat her ankles, searching for the hidden pouch. "You might not realise it now, but today you're the luckiest thief around," he added, lifting his head and groping her hips.

She frowned as Lai Ji opened his mouth to speak. Ju continued to search for his belongings all over her body. Then, he stood up and reached inside her coat. When he looked her in the eye, she slapped him hard across the cheek.

"Where do you think you're touching?" she demanded, freeing her shoulder from general Lai Ji's grip, only for him to grab hold of her again.

"I'm touching where my coins are! Now give me back my coins!" Ju exclaimed, holding his cheek and stomping his feet.

"Do I look like a concubine to you? Now, do you mind?" she pointed at her shoulder, urging Lai Ji to release his grip.

Lai Ji released the material from his hand and the young thief fixed her clothing with pride. She then cleared her throat.

"First of all, apologise!"

"Apologise for being robbed by you?" Ju retorted.

"No, for shamelessly touching me!"

"Ha!" Ju scoffed, placing his hands back on his hips. "Listen to the nonsense this woman speaks! Lai

Ji, my friend, give me that knife!" he ordered, holding his hand out.

The young thief felt uneasy, not quite sure where the real threat was coming from.

"Fine! Fine!" she said, trying to calm the situation. "I'll give you the pouch. I'm happy, you're happy, we put away the knives and life's lovely again. We all mind our own business!"

She proceeded to look for the pouch. Ju smiled with satisfaction. But after a moment of rummaging through the inside of her coat, she realised with wide-open eyes that the coins were gone.

"It's gone! I swear on my life that it was here!"

Lai Ji then lifted the pouch in his left hand and smiled, revealing his charming teeth. He moved away from the girl and threw the pouch into his friend's arms as he walked away.

"Too much chatter lets the details slip."

The young thief looked at Lai Ji in fascination, holding onto her coat. Ju grimaced at her one last time before running to catch up with his friend. She pulled her tongue out.

Ju upped his pace to keep up with Lai Ji.

"That was brilliant, my friend!" Ju exclaimed, hopping around Lai Ji. "The way you managed to get the coins without her noticing. I mean, without me noticing either… But to be honest with you, I would've done exactly the same! Did you see the look on her face when I threatened her with my knife? I don't think she's ever seen greater fear throughout her life! Let that be a life lesson to her! Thief! Who does she think she is?!"

"Let's find food. I'm hungry," Lai Ji said, turning towards the market.

"She dares to put up with The-Left-Hander-With-The-Right-Fist?" Ju squawked, as he then realised that Lai Ji was already ahead of him. "Wait, wait for me, I'm hungry too!"

Chapter II

The huge gates to the royal courtyard opened to welcome a special visitor. A middle-aged woman covered in a black cloak was waiting to be let in. Her eyes were the only visible feature as she looked up. The eunuch urged her to hurry up and she rushed inside before the gates instantly closed behind her. Once inside the courtyard, she scanned her surroundings, checking to make sure she hadn't been followed. She removed her cloak to reveal her face and greeted the eunuch with a mixture of nervousness and determination.

"Please follow me," the eunuch said, leading her with grace.

The woman followed the eunuch confidently, but there was tension in her shoulders. They arrived in front of the imperial salon, and the eunuch entered gently, speaking with a lowered countenance:

"Your Majesty, please allow me to announce the arrival of—"

"Yes, yes, tell her to come in!" the emperor shouted, cutting him off.

The woman was escorted by a young servant who immediately withdrew with a bowed head.

As she now found herself at the threshold of the Hall of Supreme Harmony, she was awestruck by the overwhelming extravagance that surrounded her. Luxurious silk flowed like water from the walls, catching the light and shimmering like a thousand stars. Fine jade glinted in the soft glow, casting a spellbinding aura over the space. The ceilings towered high above her, seemingly reaching towards the heavens, as if in homage to the majesty of the imperial court. Every detail, every intricately designed piece of furniture and exquisite art piece, was a testament to the impeccable craftsmanship of those who served the court. As she looked ahead, her attention was captivated without delay by the magnificent imperial throne. The seat of power and authority in the Dragon Dynasty was the centrepiece of the hall, its sheer size and grandeur commanding attention from all who entered.

The Dragon Throne, as it was also known, was a marvel of artistry and opulence. Fashioned from the most exquisite materials, including gold and jade, it was a breathtaking work of art in its own right. The winding carvings of dragons and clouds on the backrest only added to its majesty, each symbol representing the emperor's dominion over the land and sea.

As the woman approached the throne, a sense of reverence and awe washed over her. She knew that only the emperor was permitted to sit on the throne and to be granted an audience while he was seated upon it was a great honour. Glancing around the hall, she marvelled at the other symbols of imperial might that encircled the throne, from the banners to the pillars adorned with ornate dragon motifs.

With humility and respect, the woman drew near to the Dragon Throne, acutely aware of its great power and authority.

"You can leave us alone," the emperor spoke to the eunuch, who retreated after a deep bow.

The emperor then rose from his imperial throne and greeted the woman. His presence commanded respect, his regal bearing marked by a benevolent spirit that shone through the depths of his warm aura. Weathered by the trials and tribulations of a tumultuous era, the lines etched upon his skin told tales of past struggles and hard-fought victories. Yet, beneath his battle-scarred exterior, beat the heart of a leader unyielding in his commitment to justice. Never one to shy away from righteous battles, he exemplified courage by fearlessly leading his own warriors into the fray. However, his boundless kindness had always been highlighted in children's stories and praised through songs and poetry.

"Tell me, what did you see?" the emperor asked, standing and gesturing with his hand that he was ready to listen.

"Your Majesty, please take my life for what I'm about to say!" the woman cried out, throwing herself to her knees.

"Speak, what tidings have you brought?" he urged her to talk, implying that her visit would not have negative consequences.

"Your Majesty, please forgive me!" she cried out repeatedly, shaking her head and seemingly trying to cry.

"Say what you have to say!" the emperor lost his patience for a moment, then put his hand over his mouth, ready to cough to get over the incident.

Then, with a radical change in behaviour, the fortune teller stared the emperor right into his soul. She stood up, pushed aside her cloak, and made room for her hands to get to work, getting rid of the clothes that bothered her. She pulled out indescribable, noisy, bizarre utensils and a deep wooden bowl. Beginning to unpack multiple pouches, she took out powders of various colours, throwing them up in the air like fireworks. The emperor looked on with a mixture of curiosity and scepticism. The woman continued to take out powders, mixing them in her palms and then spinning her hands in a frightening manner.

"Air!" she cried out, and the emperor flinched. "The air… is stuffy!" She closed her eyelids as if a sudden pain pierced her heart. "My sight is darkened!" She squeezed her eyes shut even harder. "I see darkness, I see… I see..." she suddenly opened her eyes, seemingly shocked. "Now I see dust," Taking out a few more bizarre ingredients, she mixed them together. "Uncertainty!" she shouted, raising her hands. "Uncertainty… in the fog! In the darkness! My gaze is blurred!" She frowned and hastily waved the coloured powder from the air, making her cough.

"Darkness...?" The emperor held his breath.

"Yes, Your Majesty!"

"Go on...!"

The woman lifted her wooden bowl and approached the emperor's throne in a hurry.

"If you'll allow me," she said politely, bowing her head and extending the bowl.

The emperor turned to the imperial table, taking out a gold coin from the imperial box and placing it in the fortune-teller's bowl. She looked up greedily, hearing only the sound of a single coin. Bending her head again, she timidly extended the bowl.

"Ah," the emperor took a deep breath, adding another gold coin. "Now tell me, what have you seen?"

The woman, looking into the bowl and satisfied for the moment, smiled and withdrew with her head down, now focused again on supernatural matters.

"I see... through the mists of time," she said, beginning to shake her head erratically. Rolling her eyes, she went into a trance. "I see, I see, I see... I see death! A curse!" she cried out, her eyes snapping open with bated breath. "I see the death of the princess!" she exclaimed in a lower and mournful tone.

"The death of the princess?!" the impatient emperor asked, taking a step forward.

"The princess's life is in danger, and furthermore... if she remains alive, the existence of this world will be jeopardized! The continued existence of the princess will lead to the downfall of the empire!" The woman clasped her hands together.

"It can't be possible!" the emperor whispered, bowing his head slowly.

"Your Majesty, please take my life for this matter!"

"Continue..." He gathered his strength.

The woman once again lifted the wooden bowl, approaching politely. The emperor threw two more gold coins into the bowl. The woman retreated, kneeling down.

"Your Majesty, the princess cannot remain! We must fix this, we must deceive death so that the empire can continue to prosper! The princess's life in the palace means the downfall of the dynasty!"

"It cannot be true!"

"Your Majesty, is it not true that the princess has been feeling agitated in the past few nights, and that the nightmares have not given her any peace?"

The emperor had wondered up to this point how she could discern the future. Yet, as he listened, he realised that her words rang true and that she wasn't lying.

"What—what must be done? How can we save the empire? And how can I save my dearest princess?" the emperor asked, choked with emotions.

The fortune-teller raised her focus.

"There is only one way!"

The emperor waited for the answer. The woman approached with the wooden bowl, and the emperor added two more coins. She withdrew to her place, putting the bowl aside. Assuming the same dramatic posture again, she said:

"We must ensure the safety of the princess and the prosperity of our empire by sending her far away, beyond the reach of the curse. She must never return to this land, lest the curse befall us all."

"But, my dearest princess... How can she be at fault?"

"The princess isn't guilty, Your Majesty!" She bowed her head almost to the ground. "An ancient curse has fallen upon her, and nothing can save her... Except for escaping death!"

"An ancient curse?"

"Your Majesty, forgive me! The curse is almost indestructible and endures over time. Moreover, it captures souls and imprisons them between eras, tying them up, and throwing them into the mists of time! Some are never to be released… The tormented soul may wander for decades, centuries, or even thousands of years, in search of freedom. It is the most painful curse of all, especially because it is based on the passage of time. The longer the spirit is trapped, the tighter it will be tied to this fate, and the harder it will be to transcend and escape!"

Pressing a hand over his chest, the emperor fell into his throne, staring blankly at the thought of his innocent young daughter's fate.

"What is left to do?" he whispered with a heavy heart, looking around.

"Your Majesty, if the princess is not immediately sent away from this empire, the curse will certainly fall upon us all, and thus the entire empire will be a space forgotten by time. However, if the princess manages to escape, there is still a chance for her to survive this life," said the woman in a low voice.

"Is there a chance?" the emperor asked, eagerly.

The woman lifted her bowl, approached him, and held it out professionally, subtly, and meaningfully. The emperor took out two gold coins and threw them into the wooden bowl.

"The potion ingredients cost me a little more, I didn't manage to get them at half price," added the woman, making a brief negotiating grimace.

The emperor threw in more coins without counting them.

“What potion are we talking about?”

“Your Majesty, I possess the Potion of Time. Throughout the journey in an attempt to escape, the princess is not allowed to be harmed. Not even bitten by a mosquito, because the curse will be cast upon the entire empire if it happens! Therefore, if the young princess is in danger of death, she will have to swallow this potion, out of loyalty and belief in this dynasty!"

"But... if this potion will save the empire, what will happen to my princess?"

"Your Majesty, please take my life, but I must tell you that the princess will not be saved. The curse that follows her will find her! Therefore, she must be guarded at all costs and must safely leave these lands, Your Majesty!"

The emperor clenched both fists, trying to hide his tears.

"I want to be left alone!" he whispered.

The eunuch entered the hall without delay.

"Your Majesty!" he exclaimed, asking for permission to escort the fortune teller, who had already begun to gather her tools from the floor.

The emperor fell back on the soft backrest, with a lost gaze and teary eyes.

The imperial throne room had suddenly become a cold and hopeless prison. The happiness of his life, his beloved and beautiful daughter, was to defend the empire at the cost of her life. This was certainly a path that an emperor father could be proud of, but at this time, the innocence of the princess had to be protected.

Looking at the vial in his palm, a few hot tears fell from his chin. He was aware that a safe escape was the only chance for the girl. Even if that meant she would never see her father again. Even if she had never done anything to deserve such a fate. But if this attempt were to fail, the Potion of Time would cast his only and precious princess into the darkness of time, for tens, hundreds, thousands of years, maybe forever.

Chapter III

Satiated, Ju counted his coins to pay for lunch. Lai Ji stood up, but before he could make another move, a messenger from the imperial court pushed his shoulder to make him sit back down. While holding his other hand over his sword's scabbard, the messenger greeted him with seriousness. Ju sceptically rushed to pack his coins.

"Just because I've had a hearty meal now doesn't mean I haven't done anything since morning. These coins are my payment from last month, I didn't steal them. Actually, someone else stole them from me, but that's a story for another time. The fact that I'm having lunch now doesn't mean I wandered off on my own last night. And what I want to make clear is that I didn't drink, not even a drop of alcohol. And I wasn't with the courtesans! But I think that's obvious! It's more than clear, right?" Ju made sure to exclaim all at once, while holding one hand over his coins, afraid of being falsely accused.

The messenger avoided him and redirected his serious attention to Lai Ji.

"His Majesty summons you to the imperial court. We must be there immediately. We must hurry, at the cost of our lives!"

"His Majesty?!" exclaimed Ju, jumping up hastly.

The messenger widened his eyes, trying to ease the agitated exchange of remarks by lowering his tone:

"Let us depart!"

"His Majesty wants the two of us?" Ju whispered, curious to learn more.

The general started walking and Lai Ji followed him close behind, without saying a single word.

"Wow! Requested by His Majesty in person!" Ju whispered excitedly, giggling like a child.

Then assuming a serious posture, he arrogantly followed the two.

Following imperial orders, Lai Ji was heading towards the imperial court, still unaware of the tragic fate of his devotion.

In the seclusion of her private chambers, the princess sat perched atop a bed as soft as clouds, her mind occupied with the uncertain future that loomed ahead. She raised a delicate hand to her fine hair and drew in a deep breath, her thoughts momentarily adrift. With the gentlest touch of her fingers, she began to remove the intricate ornaments that adorned her body, placing them carefully in boxes of refined design, where they would undoubtedly rest untouched for eternity. She then retrieved her silken garments, arranging them with the utmost care, lingering over each piece as if to imprint their texture and beauty in her memory. Finally, she donned a simple, unassuming attire and combed her hair with the gentlest of strokes, as if savouring every moment of the quietude that enveloped her.

However, her hands trembled with a mix of fear and determination. Without her father's knowledge, she had sought out the eunuch and coerced him into revealing the full story. Now, the young princess's only desire was to locate the elusive Potion of Time, hidden away in her father's chambers. She knew he would go to great lengths to safeguard it, for he was fiercely protective of her, his only daughter. But the princess understood the gravity of the situation and the role she had to play in saving the empire. If her vanishing into time and space was the sole means of achieving this, she was willing to make the ultimate sacrifice without a second thought. She braced herself for the arduous task ahead, for she knew that time was of the essence.

As Lai Ji stepped into the hallowed halls of the imperial court, he couldn't help but be filled with awe as he took in his surroundings. The cherry trees swayed in the breeze, petals falling like snow around him. Meanwhile, the princess emerged from her chambers, gliding effortlessly towards the opulent imperial throne room. With a heavy heart, the emperor stood waiting. His face was etched with regret, seeking solace in the numbing embrace of wine.

Ju marched with a sense of pride, his pupils twinkling with excitement. "Lai Ji, my friend, I've served as an imperial soldier for what feels like a lifetime, but I never imagined I'd have the chance to stand before His Majesty in person. The honour is truly mine! But wait... you don't suppose we're being summoned here to face punishment, do you? Perish the thought! I refuse to believe that's the case!" His words elicited a weary sigh from the messenger, who closed his eyes and shook his head in exasperation.

Lai Ji remained silent, his heart pounding as they approached the entrance to the throne room. A hush fell over the young men as they waited for the eunuch to announce their arrival. The doors swung open to reveal a grand view of the imperial throne and the two bowed their heads respectfully as they made their way inside, dropping to their knees in unison.

The emperor's discerning focus swept over them, scrutinising their every move and attempting to assess whether his decision to summon two young soldiers had been wise. After a moment of intense contemplation, he nodded to himself, satisfied with his choice.

"You may raise your heads."

Both remained motionless, with their palms glued to the ground.

"Stay still!" Lai Ji whispered to his friend when he tried to look towards the emperor.

Lai Ji then bowed even deeper, so Ju also leaned down, resting his forehead on the ground.

"Your Majesty!" exclaimed Lai Ji, pressing his forehead against the back of his hand.

"Your Majesty!" Ju shouted theatrically, lightly hitting his forehead on the ground.

"Worry not, now you may stand up!" the emperor added once again.

"Show your respect!" Lai Ji ordered Ju in a whisper when he tried to rise once again.

"Your Majesty!" Ju exclaimed in return, hitting his forehead on the ground.

"Fear not." the emperor calmed him.

Lai Ji gave an approving nod and made to rise, but Ju remained prostrate on the ground, his forehead repeatedly meeting the polished marble in a desperate attempt to conform to the court's strict etiquette. Lai Ji couldn't help but steal a furtive glance at his companion, watching as Ju persisted in his painful self-flagellation. With a resigned sigh, Lai Ji realised that no amount of coaxing would convince Ju to desist from his self-punishment.

"Fear not!" the emperor reassured him again. "Kindly desist from your current course of action."

Lai Ji's gaze remained fixed on his friend to the right, who emitted a consistent noise with each thrust.

“Stop it now!” Lai Ji warned him in a whisper so that no one could hear their conversation. "Stop it!" he muttered under his breath, then resumed his respectful position, with his countenance lowered.

Ju continued to beat the floor.

“I said put an end to this at once, for Heaven's sake!” the emperor exclaimed, raising to his feet.

Everyone in the room flinched. Ju looked up, now scared. The emperor sat back down and cleared his throat, trying to appear calm again and erase the uncontrollable outburst from the memories of all present.

“Fear not, you can stand up.”

Lai Ji obeyed the order.

“Are you unharmed?” the emperor asked, truthfully concerned.

Ju stood up laughing, scratching the back of his head.

"I'm hard-headed. I'm fine."

Lai Ji closed his eyes for a moment. He turned his head slightly to the left, avoiding looking at his friend for a moment until the mix of emotions he felt towards him would disappear.

"General Lai Ji!" the emperor called.

Lai Ji quickly lowered his head.

"Yes, Your Majesty!"

"General Ju!"

"Yes, Your Majesty!" Ju exclaimed, doing exactly as his friend.

"An unstoppable curse has befallen the kingdom."

The two winced.

"The princess's life is in grave danger!"

Lai Ji dared not blink.

"Your Majesty, we will defend the princess's life at the cost of our own!" exclaimed Lai Ji with loyalty, without raising his gaze.

And with those words, a tragic fate was sealed for all eternity.

Meanwhile, Princess Fei Yan hid behind the delicate curtains, observing the scene with a heavy heart. She knew the danger she was in all too well. She extended a finger, pulling back the silk curtain just enough to see the young general who had pledged his loyalty to her father. She felt tears sliding down her cheeks. But seeing the determination etched on his face, she felt a surge of warmth inside her.

Clutching the vial she had stolen from her father, she held it close to her chest. She would leave the empire to sever any ties to her people, then she would take her own life. Trying to escape the curse seemed almost impossible. She had no intention of letting her own selfishness punish an entire dynasty. Surely, a once-lost soul could suffer in solitude, she thought, and with the passage of time, fade into obscurity. So no other spirit would have to weep for her. She could continue to wander in peace.

As the two loyal subjects bowed before the emperor, the princess retreated further into the shadows, steeling herself for the task ahead. It would not be an easy journey, but she was determined to see it through, no matter the cost.

"Rise, please," said the emperor in a gentle tone.

Lai Ji stood up, his attention involuntarily drawn to the silk curtains where the princess remained observant of him. With a suddenness that took him aback, she pivoted her head and vanished, as if she were nothing but a mirage.

Lai Ji's heart raced with anxiety as he blinked nervously, scanning the room for a glimpse of the princess. His gaze eventually fell to the ground, his head lowered in shame as if to hide from his own thoughts. The princess's allure was captivating, but Lai Ji, a general of unwavering discipline, knew all too well the weight of the sin he had committed in the brief moment their eyes met. He was torn between the overwhelming despair of his wrongdoing and the unrelenting questions that plagued his mind.

As they left the imperial court, Ju's emotions were boiling over. He was in a frenzy, explaining the situation in his own idiosyncratic way, flailing his arms and becoming overly theatrical in his gestures. Meanwhile, Lai Ji strode along with his head down, his posture that of a resolute general. Despite his commanding presence, his mind was a flurry of conflicting thoughts and emotions. He couldn't help but feel overwhelmed by the weight of the situation and the pressing questions that plagued him.

"Are you even listening?" Ju raised his voice. "What I was just saying is that there's a legend about a Potion of Time, which is said to possess unparalleled healing properties. Apparently, it's the only cure potent enough to counteract the effects of this particular curse."

Lai Ji shifted his attention towards Ju.

"Now, I hope that you agree that it seems rather absurd for us to wage a battle against destiny in such a manner."

"We shall endeavour to combat this affliction and endeavour to secure the safe return of the princess!" exclaimed Lai Ji, all of a sudden strongly indignant at his friend's words.

"Calm down, friend. You don't have to shout at me!" Ju talked under his breath.

"We'll defend her at any cost!" added the young man before hurrying up.

"Fine, I got it!" Ju shook his head. "What did I do to make him react like that?!" He followed his friend with a questioning look.

Chapter IV

As the sun set, Ju hugged his sister and older brother tightly, promising them that he would return unharmed. His parents, their hearts heavy with worry, embraced him with bitter-sweet love, hoping for his swift and safe return. Ju felt a pang of guilt for deceiving his family once more, but he knew it was for their own protection. He spun another tale, telling them he had been sent to the far edges of the empire as a soldier to oversee trade exchanges. With a cheerful wave and a proud salute, he turned his back on his humble home, drawstring bag securely in place, and set out down the dark path that would take him on a journey of unknown duration. He vowed to make enough money to ensure his family could feast on boiled meat daily upon his return.

In solemn silence, Lai Ji gathered his essentials and doused the flickering candle before departing the room. With no loved ones left to bid him farewell, he marched resolutely towards the predetermined meeting spot, casting one final glance into the enveloping darkness.

In close proximity to the imperial court, Princess Fei Yan emerged from the palace accompanied by a small entourage of servants and one of the emperor's most trusted generals, who only had permission to operate within the palace walls. The princess, veiled to conceal her identity, cast a final glance over the towering walls, her heart heavy with the memory of her father's countenance.

Resting against the plush back of the imperial chair, the emperor gazed aimlessly towards the hall's exit. A frigid, desolate air permeated the room once again. Despite the eunuch's attempts to speak, the emperor remained lost in thought, detached from his surroundings. The eunuch eventually resigned himself to silence, letting out a heavy sigh.

"My princess... I... I will never see my princess again..." the emperor whispered, raising his head and snapping back to the present moment.

"Your Majesty!" was all the eunuch had to say while bowing his grieving head.

As the servants bid farewell to their cherished princess, they implored her to flee unscathed and find happiness in a distant land. Lai Ji swiftly joined the group, offering a salute but avoiding direct eye contact with the youthful royal.

"Princess!" exclaimed Ju, almost running towards the group. "Princess, I have this honour!" he let out a shout as he saluted.

The princess offered a slight nod in greeting, surprising Ju with her graciousness. He smiled in awe, then turned to Lai Ji, who now had let go of some of his tension. The princess's expression remained inscrutable, leaving Ju puzzled. As the imperial soldier brought forth three horses, he helped the princess mount the sturdiest one, while Lai Ji and Ju silently mounted their own steeds.

As the servants bid a reluctant farewell, the princess nodded her head in acknowledgement. Casting a cold glance back at the palace, she spurred her horse into a gallop. Lai Ji expressed his gratitude to the soldier before setting off in close pursuit of the princess, determined to keep a watchful eye on her. Ju, wide-eyed and astonished, waved childishly at the imperial soldier, who rolled his eyes and reacted with familiar exasperation as the messenger on the previous day. Chuckling to himself, Ju spurred his horse to follow the others.

As the princess and her two companions slowly departed, the servants and the soldier bowed their heads. They were left behind with a desolate palace, emptied of all that was most cherished across their land.

Not long into the journey, Ju began to moan and contort his face in a way that was unbearable no matter how he positioned himself.

"Friend, nature's calling!" he exclaimed while suffering, looking for Lai Ji's attention.

Lai Ji avoided eye contact and the princess pretended not to hear.

"I'm being really serious!" Ju exclaimed, unable to bear it any more.

He was deserving of sympathy.

Ju sought solace near a bush not too far from the bustling day taverns, relishing in the peacefulness of the night.

Lai Ji helped the princess dismount her horse, while she let out a deep sigh and gazed up at the sky. Meanwhile, the young general feigned preoccupation with the saddle, concealing his ability to hear her melancholic breaths.

"Thank you," the princess whispered. She delicately unveiled her face, which glowed in the gentle embrace of the moon's brilliance. With a graceful motion, she directed her attention towards Lai Ji.

The young general dared to take a closer look at the princess. Her pale skin, the delicate contour of her lips, and her genuine eyes were all highlighted by the soft glow. In response, she smiled silently.

Suddenly, faint footsteps could be heard approaching.

"Look at how life brought us on the same path again, General," exclaimed a young and confident voice coming from the darkness. "General, isn't it?"

Lai Ji inspected the girl and immediately recognised her as she was once again dressed in men's attire.

"You!" Ju exclaimed, pointing his index finger at the young girl.

She rolled her eyes and clasped her hands in front of her, trying to avoid him.

"What's the thief doing here?! Ju asked, agitated. "Why are you here?"

"Young General, I—," the girl tried to speak to Lai Ji, not knowing how to begin.

Lai Ji turned his back and began searching through his saddlebag.

"Why are you pretending to be shy? Do yourself a favour and go your own way!" Ju suggested.

The princess listened with an air of detachment and reserve, seemingly unaware of what was being said. Lai Ji turned around and handed the girl her hairpin, the one she had lost in the market. This was meant to be his first and last gesture of friendship, a sign of farewell.

"General! My hairpin has been with you all this time?"

Lai Ji nodded in approval, trying now to avoid further discussion and prepare for departure.

"But who's the beauty?" she then asked, looking towards Princess Fei Yan.

"Be careful of what you say, you loud-mouthed thief!" Ju warned her, promptly pointing his finger. "Get lost, before you rue your further decisions!"

"As the Heavens allowed us to cross paths again, I would personally choose to honour its glory by maintaining my silence towards you," she replied, turning her back to Ju.

As the princess observed the childish argument unfolding before her, a restrained smile played upon her lips. Despite watching their every move, she felt a sense of alleviation in their company. Ju took a deep breath, gathering his words for his next remark. Meanwhile, Lai Ji helped the princess to mount her horse and prepared the saddle for their departure. The girl looked on with curiosity, eager to examine every one of Lai Ji's moves.

"Wait a minute," Ju exclaimed, his surprise evident. "Since when have we become so friendly to even talk to each other?" He turned his gaze towards the young woman before him. "Please, don't tell me—" he trailed off, his eyes widening in shock.

"Don't tell me that you've fallen in love with General Ma Lai Ji!" he exclaimed, staring at her in disbelief.

"Ma... Lai... Ji…" the girl let out a soft whisper, savouring each syllable. A radiant smile spread across her face, as she absorbed the information with unbridled happiness.

Lai Ji turned his head, clearly taken aback by the sudden revelation. Princess Fei Yan couldn't help but flinch in curiosity, although she quickly concealed her reaction.

"Ah, please! You can't do that! Not now!" Ju laughed in her face. "Not now, when the general has to protect Princess Fei Yan's life!"

Lai Ji opened his mouth, intending to halt his friend's actions, but by then it was already too late.

The girl grew pensive as she whispered, "Princess Fei Yan?" A spark of excitement flickered in her gaze as she looked at the princess. "Princess Fei Yan!" she exclaimed in awe. "It really is her!" She let out a gasp of amazement.

"Shut up! How dare you?" Ju warned her as if nothing that had just happened was his fault.

Lai Ji closed his eyes and sighed.

"Let's not worry. We shall make our exit in a quiet manner," the princess spoke in a soft voice.

Hearing the princess talk piqued the girl's interest even further.

"How exquisitely elegant and refined in her manner of speaking!" the girl exclaimed with a note of admiration. "One can only surmise that she must indeed be of royal blood!"

"She is the princess herself! So come on, make yourself invisible! We have an empire to save!" Ju commented impudently, with a lack of respect and disregard for decorum.

"Ju!" warned Lai Ji, so he wouldn't let his words slip again and handed him the reins. "It's time to go!"

"But where are you taking the princess? Don't tell me you kidnapped her?! Or did she run away willingly?"

The princess frowned.

"How dare you come up with such an invention right in front of the princess!" Ju was filled with a profound sense of indignation. "By slowing us down, you're putting your own life in grave danger! The princess didn't run away from the palace. The princess was forced to leave the palace. This is the only way by which we can dispel the curse!" he rushed to explain.

Surprised by the speed with which his friend had just transmitted the secret information, Lai Ji sighed and brought a hand to his forehead.

"So it's true! Such curses really do exist!" exclaimed the delighted young woman, taking a step closer.

Lai Ji stepped in front of the princess, more cautious now than ever.

"Allow me to join you," whispered the excited girl with a glance that assured utmost secrecy.

"Where, to do what?" Ju opposed in a flash, pressing his lips together.

"To accompany you."

"To steal from us maybe!"

"I promise. Now I'm on your side."

"Better be on your own side and get lost!"

Lai Ji interjected with a thoughtful sigh. "No! She will come with us."

"Do what?!" Ju retorted with a sense of betrayal, expressing disbelief that the person he chose to confide in was the one responding in such a manner.

"I knew it, General Lai Ji, I knew it!" the girl rejoiced.

Now that the secret had been revealed, Lai Ji couldn't count on anyone, including the girl, to keep quiet. He realised that the only way to prevent the rumour from spreading was for her to become part of the group.

"She'll travel with you," Lai Ji specified before turning away from Ju.

"Me and her on the same horse? Not even in my worst nightmares! Haha! No way!" Ju rebelled without any hesitation, making faces.

The girl pouted.

"It's alright," intervened the princess in a soft tone. "You can come closer, General Lai Ji."

As Lai Ji observed the princess, his expression shifted from confusion to shock. He struggled to comprehend the meaning behind her words. But as the young princess's proposal dawned on him, he humbly bowed his head and responded with unwavering loyalty:

"I beg your pardon, Princess, but such an action is strictly forbidden to me."

"Please do not fret, as you won't be doing any harm. We shall leave now," the princess reassured him.

The general peered at the princess in disbelief. Ju snatched the reins of his own horse, while the young girl nimbly mounted Lai Ji's.

"Are you sure she won't run away with our horse?" Ju tried to convince the general one last time, feeling that what they were about to do wasn't right.

The girl grimaced in response. As Lai Ji helped the princess, she gave him a subtle nod to communicate her nonchalance about the situation at hand. The young general gingerly climbed up onto the horse, trying his best to minimise physical contact with the princess while grasping the reins firmly in his hand.

"My name is Lu Lu!" the girl exclaimed, looking confidently at Lai Ji.

"We don't care!" Ju felt obligated to add before setting off at a gallop.

The map revealed a meandering and lengthy route leading to the very borders of the empire. True to the agreement, the emperor's men awaited them not far from the edge of the kingdom, ready to escort the princess to a foreign land where she would blend into the masses and lead an unremarkable existence. Despite the serene appearance of the road, lurking dangers could materialise at any moment, putting the princess's life at grave risk.

At intervals, they made stops to alleviate their hunger and thirst.

Exhausted, Princess Fei Yan struggled to stay awake while General Lai Ji assisted her down from her horse, holding her hand with care. Lu Lu stretched her arm out as well, but waited like that for a while, as Lai Ji fulfilled his duty to protect the princess. Ju had already dashed off to find relief in the bushes. Lu Lu frowned and dismounted on her own, but immediately smiled as she looked for Lai Ji's attention.

Not long after, Ju doze off, content, sated and warm next to the campfire. Lu Lu slept on the opposite side of the fire, with her hands flat on the ground.

General Lai Ji stoked the flames with a few more dry branches before settling down on a fallen tree trunk. As if the distance between them posed a threat, Princess Fei Yan hesitated before slowly sitting down next to the general. Lai Ji averted her gaze and stood up, pretending to be engrossed in the fire, adding a few broken branches to it once in a while. He felt uneasy and unsure of what to do when he returned to the princess, so he took off his garment and draped it over her shoulders.

"Please pardon my audacity, Princess, but the night may bring a chill."

The princess flashed a smile, expressing her gratitude as she adjusted her clothes, seeking warmth and closeness. The mesmerising sparks of the campfire captured both of their attention, holding them in silence. As the princess leaned her head against General Lai Ji's shoulder, he was startled, gazing at her face, which held a pleasant smile without a single word spoken.

The forest's hidden corners suddenly lit up with the appearance of playful fireflies, their twinkling lights illuminating the surroundings with a magical glow.

Morning arrived unexpectedly early and the leaves rustled with a refreshing crispness. Lai Ji slept with his back against a tree trunk. The princess dozed off with her head resting on her knees, while Ju and Lu Lu lay sleeping on the ground.

Though morning in the forest brought with it a flurry of sounds, the snapping of branches underfoot could only signify the approach of a person.

Lai Ji shook his head, briefly parting his eyelids but otherwise remained still. As he sensed the precise approach of three people, he immediately remembered that his sword was attached to the saddle of his horse. He let out a deep sigh, disappointed in himself.

The sound of a knife being unsheathed woke Ju. The princess stirred from the muffled sound of a fist hitting something.

“If you don't know how to hold a knife, just give up on what you're doing!” Ju gave a quick lecture to one of the thugs he was holding down to the ground.

Lu Lu stood up in fright, feeling another thug’s cold knife against her warm skin. Lai Ji pushed the princess behind him.

“Ah, you can kill that one. You’d in fact do us a great favour if you got rid of her.” Ju encouraged the thug, dismissively waving his hand at Lu Lu.

Impatience grew within her, while the bandit's terrifying laughter sounded through the forest. Lai Ji carefully measured his steps towards his sword, holding the princess tightly against him. Ju lifted the thug, whose hands were now bound behind his back with a piece of clothing. Meanwhile, the other thug menacingly held Lu Lu's life in his hands.

"Come on, let's make a deal. Give me that one and you can take him!" Ju bargained, shoving the bound bandit forward, causing him to stumble and fall to his knees. "Release her now," he demanded, pointing towards Lu Lu.

As the bandit with the pointed sword kept a watchful eye on Lai Ji, he signalled to his comrade to release the captive Lu Lu. She wasted no time in running towards Lai Ji, her move suddenly shifting the attention of all onlookers towards the princess. The thieves couldn't contain their satisfaction at their apparent find.

In a swift and unexpected move, Lai Ji shoved the princess towards Lu Lu, causing them both to let out a piercing shriek as they tumbled to the ground. Springing forward, he closed the distance. The bandit's grip on his sword weakened after a single blow from Lai Ji, causing his sword to clatter to the ground. However, before it could be seized by anyone else, his accomplice snatched it up, leaving the injured bandit to groan in pain. Meanwhile, the bound captive struggled on his knees towards the nearest tree, desperate for a chance to escape or to simply be left alone.

Lai Ji signalled to Ju with a subtle look, reminding him of the sword still securely tucked away in the horse's saddle. Ju nodded in approval, while Lu Lu held the princess protectively by her side, watching in excitement as Lai Ji dispatched the bandits one by one.

With a flick of his wrist, Lai Ji plucked a long bamboo pole from the ground, wielding it like a staff. He spun it around with lightning speed, creating a whirlwind of motion that kept the thieves at bay. Each strike was carefully choreographed as if he was performing an intricate dance routine. He weaved in and out of their attacks, effortlessly dodging punches and evading their desperate lunges.

Meanwhile, the princess observed each manoeuvre with caution, while Lu Lu supported the action with a combination of grimaces and gestures that imitated the general's movements.

As Ju approached the horse, he drew out the sword from its sheath with a quick, powerful and theatrical move. He plunged the blade into one of the nearby trees.

"What the hell are you doing?!" Lai Ji's eyes widened in alarm as he realised that the bandits outnumbered him more than he initially thought.

"Don't worry, friend!" Ju shouted back, then grunted as he struggled to dislodge the stubborn sword. "Stupid cursed blade!" he muttered under his breath, his frustration mounting.

Bracing his foot against the tree, Ju grappled with the sword, but it refused to budge. Seeing his struggle, Lu Lu rushed to his aid with the princess hot on her heels.

"Get a good grip and pull with all your might!" Lu Lu commanded, seizing the hilt of the sword.

Together, they strained against the stubborn blade, but their efforts, along with their exhortations and grimaces, seemed to make little headway.

"Join us, princess!" Lu Lu implored, and the princess hastened to comply, looping her arms around Lu Lu's waist and adding her strength to the fray.

"Damn cursed sword!" Ju growled through gritted teeth, until, with a final, collective cry, the sword was wrested free from the tree's grasp.

General Lai Ji was saved from being stabbed by a knife at the very last moment by Ju, who swiftly placed the sword at the throat of one of the bandits. Ju savoured his victory with wide eyes as Lai Ji breathed a sigh of relief and made his way towards the princess. The princess smiled and this gesture instantly calmed Lai Ji. As she reached out to touch a scratch on his cheek, Lu Lu scrutinised the two of them carefully. She then moved her attention towards Ju and rapidly walked towards him. She aimed at one of the bandits and pushed aside the mask covering half of his face.

"Uncle?!" she exclaimed, taken aback, her focus on the thief before her.

"Uncle…?!" the two generals chorused.

With a subdued and guilty countenance, he tried to avoid his niece's penetrating scrutiny.

"How dare you show up here, Uncle? You nearly got us all killed!" she hissed through gritted teeth, feeling a mix of indignation and disbelief at her uncle's actions. Despite the danger he had put them in, he now stood there, unnervingly calm as a sheep.

Lowering his sword, Ju watched as Lai Ji approached cautiously. It seemed that the bandits had abandoned their hidden intentions.

"Uncle, I explicitly warned you to steer clear of these areas." she ensuring her words were heard by him alone. "You're making me look bad! Seek out other places and unsuspecting individuals to swindle, understood?"

With a sudden burst of theatrical laughter, she then turned to the generals, signalling that she had the situation under control.

For several more days and nights, they journeyed on. Ju's criticism of Lu Lu persisted, as he constantly berated her for being bothersome and useless.

As evening approached on this particular day, the road remained long despite their proximity to the end of the journey. Ju and Lu Lu were still preoccupied with outdoing each other's bravery and they galloped ahead of the general, who stayed behind with Fei Yan.

The sun began to dip below the horizon and a hush descended upon the two. Their surroundings gradually grew darker. Yet even from the distant hill, the outline of their forms could still be perceived.

With a gentle motion, the princess extended her fingers and tenderly brushed her hand against the general's palm.

"Thank you," she whispered. "Thank you for trying to save my life."

Lai Ji's hand tightened around the princess's, but he remained silent. Nightfall had settled completely. For the first time, the general was entranced by the moment, his mind consumed with the desire to abduct the princess and flee far away with her, despite the curse that surely pursued them. But the promise he had made to the emperor, even at the cost of his own life, snapped him back to reality. Despite the circumstances, he pulled her closer as he adjusted his grip on the reins, vowing to protect her endlessly.

As the thick black fog of the curse encroached on them with alarming speed, threatening to claim the soul it coveted, the two of them carried on enveloped in silence.

The following day, their journey was nearing its end.

As they made their way through a bustling food market, the four of them approached the meeting place where the emperor's men were already waiting.

Merchants serenely peddled their pristine produce, while skilled restaurateurs expertly prepared delectable dishes. Joyful villagers revelled in mirthful feasts, blissfully savouring their meals, completely oblivious to the lurking perils that surrounded them.

Though the three soldiers were confident and well-prepared to escort the princess, Lai Ji felt an unsettling sense of confusion. He knew he would never see the princess again. Ju and Lu Lu were stricken with grief from the moment the princess dismounted her horse. As General Lai Ji offered his assistance, the princess's delicate hand remained in his grasp. Fei Yan attempted to slip away, but Lai Ji refused to let go, watching her through tears. Finally realising that it was time to bid farewell, the general reluctantly released her hand and the princess turned away. The emperor's soldiers saluted briefly, then made way for the princess to step forward. Placing her hand over her heart, where she had hidden the Potion of Time, she turned to look at the three, watching as General Lai Ji gradually fell further behind.

Days and nights away, the imperial court was now consumed by bloodshed as the princess distanced herself further from the empire. Rebels had seized control of the palace, slaughtering all who opposed them. The surroundings were drenched in blood.

Amidst the chaos and devastation, the emperor had lost all of his men. He was left with only his most faithful general, who stumbled into the imperial salon wounded. With a steely resolve, the emperor rose to his feet, determined to protect his empire until his last breath. He clutched his sword with unshakeable strength and strode out of the salon alongside his general, ready to fight to the bitter end.

Caught in a maelstrom of fury and despair over his grievous loss, the emperor ruthlessly dispatched every rebel who dared to cross his path. Despite his and his general's undaunted bravery, they eventually realised that there was no escaping the inevitable. They were hemmed in on all sides.

With a mighty battle cry, the loyal general breathed his last, his warm blood splattering onto a frigid stone, as a masked rebel's sword sliced his throat. His final gaze turned to his emperor. His ultimate remorse was that he could no longer provide him with ample protection.

Rising to his feet, tears streaming down his face, the emperor slew all who stood before him, avenging the life of his faithful general.

A sword then plunged deep into his gut.

As he struggled to move, crimson blood erupted from his mouth. Discarding his sword, his restless eyes scanned his surroundings, seeking the image of his cherished princess, yearning for one last glimpse of her before his demise. Collapsing to his knees, immersed in his own blood, he fervently hoped that Princess Fei Yan was now far from these treacherous lands.

Soon after parting ways, the trio embarked on their journey back, unaware of the turmoil brewing in the court. Walking at a leisurely pace, with their horses by their side, Ju and Lu Lu lapsed into a solemn silence, overtaken by a sudden sadness. Lost in his thoughts, Lai Ji wore his melancholy on his face.

"Regardless, I pray for the princess's safe arrival past the border. Though I already miss her terribly. And yes… I know it's not proper to voice such feelings," Ju bemoaned to himself.

Lu Lu turned her attention towards Lai Ji.

"Now that everything has come to a close and all is well, I find myself famished!" Ju exclaimed, making an animated gesture. "No joke now, I'm starving! What about you, Lai Ji my frie—?"

Ju noticed Lai Ji mounting his horse and heading in the opposite direction.

"What are you doing?" Ju cried, taken aback as he and Lu Lu trailed behind.

Lai Ji's mind raced with flashbacks of the suspicious glances cast his way by the border generals. Now, with a growing sense of certainty, he knew that something was gravely amiss. The princess was in danger. He felt it keenly.

In the heart of the vibrant food market, amidst the mesmerising sights and sounds, the escorts guided the princess through the lively crowd. One of them suddenly took a firm grip of the princess' delicate elbow, propelling her forward with an unexpected urgency.

In a moment brimming with astonishment and righteous indignation, the princess came to an abrupt stop and focused her penetrating attention on the man.

"How dare you?" she exclaimed, her words resonating with a potent blend of defiance and outrage.

As the weight of the princess's accusatory words lingered, a derisive snort escaped the offending escort, instantly spreading like wildfire among his comrades.

“Come on, Princess, no need to be rude.”

An icy chill embraced them, carried by a sudden shift in the wind.

With calculated swiftness, the group opened their sachets and ensnared the princess in a taut rope. Bundling the cords hastily, they began to drag her out of sight. Little did they realise that by holding the princess captive for too long, they risked unleashing the Curse of Time upon themselves, and with it, the entire Dragon Dynasty.

However, summoning an extraordinary display of fortitude, the princess seized hold of a scorching-hot pan that lay within reach, emanating its sizzling heat from a nearby restaurant. With an audacious act, she cast aside the searing contents, unleashing a scalding cascade upon the faces of the rebellious forces, breaking free of their hold. Their anguished groans echoed as she vanished from their grasp, leaving them bewildered and in pain.

As the rebels came to their senses and scoured the crowd with ruthless intensity, the sky overhead grew ominously dark, portending a gathering storm.

The princess clutched the vial tightly and ran as fast as her feet could carry her, blindly fleeing the market square.

Meanwhile, Lai Ji drew nearer to the agreed meeting point and dismounted his horse without hesitation. Casting his gaze around, he found himself in a deserted, desolate landscape. Ominous storm clouds loomed overhead, gathering with an air of foreboding.

The princess, by some stroke of luck, had made it out of the market and was now resting on a bed of soft grass, the raindrops pounding down heavily upon her delicate features.

The general ran wildly, without direction, lost in the fury of the storm. The rumble of thunder shook the very earth beneath his feet, heralding an uncertain future for them all.

"Princess!" distressed and unsure of what to do, Lai Ji cried out.

The pounding rain drowned his voice, rendering it a mere muffled echo. Wiping his wet face, he shouted again:

"Princess!"

But to no avail.

Opening the vial, the princess wept as her tears mixed with the raindrops.

"Princess!" the general bellowed with all his might, and the reverberation of his voice reached Fei Yan just as she swallowed the last drop of the Potion of Time. Dropping the vial, she stood up and searched around her for the general.

Drenched and wide-eyed, Lai Ji found the princess standing only a few paces away. For a brief moment, she smiled at him before her expression turned tragic.

"Princess…!" he called, drawing near.

Fei Yan shook her head, backing away as a black whirlwind slowly encircled her.

"Princess..." Lai Ji whispered fearfully.

Both of their eyes filled with tears. Lai Ji rushed over, seizing the princess's hand. Attempting to conceal her pain, she smiled bravely, acknowledging his gesture no matter how difficult it was for her.

"Princess, no!" objected the general, at a loss for how to save her.

The black fog continued to increase in volume and menace, gradually forcing the general away. Nevertheless, he persisted and drew nearer to her despite the struggle. The thunder and the curse conspired to create a perilous storm.

"Princess, you cannot leave," cried Lai Ji, struggling to meet her gaze.

"General Lai Ji," she responded simultaneously, determined not to waste a moment, unsure of when or how she would vanish. "General Lai Ji, I'll wait for you," she whispered with a smile.

"I won't let you leave, Princess!" he warned.

Fei Yan smiled through her tears, aware that she had to relinquish his hand.

"I'll wait for you for a year, ten, a hundred, a thousand… I'll wait for you for eternity! I hope to meet again in our next lives." Fei Yan whispered as she pushed the general's hand away.

Lai Ji stood frozen, unable to look away from the swirling black vortex that engulfed the young princess before him.

Fei Yan vanished, swallowed up by the merciless passage of time.

"Princess," he said one last time, acknowledging the cruel reality that he was now alone, the princess stolen away by the Curse of Time.

Torrents of rain poured down upon the empire, cleansing away the blood and tears, washing away the remnant echoes of joy.

PART TWO

Chapter I

2000 years later, Hong Kong

As rush hour hit, even villains grew weary.

The narrow roads were transformed into a labyrinth of movement, filled with a dizzying symphony of screeching tires, blaring horns and the shouts of street vendors. Neon lights flickered above, casting an otherworldly glow on the winding streets as if daring those who walked below to enter a realm where danger and adventure intertwined.

Amidst the sea of people, each rushing to their own destinations, the scent of sizzling street food wafted through the air and mingled with the aromatic blend of spices and incense that hung delicately from nearby temples. The mixture of sounds reverberated off the towering skyscrapers, lending an air of urgency to the scene. Pedestrians manoeuvred with agile grace while motorcycles weaved through the labyrinth with daring speed, their riders clad in leather jackets that billowed in the wind.

Beneath the frenetic energy, an undercurrent of anticipation pulsed through the streets. It was as if every passer-by carried a secret, a hidden story waiting to unfold. Strangers brushed past one another, their momentarily lingering gazes acknowledging the unspoken code of the urban jungle. In this world of teeming humanity, a sense of adventure permeated the atmosphere. It whispered promises of thrilling encounters, unexpected twists and the possibility of the extraordinary. It was a street that dared you to embrace its rhythm, to dive head-first into its chaotic embrace and emerge forever changed.

The symphony of incessant honking and the ceaseless flow of vehicles formed an exhilarating soundtrack that, to the discerning ears of individuals like Agent Eddy, evoked a sense of thrill and invigoration.

The car door opened almost silently, barely noticeable amidst the surrounding sounds. On the passenger seat sat a thief, his hands bound by handcuffs that looped through the car's upper handle.

"You have the right to remain silent," Eddy recited the familiar lines with a sly grin on his face. "You have the right to a lawyer...!" the young agent's voice was smooth and confident, betraying his pleasure at the prospect of getting his man. "You have the right to a pack of cigarettes. I believe you're a smoker, aren't you?" he circled the car, revelling in the thrill of the chase, before erupting into a hearty laugh that showed off his perfect teeth.

Just then, a blur of movement caught Eddy's attention. A young woman rushed by, accidentally colliding with his shoulder. He turned to look at her, confused and momentarily caught off-guard.

But in the blink of an eye, she was gone.

Without a second thought, Agent Leo bolted after her. His shouts carried through the alleyway as he raced to catch up. His heart was pounding in his chest and he could already feel the burn in his lungs. But he wasn't about to give up. Not now, not ever.

“Stupid thief, give me back my wallet!"

As the adrenaline faded, Eddy took a deep breath and realised that sweat had soaked through his shirt.

"I should take a shower."

Turning his attention back to the arrested thief in his car, Eddy's eyes glinted with a warning.

"You stay put, understand? Don't try anything stupid."

He then whipped his head around to face the direction where the two had bolted.

As he chased after Leo, Eddy was forced to thread through the throngs of people crowding the busy street. The girl was a blur of speed, slipping past the crowd with the skill of a seasoned undercover agent. Leo was forced to stop halfway and gasp for air. Eddy never lost sight of her, his attention fixed on her every move.

She weaved through the crowded streets hoping to disappear into the masses.

But fate was not on her side.

The red pedestrian light marked the end of her professional escapade. Eddy closed in with a grin, the roaring traffic trapping her like a cornered animal.

"If you come any closer, I'll jump!" she threatened, her hand poised to make good on her words.

Eddy let out a hearty laugh, throwing his head back and planting his hands firmly on his hips.

"And where do you plan on jumping, if I may ask?" he replied, his tone polite but laced with amusement at her absurd threat.

"In front of a moving car, that's where!" Her expression flashed with fierce determination.

With a theatrical flourish, Eddy extended his arm towards her, inviting her to go ahead. Taken aback by his cool demeanour, the girl hesitated. Eddy moved his left hand, demanding the return of the stolen wallet.

Panting heavily, Leo managed to finally catch-up. He leaned on his friend's shoulder and lifted his fist.

"Give it back! Now!" Leo growled, making it clear that he wasn't joking.

She clung to her side purse with a fierce grip, her eyes darting between Leo's smirking face and Eddy's calculating stare. The tension was palpable.

Leo stepped forward, trying to intimidate her with his imposing presence. His eyes widening as he stared her down.

"Are you not going to give it back?" he taunted, his voice laced with arrogance. "Haha! That means you've never heard of Agent Leo, the Left-Hander-With-The-Right-Fist, huh?!"

The girl burst out in loud laughter, mocking his feeble attempt at intimidation.

Leo's face darkened with offence.

"You piece of—, Eddy, hold her down. I'll look for the wallet."

Her posture tightened up as she desperately looked for a way out.

"Alright, check it out. I got another idea brewing in this brilliant mind of mine!" Leo declared. "You're gonna come with us to the station. We'll sort this whole damn mess out once and for all. No more playing around!"

Her body trembled as she searched for help in Eddy's eyes. After a brief moment of hesitation, she let out a deep sigh, trying to calm her nerves.

"Look, you and I are strangers," she said, trying to reason with Leo. "Why don't we just forget about this? If I give you the wallet back, everything will be okay, right?"

"So you admit it!" Leo barked, thrusting his index finger in her face. "Give it back to me, now!"

Taking a firm grip on her shoulder, he yanked her bag towards him and unzipped it promptly. His eyes darted back and forth, searching for his precious wallet. But it was nowhere to be found.

He turned his attention back to the girl in front of him, examining her from head to toe. The wallet had to be somewhere. He focused on her thin vest, convinced that it was hidden there.

Without a second thought, he bent down towards her and slipped his hand under her jacket. And then, he felt it. The smooth leather of his wallet, nestled snugly against her body.

"It's here!"

In a sudden move, her hand flew across his face. Taken aback, Leo clutched his wallet in one hand and held onto his stinging cheek with the other.

"Where do you think you're touching?!" She fixed her vest with both hands.

Without missing a beat, Leo straightened his back and raised his finger, ready to accuse her of a crime.

"Assault! Theft and assault!" he barked, his voice growing louder with each word.

Eddy stepped closer and slammed the cold metal handcuffs onto the girl's left hand. Startled, she jolted in fear, her heart racing with apprehension.

"Take that you piece of—" Leo cheered, but then stopped abruptly as he was left dumbfounded at the sight of the other handcuff on his own wrist.

"Eddy, what the—"

Undeterred by Leo's outburst, Eddy offered a serene smile as he ushered them both towards the car. Leo tried to pull his arm back but jerked the girl after him by doing so.

Back at the car Eddy leapt into the driver's seat, leaving Leo to follow suit. The girl, now a prisoner of their game, was dragged along in tow.

As Leo and the girl approached the car, the captured thief slouched and buried his face into the passenger seat. Captivated by the sleek, polished exterior of the car, the girl eagerly traced her fingers over the glistening door.

"What a jewel!"

"Shame it doesn't fit into your pocket!" Leo snorted.

He opened the door and stepped inside, forcefully pulling her in behind him. At that moment, she caught a glimpse of the mysterious figure in the passenger seat. Desperate to get a better look, she leaned in, but he quickly turned away, avoiding her at all costs.

"Uncle?!" she exclaimed in a whisper, miming more than speaking so that the other two wouldn't hear. The man grimaced, deliberately averting his attention from her.

"What are you doing here? Uncle, you're embarrassing me!"

The uncle acquiesced and looked away, awaiting the car to shift into gear.

Seeking to downplay the awkward encounter, the girl turned to Eddy, eager to meet the honourable gaze of the agent who had arrested her with such charismatic authority.

"Like a real man…" she thought. "My name is Li Li!" she said, waiting for a positive reaction from Eddy.

"We don't care!" Leo's voice was heard instead, pulling her next to him on the back seat using the handcuffs. "You could be called Li Li Lu Lu La La Lu for all we care!"

Li Li pouted. Leo then visibly squirmed as he turned to Eddy.

"How about you do me a favour and kindly hand over them keys to these damn handcuffs?"

Eddy pretended not to hear his friend's request and started the engine.

"Agent Eddy!" Leo exclaimed, trying to be authoritative.

"I don't have them any more." Eddy started pressing the buttons on the radio.

"Agent Eddy!" Leo childishly kicked his feet.

Li Li pulled him back this time, stopping his flailing arms and legs.

"Agent Eddy!" Leo protested, trying to make himself heard.

"Call me Eddy!" Eddy replied with a grin, as the radio music had just started playing.

Leo scowled, feeling ignored and ridiculed right in front of two suspects.

"Leo, listen! Call me Eddy!" Eddy continued to mock, bobbing his head to the rhythm of the music.

The car hit the road, heading towards the police station. Leo gave in and leaned his elbow against the car door, annoyed as the wind tousled his hair while he glared at passing vehicles.

"Call me Eddy, call me Eddy!" Eddy continued to sing happily, ignoring everything around him and drumming his hands on the steering wheel.

Later, in the police station parking lot, Leo rushed to open the car door and get out. He yanked Li Li's arm and made her run after him. Eddy helped the girl's uncle out of the car by removing his handcuffs.

Leo stormed into the office, his sudden arrival causing two officers to jump up in surprise. They watched him in confusion as he made his way towards the main area, his frustration palpable. The Chief of Police turned to Leo, his expression firm, but it didn't take long for a hint of humour to creep onto his lips.

"Where does it hurt, son?" he asked, a hint of amusement in his voice as he watched the young agent's theatrical performance.

The police station was abuzz with energy and purpose as dedicated agents carried out their duties with utmost diligence. The office, cluttered with rows of gleaming computers, had a sense of technological sophistication mixed with a touch of chaos. Plastic chairs, though modest in appearance, provided seats for weary officers engrossed in their tasks. Amidst the constant hum of conversations and the clickety-clack of keyboards, a symphony of law enforcement efforts unfolded, illustrating the dedication and commitment of those who safeguarded the city's security.

In front of Leo stood the Chief of Police, Boss, a figure in the prime of his seasoned years who carried the essence of a quintessential leader. His countenance embodied the steadfastness of a loyal mentor, while his gentle eyes mirrored the warmth of a paternal figure. Boss possessed hands weathered by the toil of a genuine warrior as if they had once waged battles teetering between life and death. His mere presence was reminiscent of a king, commanding respect and awe in equal measure.

Leo let out an arrogant laugh, briefly turning his head to the side before raising his right hand, causing the girl to move her arm as well. The other officers burst out laughing, muffling their chuckles.

"Since when did this become the damn norm?!" Leo shook the handcuff on his wrist in frustration.

"But who’s this young lady?" Boss looked at Li Li as if Leo had just arrested his very first girlfriend.

"This piece of work straight-up swiped my wallet, and in my bad-ass mission to catch her, shit went down."

The girl remained silent.

"Mid-mission, his wallet was snatched," one agent whispered to another, stifling their laughter behind their desk as the action-packed tale continued to spread like wildfire throughout the precinct. “But he didn't just let it go. No, he turned the incident into a full-blown wallet recovery operation!"

Li Li smiled with innocence as Leo stomped his feet.

"Boss, come on!"

Eddy burst into the room and hastily placed the thief on the first chair by the entrance.

"Prepare the report," he ordered one of the desk agents. Giving a quick nod of acknowledgement to his boss, he abruptly realised that he had interrupted a crucial conversation; at least from his friend’s perspective.

Li Li winced.

"Ah," Eddy muttered with a smile.

Pulling a key-chain out of his pocket, Eddy tossed it to his friend. Leo's eyes widened as he found himself holding the keys, looking to his friend for an explanation. Boss sighed while shaking his head.

"See, Boss?!" Leo argued with desperation.

"Enough! Release the girl and focus on what’s important. Now." Boss's voice was firm and commanding, leaving no room for argument.

Leo bowed his head obediently, feeling defeated as he searched for the right key.

And with that, the other agents sprang into action, suddenly more focused than they had ever been before. Eddy couldn't resist leaning in playfully to whisper something in his boss's ear.

"Boss, I think you were an emperor in a past life!"

"Is that so?" A grin spreading across his face. "Now get back to work, you rascals!" Boss straightened up, his lips still betraying a hint of amusement.

Li Li and her uncle, who had both denied any familial ties, were finally released after a tedious hour-long paperwork process.

As they were leaving the room, Leo couldn't resist the urge to toss a crumpled-up piece of paper in Li Li's direction to let her know that her presence was a nuisance. Li Li followed her uncle out while grimacing back at Leo, who was splayed out in his seat like a wilted flower. In response, Leo jumped up and raised his fist.

The girl slipped away behind the wall, stealing a final glance at Agent Eddy, who was now preoccupied with the endless stacks of papers cluttering his desk.

Chapter II

Just before lunch break, a frantic lady burst into the room and plopped down on the first chair she could find, pleading for help. Leo stood up, palms braced on his desk.

"Help me, someone's trying to kill me!" She clutched Leo's hand.

"Please calm down, you're safe here." he reassured her, signalling that he was ready to listen to her story.

As soon as Boss stepped out of his private office, he scanned the room. With a stern gaze, his eyes locked onto Eddy's. It was for the reason Eddy had suspected. Boss had a problem on his hands that he didn't want to bring attention to in front of the others. Eddy knew what he had to do. He calmly rose to his feet and followed Boss into the office, shutting the door quietly behind him.

Boss sat back in his chair, his expression turning from one of worry to one of assurance as he gave a slow nod.

"It's time. We'll begin," Boss declared, his tone firm and determined.

Eddy felt a sudden surge of adrenaline as he realised that the moment he had been preparing for had finally arrived.

Boss pulled a large curtain aside to reveal a wall covered in research and evidence. The sight was enough to make Eddy's heart skip a beat.

Boss's voice was heavy with frustration as he spoke, his eyes fixed on the wall panel in front of them. "Without concrete evidence, we can't incriminate them," he explained, his finger jabbing at the panel as if trying to will the evidence to appear.

Eddy could sense the tension in the room rising, while he struggled to comprehend why his boss was making such a big deal about it. Boss's words lingered like a warning, a reminder that they were up against a powerful enemy who knew how to cover their tracks.

"They transferred 70 million dollars to a Swiss account," Boss continued, his voice dripping with disdain. "But the recipient's name has changed three times already. These are the latest funds they've transferred. We could monitor them until here," Boss pointed at a spot on the wall. "Then the trail goes cold somewhere around here."

Eddy knew that they had to act fast if they were to have any chance of catching these criminals. The clock was ticking, and they had to find the evidence they needed before it was too late.

On the other side of the thick, concrete wall, the buzz of police headquarters continued uninterrupted. Leo perched on his chair with both feet and typed away furiously at his computer, his eyes darting back and forth between the screen and the woman sitting across from him. Every so often, he paused to glance up at her face, trying to read the subtlest of expressions as she described the wanted criminal. Sweat beaded on his forehead as he struggled to create a realistic composite sketch, his fingers flying over the keys.

"With or without a moustache?" Leo tried to clarify, struggling to reconstruct the criminal's face through a police sketch.

"He had no moustache... nor hair on his head!" she confidently clarified.

"He was bald?!" Leo exclaimed in surprise.

"Yes, absolutely barren up there!"

"Listen up, ma'am! Just a couple of minutes back, you were yapping about him sporting a beard!"

"When did I say that...?" she muttered, shaking off any blame. "Here, look, the nose was thinner."

Leo sighed, looking back at the screen.

"Forehead higher, not that high, just wider... Here, eyes smaller, but with big pupils, nose more crooked, but thinner. Here... No, his head was quite small."

Leo gritted his teeth, hanging on every word of the witness as he twisted and contorted the sketch.

"But he had very bushy eyebrows! Just like his moustache!"

"You just said that he didn't have a moustache!"

"When did I ever say that?" the woman muttered, shaking off any blame. "I just said he had big and terrifying eyes."

Leo's anger boiled over, causing him to lose his composure as he furiously pounded the keys, destroying the entire image in a fit of nerves.

"Oh shit, now he looks like my ex-husband!" exclaimed the woman, staring at the screen. "Get rid of it!"

In Boss' private office, Eddy sat fixated on the investigation board, his fingers tapping with purpose.

"This implies that they're presently hiding under the guise of this organisation that purportedly supports families with prematurely born children."

"This is nothing but a cover-up! The money is being funnelled into seemingly non-existent accounts, only to be transferred to unchecked locations later on. This is the crucial moment for us to step in. We need concrete evidence that the funds are being illegally multiplied within that building and transferred out straight away, erasing any traces of wrongdoing in the process."

Eddy's head bobbed up and down in silent agreement, his hand rising to his mouth as he nervously gnawed at his thumbnail. But when he lifted his head, his expression turned deadly serious.

"We'll take care of this."

Back in the main office, as the woman vehemently gesticulated, recounting how the attacker had attempted to strangle her, Leo's attention was drawn away by Eddy's pensive departure from the covert office. Despite nodding at her in agreement, Leo's mind was now fixated on his wooden desk, contemplating the looming possibility of the pre-planned secret operation beginning imminently.

"And even though he was much taller than me, he only reached my shoulder… this tall," the woman continued, standing up and showing the possible height of the attacker.

"Are you saying that he was much shorter than you?" Leo asked, already bored with the case.

"When did I say that?" the surprised woman asked, tilting her head in suspicion.

"In fact, you didn't," Leo reassured her. "But since you already got yourself standing up, would you mind kindly sauntering over to my partner right here? He's all set to take care of your case, straight up," he added, pointing to one of the agents sitting at the desk next to him.

As soon as the agent heard this, he shook his hands nervously, clearly indicating that he wanted nothing to do with the complicated woman. However, she meanwhile already settled herself comfortably in front of the agent's chair. Despite his disappointed sigh, he politely started listening to everything she had to say.

Leo quietly made his way over to Eddy, taking note of the expression on his face.

"Do we have details?"

"We're ready to go."

Leo nodded fervently, filled with a sense of profound readiness to embark on another mission.

The clock on the wall showed 2:15 am.

It was a dark, quiet night and the tension in the secret offices of the police headquarters was palpable. Undercover agents, all geared up, gathered around a dimly lit table. The sound of papers shuffling and hushed conversations surrounded them as they meticulously analysed the final plans.

Leo fussed around as one of the agents helped him prepare his microphone and bulletproof vest. Eddy held his right hand over his ear, checking the sound quality. Every detail mattered, and they all knew it.

Suddenly, one of the youngest agents stood up triumphantly, declaring that he had hacked into the surveillance camera database. The room erupted in cheers as they examined every angle of the building's courtyard. But their elation was short-lived as the young agent sighed in disappointment—the cameras weren't connected to the interior of the building.

Despite the setback, Boss encouraged his team, assuring them that they were doing great. Eddy checked and double-checked all of his hidden microphones and cameras as he tried to get used to the footage of the location they were to approach at dawn.

As they continued their preparations, the door burst open and a confident young woman strode in. Leo couldn't help but gasp.

"Oh la la," he exclaimed, with no intention to sound frivolous.

Boss frowned but refrained from giving Leo a lecture.

"I'm Agent Fei, Espionage Division," the young woman introduced herself, already equipped with the necessary gear and detailed documentation of the situation.

"Agent Fei, this is Agent Eddy," Boss said, making the necessary introductions. "Eddy will be leading this operation," he added with a stern look on his face. "I have full confidence in you."

Fei briefly bowed her head and Eddy respectfully acknowledged her with a nod, without saying a word nor being distracted by the young woman's beauty. Leo couldn't take his eyes off her, his admiration apparent. He strode confidently towards Fei with a smile on his face.

"I'm Agent Leo," he introduced himself extending his right hand.

The young woman greeted him politely but kept her distance, turning her attention to the computer where the surveillance cameras could be monitored. Leo stood there for a moment, hand still outstretched, before awkwardly withdrawing it. He scratched the back of his neck, trying to play off the awkward moment.

Eddy double-checked his equipment and confirmed that they were ready to commence the mission. Fei, dressed like a savvy businesswoman, was handed the additional microphones to carry out the operation. As for Leo, he had to switch into a modest black suit that wouldn't make him stand out.

Chapter III

As the sun began to rise, the car carrying the three agents crept towards the billionaire's villa-like building that was supposed to house a charitable organisation. Fei stepped out of the car, carefully scanning the area for any signs of danger. With a simple flicker of his eyes, Eddy signalled to Fei that he was heading off behind the towering walls. Leo was left standing there, his mouth agape, stunned by the sheer opulence of the imposing gate.

"Let's get going," Fei whispered to Leo, her face expressionless.

Without a second thought, they strode up to the intercom with smiles that were polite but determined. The guards scrutinised them through the surveillance cameras. Eventually, the massive gates creaked open to reveal a sprawling courtyard filled with fountains and hedges, with twisted shapes that didn't always resemble any recognisable animal.

As they walked towards the main entrance, Leo couldn't help but gawk in amazement. Fei was all business, her mind racing with a plan.

"Let me take care of this," she said, turning to Leo with a quick, sharp glance. "You just stick to the script. You're the foreign husband who only speaks foreign languages."

"But I don't know any foreign languages!" Leo protested in a hushed tone.

"Then make one up," Fei whispered back, making a face that suggested there was no more room for argument.

The double door creaked open and a surly employee of the organisation stood before the two agents. Despite his posture denoting wide open arms as he was holding the double doors, he looked less than pleased to see the two. Undeterred, he forced a smile. They returned the fake politeness.

Meanwhile, Eddy prepared his tools. Leaning against the wall, he surveyed the building's sensor surveillance cameras, waiting for the green light from his team. A beep signalled that the coast was clear.

“Clear.”

“I’m heading north,” Eddy announced his next move to the team at the head office and leapt over the fence, adrenaline pumping through his veins.

As he landed on the other side, he scanned the luxurious surroundings, amazed by the extravagance. He nodded to himself, acknowledging that anyone would kill for such a life. The team's eyes were on Eddy as he crept closer to the building. The cameras stationed in the corners of the courtyard went blank for a few seconds, and then, to their relief, the transmission resumed without showing any hints of intrusion. Eddy was now standing against the expensive stonework, his hand tracing the intricate patterns as he looked up at the towering windows.

Still at the main entrance, Fei and Leo maintained polite smiles as the guard gestured at them.

"What's your business here?" he asked, scanning them sceptically.

Fei took a firm stance, subtly trying to convey her modest intentions.

"We're here to make a donation to save the lives of these innocent children," Fei spoke with a gentle tone. "My name is Lee, and this is my husband," she said, pointing to Leo.

"Lee," Leo stuttered, nodding politely.

The guard's suspicions heightened as he scrutinised Leo from head to toe. He couldn't shake off the feeling that something was off about him.

"*Carpe diem,*" Leo then exclaimed with a quick and elegant move of his arm.

Fei turned her attention away from Leo, closing her eyes tightly in an effort to conceal any hint of a grimace that might blow their cover. The guard furrowed his brow, unable to comprehend the meaning behind Leo's words.

Fei stepped in to smooth things over. "My husband just arrived from overseas," she said convincingly, flashing a reassuring smile.

The guard's expression softened as he finally pieced things together.

"Alright, come this way." He motioned them to step in, leading the way into the massive hall.

As Fei entered with a slight bow of gratitude, Leo stopped at the threshold next to the guard's ear, adopting an elegant expression.

"*L'effort est ma force,*" Leo conveyed convincingly, thanking him for the hospitality.

Fei hurried towards the centre of the room. Putting two fingers to her forehead, she sighed, regretting to have accepted a mission with an agent she had never met before. Leo joined her, fascinated by the gilded stairs and lavish paintings hanging on the white walls.

"Wahhh... Why you suddenly so serious, huh?" he whispered, noticing her tense expression. "Don't you scroll through social media? It teaches you a thing or two, I'm telling you. It helps when you're in need, you know what I'm saying?"

Looking sharp in his fitted suit, the guard caught up with them, overtaking their steps and expertly gesturing in the direction they should head.

Fei cast a quick glance over her shoulder at her colleague before muttering under her breath with a wince of displeasure:

"*Carpe* shit! *L'effort est ma force* my ass!"

Fei then struck a determined pose, flashed an elegant smile, and picked up her pace, tailing the guard with calculated steps.

Meanwhile, Eddy untied his rope and propped himself up on the third-floor windowsill, slowly pushing open the already unlocked window to peer inside the room. The area appeared to be unoccupied.

Adjacent to the room, a group of five guards were monitoring the security cameras while nonchalantly smoking cigarettes and engrossed in a game of cards. One of them caught a glimpse of a flickering light on the surveillance monitor and signalled to the other to investigate the matter.

Eddy leisurely strolled into the empty room, adjusting his vest and dusting off non-existent dirt. He scanned the peculiar shapes on the walls and the lofty ceiling. Without warning, he suddenly heard the clanking footsteps of a guard passing by the open doorway. The sound abruptly ceased, as if the guard had vanished into thin air.

The guard reappeared from behind the wall and peered into the room. He spotted the open window in the empty room.

The man strode across the threshold, suddenly twisting his head with a dramatic expression as he spied Eddy's shadow lurking by the wall. Whether from shock or from the impact of Eddy's punch, he crumpled to the ground in a heap. Eddy sprang into action, catching the guard in his arms and easing him gently to the floor with the precision of a seasoned veteran. With the finesse of a museum curator, he gingerly positioned the limp body against the wall like a delicate porcelain figure. He nodded to himself, confident that the man would remain in a deep slumber for quite some time.

Eddy slipped out of the room, shutting the door with a barely audible click. He peered over the balustrade of the grand staircase and caught the sound of Fei's mellifluous voice, along with the footsteps of Leo and the guard, as they made their way towards the adjacent chambers. Glancing around, Eddy headed along the corridor.

Fei and Leo were invited into the office of the so-called President of the organisation. The doors closed behind them, leaving the guard outside.

The President stood up, wearing the same fake smile as Fei. With an elegant gesture, he invited the two visitors to sit down.

In the background, a vintage turntable played "The Marriage of Figaro" on repeat.

"Excuse me for a moment," he said gently, then immediately left the room.

With a sense of comfort settling over him, Leo sprang up from his seat and took a curious tour of the room, running his fingers over the old, ornate furniture and examining each and every frame of the valuable paintings hanging on the walls.

One particular Renaissance painting caught the eye with its riotous portrayal of a nobleman engaged in an absurd activity. The golden-plated figure, resplendent in his regal attire, balanced precariously atop a unicycle, his expression caught between determination and sheer panic. With each stroke of the artist's brush, the motion of the unicycle seemed frozen in mid-air, defying gravity and reason. Nearby, a scene unfolded with a group of well-to-do gentlemen engaged in an extravagant feast, their faces contorted in expressions of exaggerated gluttony. Their mouths gaped wide open, attempting to devour monstrous delicacies that defied both taste and logic, while the table groaned under the weight of their extravagant indulgences.

As the President stormed out of the room, his gait was no longer elegant and his eyes blazed with fury as he made his way towards the guard who was waiting at a distance.

"Why the hell have you brought them to me, huh?!" the President roared, his face contorting with anger. "You know damn well that we accept donations only through accounts and never in person!"

"Sorry, chief, but they were extremely insistent," the guard responded, his voice tinged with anxiety. "It would've raised suspicion if we hadn't allowed them in."

The President sighed and rolled his eyes.

Inside the office, Leo settled onto the sofa and noticed a plate of crackers on the glass table. His greed got the better of him as he eagerly leaned over the small plates. Fei slapped his hand.

"Ouch!" Leo withdrew his hand with a start, then his lips curled into a mischievous smile. "Do I really deserve such a stern punishment?" he asked with a hint of playfulness, his expression taking on a suggestive tone.

Fei frowned, avoiding his gaze.

"You're aware that those snacks are merely for display, not for consumption," Fei replied sternly. "Moreover, we can't trust anyone," she added, her tone heavy with responsibility.

Leo contorted his face in a pouty grimace, sighing like a child who had been sent to a corner for misbehaving.

Just then, the President strolled back in with an amiable smile and the performance of "The Marriage of Figaro" resumed. Fei replied with a graceful smile.

"So, if I understand correctly, you're interested in making a donation," said the President, turning to Fei.

"Absolutely," Fei approved, her slow and elegant blinking adding to her composed demeanour. "My husband and I have recently arrived from abroad and have decided to contribute a small portion of our income to this organisation."

"What a lovely thought," the President approved, causing Fei to flash a charming smile and tilt her head. "So, what's your profession?" he then inquired, glancing over at Leo who had meanwhile been gawking at a portrait on the left side of the wall. The person in the painting exuded such an intense presence that it was practically impertinently obscene.

Leo recoiled in disgust at the portrait, before refocusing on the conversation, realising he was asked a question. Fei cleared her throat.

"My husband's language skills are not exactly up to par, as he's just returned from his time away in Germany for… personal reasons," she chimed in, indicating her desire to steer the conversation forward.

"Buy us some time, I think I've found something," Eddy whispered into their hidden earpieces. Fei blinked in agreement. Leo, now playing along with the plan, sprang to his feet with a flourish upon realising that the President was still eyeing him expectantly.

Approaching the President, Leo slung his arm over his shoulder, coaxing him up and guiding him towards the wall adorned with bizarre and disturbing portraits of unknown individuals. Leo scowled at one particularly grotesque portrait, feeling a nauseating sense of befuddlement. With a resigned air, he turned his attention back towards the President while still gripping his shoulder and let out a drawn-out, weary sigh.

"Hitler *mein Freund, carpe diem*!"

The President jerked back in surprise at Leo's words, while Fei, appalled, pressed her fingers to her forehead and closed her eyes, trying to collect her thoughts.

As "The Marriage of Figaro" played out throughout the mansion, Eddy stealthily infiltrated the secret section of the building to hunt for the evidence they needed. Unfortunately, there was no indication of any evidence thus far suggesting that the illicit money transfer was occurring from this location. Standing outside a closed door, he pressed his ear to the thin wood, straining to eavesdrop on the conversation inside.

"Listen up, pal. We ain't playin' around here. We're gonna grab ourselves a fat stack of cash, courtesy of a sweet loan for those fancy renovations. And you know what? We're gonna move that dough in hush-hush style, like shadows in the night. No one's gonna know what hit 'em." a smooth voice spoke.

Focusing so much on trying to hear the conversation, Eddy heard the approaching footsteps in the hallway next to him a few seconds too late. A guard rounded the corner and spotted him. They shared an intense moment of connection before the guard charged at him like a rugby player. With nowhere to run, Eddy lunged forward with his elbow to catch his opponent squarely under the chin. Carefully catching his limp body, Eddy propped him against the wall and left him to his well-deserved rest.

"What sustains you guys all day in this place, milk and cereal?" Eddy whispered, slightly judgemental. "Spinach, more spinach and proper protein is what you guys need," he added to the guard, who was too far away in his dreams to hear anything anyway.

Back in the President's office, Leo put on his thinking cap and plopped back onto the couch. The President gestured for Leo to help himself to the crackers, pointing twice at the plates, just in case the German visitor was a bit slow on the uptake. Leo leaned in to grab a cracker, while making a face at Fei, proving her initial suspicions about the snacks wrong.

"Scurry off now! Their cars have pulled up at the gate!" one of the agents back at the office announced through the microphones.

Leo jolted to his feet. Fei, who also received the message, chuckled nervously, glancing over at her pretend husband.

"I believe it's time for us to depart. We'll inform you once we've completed these forms. Hopefully, our visit hasn't been too disruptive!" she said with a hast smile.

"Not in the slightest!" the President lied through his teeth, lacking professionalism in his voice.

Fei and Leo headed towards the door, ready to leave.

At the other end of the building, Eddy quickly deployed his climbing tools and jumped back through the open window, sliding professionally towards the bottom of the building. As a preventive measure, he avoided the cameras as best he could and climbed over the fence.

Fei and Leo elegantly left through the front gate without arousing suspicion.

"The Marriage of Figaro" continued as the President emerged onto the gold-plated hallway. He grabbed the first guard by the neck.

"Which one of you losers let these two in?!'

With a collective exhale of relief, the trio piled into their car, feeling like they'd just dodged a bullet. A lot of bullets, in fact.

At that same moment, Leo's attention was drawn to the swarm of expensive cars amassed at the gate. Amidst the slick-suited, shifty-eyed men loitering about, he spied a familiar figure skulking around, as calm as a summer breeze.

“Isn't that the damn thief?!” Leo shouted, squishing his face against the car window like a kid at the candy store.

Fei and Eddy swivelled their heads to see the parade of dapper-yet-shady guys exiting their fancy cars and sure enough, there she was—the light-fingered Li Li—slipping a couple of wallets into her jacket pocket.

"Ah, come on now, that's just low-hanging fruit," scoffed Leo, itching to hop out of the car and put a stop to her thievery.

Without any further words, Eddy hit the gas, making Leo bump his forehead against the window.

Chapter IV

The agents pulled into the subterranean parking lot and headed for the police department.

Leo trailed behind Eddy and Fei, his heart racing with anticipation of what was to come. As they approached the sliding doors, Leo's eyes narrowed as he watched Eddy chivalrously hold the door open for the young agent, who thanked him with a subtle nod. Leo shook his head in disbelief at Eddy's gesture, feeling more suspicious than ever.

As they entered the top-secret offices, a hush fell over the room and the agents knew they were in for some serious debriefing. Tension crackled and silence quickly gave way to a frenzied buzz.

"It looks like our best shot at cracking this case lies just around the corner. I've got a hunch that the evidence we need is practically begging to be discovered!" Eddy said with confidence.

Boss gave his approval, summoning the team to a table near the wall. Heads bent over diagrams and documents, they discussed and gestured with intense focus. Leo, however, opted out of the activity, knowing that non-stop work could lead to burnout. As he was hanging around the group, a low grumble emerged from his stomach, causing him to rub it and flash an innocent smile. Eddy too felt hunger pangs and swallowed hard. Boss chuckled.

"You all deserve a break. Get out! Find yourself some food."

Fei gazed at Boss wordlessly and he nodded in acquiescence, his smile filled with affection. Leo's face broke into a foolish grin as he signalled to his friend, indicating that he would take charge of selecting the restaurant this time.

In the parking lot, Leo couldn't contain his excitement and slid into the passenger seat, mentally reviewing the menu options. Eddy held the door open for Fei, exhibiting calm politeness. As Eddy buckled up, Leo flicked through the radio stations, making sure to avoid anything he disliked or anything that might encourage Eddy to burst into song or dance.

As they entered the restaurant they often frequented, Leo scanned the area for the table closest to the cash register, pulling out his chair. Eddy gestured towards a more secluded table and Fei nodded in agreement, both passing by Leo's preferred table without even acknowledging it. Leo reluctantly replaced his chair and prepared to join the others, eyeing them suspiciously without saying a word.

At that moment, he glanced out the window and spotted Li Li strolling by, reaching the door and entering the restaurant. He snickered arrogantly, twirling his tongue around his teeth. Eddy and Fei studied the menu, coming to a consensus on what to order. Li Li grabbed her chair from the table next to the cash register, taking a sip of the tap water that had already been served to her prior to ordering.

"Ha!" grunted Leo, shutting his mouth and now chewing on air. "That's why I said we should sit at that table!" he exclaimed, pointing his finger at Li Li's glass of water, but no one paid any attention to him.

As he turned his head halfway, he jumped when he caught sight of Li Li noticing them out of the corner of her eye.

"Agent Eddy," she whispered, her smile involuntary as she gazed at Eddy, who had just handed the menu to the waitress and was informing her of their orders.

Brimming with enthusiasm as she took her glass, she rose from her seat and made her way towards their table. Leo caught sight of her gesture, his eyes widening in surprise, but it quickly became apparent that he was of no consequence to her; all of her attention was fixed on Eddy. In a diabolical move, Leo pretended to be careless and extended his leg, hoping to trip her up. Just as he thought he had succeeded, Li Li arrived, bursting with energy and holding her glass in hand.

"Agent Eddy!" she exclaimed joyfully, offering a greeting to him, all while stomping over the tips of Leo's toes without even noticing.

Leo gritted his teeth and balled his fists, determined not to reveal the pain caused by his own wrongdoing.

Eddy recognised the girl. He looked up as she placed her glass on the table and took the only free chair, situating herself between Eddy and Leo. She was nearly face-to-face with Fei, who smiled in a friendly manner.

"Looks like we meet again!" Li Li looked at Eddy, who responded with sincerity.

"Indeed we do."

Leo still stared regretfully at his shoes, biting his lower lip. Suddenly, he raised his head with a serious expression.

"Who said you can sit here?!"

Li Li examined Leo's face without saying a word, then passively turned her head and flashed a smile at Eddy, seemingly oblivious to Leo's question. Outraged, Leo prepared to say something, but the waiter interrupted him by bringing plates and bowls of food. While the food was being served, Li Li admired Fei in silence. Once the waiter left, Li Li slowly leaned her head towards Eddy and whispered:

"Who's the beauty?"

Fei's lips curled upwards, a hint of amusement in her expression. Li Li's own smile faltered slightly, feeling a tinge of embarrassment as she awaited a response that never came.

"Let's eat," Fei interjected, gesturing towards the plates. "We've ordered more than enough."

Li Li eagerly grabbed a plate for herself, while Leo maintained a cautious distance, pulling his chair away and patting his chest, nervously checking for his wallet. Just in case.

An hour passed by fleetly and Li Li threw her napkin over the remnants of her meal. Leo released a contented sigh, his stomach full to the brim.

Eddy whipped out his wallet alongside Fei, both eagerly anticipating the bill.

"No worries," Eddy reassured Fei, his voice full of conviction as he stood up. "I'll take care of it."

Fei shook her hand.

"I'll get it."

"Let's go Dutch," Li Li chimed in, rifling through her purse.

Fei's smile broadened and Eddy nodded in agreement.

"What," Leo questioned, his brow furrowed in confusion as he scratched his head. "Paying in euros?"

Eddy shut his eyes tight, feigning ignorance of the commotion. Fei clamped her hand over her mouth, attempting to suppress her laughter. With a derisive curl of her lip, Li Li swivelled her head to Leo, scrutinising him from top to bottom while dragging her tongue over her teeth.

"That means I pay my shit, you pay your shit!" Li Li spat in Leo's direction, fixing him with an intense stare.

Fei's laughter erupted, but she managed to quell it straight away. Leo nodded, content that he comprehended the task at hand. His countenance then abruptly changed when he registered Li Li's vulgarity. Prepared to protest, his objection was cut short by Li Li's action as she produced several wallets from her purse.

Eddy recollected the scene outside the villa, where Li Li had swiped the wallets from the mobsters. Without a second thought, he seized the two wallets from her grasp, flipped open the first one and rummaged inside. Li Li stared at him with caution.

"Seems like you're covering the tab today," Leo declared confidently, snickering at her prior statement.

Upon discovering IDs and credit cards, Eddy raised his head to look at Li Li.

"If I were to compensate you for these, what amount would you consider fair in return?" he inquired.

Li Li and Leo both flinched but for distinct reasons. Fei grabbed one of the wallets, unearthing an ID among a few receipts. Then Leo also caught on to what was happening.

"Why pay her anything?" he retorted sardonically. "Let's consider them as evidence!"

"Lunch," Li Li suggested, glancing towards Eddy who instantly agreed to pay for her meal.

Leo meanwhile picked up one of the ID cards and examined the face of the owner, attempting to connect the photo to the incident in front of the villa.

"Arnold von Weißenberger...?!" Leo exclaimed, raising an eyebrow in surprise. "Is this guy a Disney character?" He grabbed the other ID from across the table. "Kevin Lee?" he read with a thin, ironic voice. "That's the shorty who got out of the car last, the slick one with sunglasses!" He immediately remembered.

Eddy snapped his fingers in agreement, "It's possible the documents are fake."

Fei gathered all the bank cards together with a serious expression.

“How do you know that?” Leo tilted his head.

“If you don’t mind me interfering,” Li Li whispered as she leaned closer. “What are we talking about? Do you know these guys?”

"Somewhat," said Eddy, taking a thoughtful pause.

"But it's none of your business, thief!" Leo felt like adding in order to emphasise his importance.

"Oh, I know!" Li Li exclaimed excitedly, clasping her hands together. "You're on their trail!"

"OK, it's time for you to leave," Leo suggested, grabbing the shoulder of her blouse with his fingertips and attempting to make her stand up from the chair.

"Wait a sec," interrupted Eddy.

"Do you have some insider knowledge on these mysterious folks?" Fei spoke just as Eddy wanted to ask the same.

"I might know a thing or two," murmured Li Li with a clever look on her face.

Leo withdrew his hand.

"What do you know?" Eddy rushed to ask.

This time, Li Li sank comfortably into her seat, taking on the demeanour of a prominent personality.

"Well, it depends on how we look at it…"

"Get to the point!" Leo's impatience had reached its limit.

"Alright," she responded curtly before straightening her back. "I'm not really sure who they are, but here's what I've picked up: they're loaded. I mean, come on, have you seen the cars they drive? Those ain't no beat-up jalopies. These folks have got some serious dough. I know for sure, from the day when I… Well, when I was there. To, you know…"

"Don't worry. You've done us a great service this time around." Eddy said with a reassuring smile. "But we'll make sure to hold onto these wallets."

Li Li nodded but her curiosity was far from satisfied.

"Hold on a minute, guys. Do you think these people are robbers? Organised crime? Could there be counterfeit money involved?" Her smile widened with intrigue.

The three agents exchanged glances but remained silent, causing Li Li to become even more suspicious.

"You must be undercover! Can I join in on the action?" she whispered filled with excitement.

Fei and Eddy both looked up at her as she leaned even closer.

Leo tried to calm her down, looking at her with a hint of disdain, "Do you think this is child's play? Mind your own business, okay?"

"Yes, let's get to the station first," Eddy replied instead, taking out some money from the mobster's wallet as payment for lunch, sure of the fact that there were enough banknotes left to use as evidence.

Leo squinted his eyes.

As they piled into the car, Li Li made a beeline for the passenger seat. Eddy carried on in silence as he leaned forward to turn on the radio.

"Move to the back, that's my seat!" Leo barked, standing in front of her and gesturing with his thumb.

Li Li stubbornly remained in the passenger seat, arms crossed and ignored Leo's demand.

"Do you hear me?!" he insisted, impatiently tapping his fingers on the convertible door.

Eddy didn't say a word, his attention fully absorbed by the music playing on the radio. Leo turned to him for support. Fei could only sigh in exasperation, hoping the childish argument would soon come to an end.

"If she doesn't get off my seat," Leo's voice rose in frustration. "I'm not budging from this damn spot," he declared while pointing menacingly at the pavement.

Eddy continued to bob his head to the music, oblivious to the tension in the car.

"Do you hear me?" Leo shouted. "Hey, cut the music! Tell her to get off my seat right now, or we ain't going anywhere!"

Li Li remained steadfast in her disregard, deliberately casting her focus towards other vehicles and structures that held no allure for her. Eddy had meanwhile developed a fervent passion for rap and hip-hop, his every word accompanied by intricate gestures and lively dance moves. He immersed himself in the rhythm, savouring each beat without so much as a glance at his surroundings.

"Oi, Eddy! It seems like you've been straight-up mocking me lately! We're losing touch! I can't figure you out any more, I really can't!" Leo protested, disapprovingly shaking his head at his friend's behaviour.

Fei chuckled looking at Leo, who seemed to be the one out of touch.

"Eddy, I can't stand you any more," he added, childish in his anger, but still serious.

Distracted, Eddy shook his head, theatrically mimicking:

"You seem to be alone. How's the weather out there? I'm gonna have fun over here..."

Leo scoffed in annoyance, placing his hands on his hips and looking down in frustration, fully aware of the irony he was just trying to address.

Eddy forcefully started the car with a rough jolt. Fastening his seatbelt, he revved up the engine. Leo flinched, watching helplessly as the vehicle rapidly drove along the small street towards the main road.

Nervously, Leo threw his hands up in an attempt to signal the car to halt. Eddy slowed down a few meters away, giving Leo just enough time to catch up. Leo sprinted towards them, the wind tousling his hair. He hopped wordlessly onto the back-seat next to Fei, now barely caring about the cramped space and blaring music.

Back at the police station, the two computer agents looked up inquisitively as Eddy walked in with a grin on his face. He placed two wallets on the desk, grabbing everyone's attention.

"IDs and bank cards," Boss noticed, rifling through the wallets.

Eddy made a playful gesture, flashing a peace sign.

"Don't be ridiculous and check these," Boss rebuked while smacking him on the head.

"Sir, yes, sir!" Eddy exclaimed, saluting militarily.

Boss shifted his gaze to Fei, wiggling his eyebrows quizzically at Li Li. Fei shrugged in response. Leo rolled his eyes and let out a sigh, moving to the seat next to the youngest agent. Eddy brought a chair closer and urged Li Li to sit down.

"She's the one who provided us with the evidence and she's also a witness."

Li Li complied, her curiosity piqued. She now scanned the room instead of the people. Boss approached her with a kind disposition.

"Where did you get those wallets?"

Her smile remained genuine as she took a brief pause without saying a word.

"She stole them," Leo interjected with a nonchalant shrug, scanning the room for any reactions. "Where else would she have the damn wallets from?"

"Let's set that aside for now," Boss interrupted, gesturing to move past the accusation. "Please, tell me how you obtained them."

Li Li raised both hands, pinching her fingers together to mimic the motion of retrieving an object from one place and placing it in another. Leo let out a scoff of arrogance. Boss nodded.

"And where did this take place?"

"In front of the villa of those peculiar wealthy people, the ones with the black jackets and fancy cars." Li Li responded with confidence. "I've been told by reliable sources that their piles of cash don't all come from reputable sources."

"How do you know that?" Fei interjected.

"Ey, how do I know! I said reliable sources! You can trust me on that. None of us will starve in such situations!" She paused for a moment before continuing with a hint of indignation, "And let's be real, the vast majority of those wealthy people don't even deserve a glass of water a day!"

"From now on, please stay away from that place and those people," Boss repeated with a note of caution.

"It's about dirty money, right?! They're bad guys, aren't they?" Li Li burst out with her questions, her curiosity getting the best of her.

Boss looked up, glancing over at Eddy who just shrugged. He turned his attention to Leo, who excused himself by raising his hands in mock surrender.

"I didn't say a word! She figured it out on her own. You might think she's lacking a few bulbs at first, but she's actually got tricks up her sleeve you wouldn't even believe," he added, making a genuine effort to compliment her.

Li Li frowned before raising her chin.

"I may not know how to catch them, but I sure know how to steal from them," she said confidently while giving herself a nod of approval.

"Oooh!" exclaimed Leo, genuinely impressed this time. However, he quickly reverted back to his sceptical mindset. "But we can't trust her!"

A nearby agent interrupted the conversation, holding up one of the IDs and wondering aloud:

"Arnold von Weißenberger? What's this, Russian?" he said as he examined it closely.

"I know, right? That's what I was just saying!" Leo felt compelled to intervene. "Did I already mention that this guy came from Disneyland? Come on, give it to me, let me show you!"

Leo snatched the ID card from the young man's hand and held it up to his own face, placing his index finger on the photo.

"You see, this look, I don't know how to describe it... Nordic…" Leo adopted a philosophical tone as he tried to explain. "It reminds me of... Of…" he gestured as if trying to jog his memory. "Of...

Terminator! That's it!" he exclaimed, pleased to have finally made the connection.

The young agent and his partner nodded their heads in apparent agreement.

Leo proceeded, noticing the sudden air of superiority he had just received, "And this little guy right here," causing Eddy to let out an exasperated sigh. "Kevin Lee!" Leo held the ID card up like a salesman presenting a new brand of sports deodorant. "The masculine type with sunglasses who hides his true fears behind the tinted lenses." Leo paused for effect, allowing the information to sink in before continuing with short, impactful statements. "Don't be fooled by appearances!" He held up a finger. "This guy may be small, but he's quick on his feet."

The two young agents murmured in agreement, now clearly impressed by Leo's confident delivery.

"Picture this: Even when our man takes off his glasses, guess what? Bam! He's still rocking a mask! Yeah, I call it the mask of deceit, folks! Don't let that smooth talk or his icy stare fool you! That is, if he's not wearing sunglasses, you know, the eyes must be visible... whether they look fierce or not…"

Placing the ID card on the table adjacent to the first one, Leo paused to compare them, noticing the stark black-and-white contrast between the two mafiosos' photos: blond versus brunette, Nordic versus dark brown.

"Very interesting indeed." Leo expressed his approval with an air of intellectual enthusiasm, as he expertly organised the stack of IDs. "Little Kevin Lee, you can go on top," he said in a gentle tone, placing a calming hand on the topmost ID.

Turning to Eddy, Leo assumed his teaching persona once again, drawing the admiration of the young agents who watched in awe.

Grasping Eddy's shoulder, he presented the new victim with a twinkle in his eye, "This man is the epitome of charm!" As he studied Eddy's perfectly measured hairstyle, he placed a finger on Eddy's temples, turning his head left and right in a demonstration. "Natural black hair, untouched by dye, it's a testament to his self-confidence and strong personality." He even lifted a strand of hair, as if offering it as a secret gift for wig-making. Drawing attention to Eddy's features, he pointed out his big, round eyes. "Check it out! We're talking about the ideal features for someone who ain't too tall, just average in height. And let me tell you, this dude got charm oozing outta every pore, plus a style game that's off the charts! Guaranteed to make heads spin wherever he steps foot. I'm talking about a straight-up masterpiece, folks! Oh, and peep that lightly bronzed complexion, like he's been lounging on a beach catching some rays. And them arms? Oh, they're well-toned, my friends, ready to flex and impress!" Leo continued, squeezing the muscles in Eddy's left arm. "It's a real shame, I'm telling you! My man be rocking a vest and I'm just dying to talk about his impressive six-pack. It's the real star of the show, no doubt about it!"

Fei let out a brief chuckle, captivated by the ongoing presentation. Eddy, on the other hand, withdrew his arm from his friend's grip with a tinge of embarrassment.

"Give it a rest now."

But when he looked up and saw Fei smiling and even amused by Leo's antics, he sought her gaze and let out a laugh acknowledging Leo's exaggeration.

With a big smile, Leo then turned to their boss and patted him on the shoulder.

"And finally, we have our boss! He's got this gentle and immortal soul. It's been his guide through a life of epic accomplishments, standing the test of time!"

"Alright, that's enough, you charlatan! Get back to work." Boss interfered, signalling for each of them to refocus their attention.

Leo apologised with a respectful bow and the rest of the agents obediently returned to their designated positions, ready to resume their mission. The hardest part had yet to begin.

Chapter V

48 hours later, the entire operation had taken a completely different turn.

As the trio of agents arrived at Boss's doorstep, their focus narrowed on the entrance. Among them was Li Li, whose remarkable level of dedication was apparent. It was evident that Boss had been conspicuously absent for the past 48 hours, intensifying the intrigue surrounding their visit.

The elegant fence encircling the front yard complemented the vibrant rows of flowers, while a delicate artificial stream flowed gracefully from the fountain. With the arrival of spring, the once dormant trees bloomed beautifully as if stirred by nature's gentle caress.

Leo whistled a happy tune as he pressed the doorbell. The door creaked open and Boss appeared. Eddy nodded politely. With the door opened wide, Boss cordially welcomed them into his well-lit living room.

As Eddy sank into the comfort of the couch, he noticed a slight tension in his boss's demeanour.

Quick to respond, Leo took a seat beside Eddy, skilfully manoeuvring to ensure that Li Li didn't come between them.

Li Li pulled a chair from the table next to the windows, revealing a scene that appeared undisturbed for a long time. The tablecloth was neatly draped, suggesting a meticulous touch. Despite the layer of dust on the artificial flowers, their strategic placement suggested someone had taken the time to arrange them with intention.

Fei gently grasped Li Li's hand, a clear signal that brooked no resistance. Li Li's initial shock was hidden behind a vulnerable expression, as Fei's gaze held her attention. Yielding to the unspoken request, Li Li carefully pushed the chair back into its original position.

Fei gestured for Li Li to take the seat beside her on the couch. Meanwhile, Boss claimed the solitary leather couch on the opposing side of the glass table, a physical barrier emblematic of the strange tension that now lingered between them.

"I'll cut to the chase."

Leo's once friendly and carefree smile disappeared as he sensed that something was amiss. Boss's grave tone of voice was new to all of them and it left them all feeling unsettled. Li Li listened with rapt attention as Eddy was about to ask if everything was alright. Boss bowed his head, clasping his hands between his knees as if giving up on everything he had ever known.

"It's the Triads." Boss finally whispered, looking up.

Eddy's expression shifted from surprise to concern, his once-broad smile now replaced with a look of worry. Leo furrowed his brow, attempting to make sense of the situation by piecing together any relevant information from the previous case. Li Li's attention remained completely fixed on the conversation and as her left hand began to tremble, she balled it into a tight fist. Fei observed the group in silence, taking in the weight of the situation. Eddy corrected his posture as he prepared his voice to speak:

"We'll catch them. It's not like we're dealing with them for the first time." Eddy met his boss's eyes with conviction.

"No." Boss shook his head. "No, this time it's different."

"Don't worry, Boss. Trust us, we'll catch the bastards." Leo waved his hand as he bounced around in his seat.

Eddy nodded in agreement. "Piece of cake. What's the plan?"

Boss's face turned red with anger as he took a deep breath, his chest heaving with emotion. With a sudden burst of fury, he slammed his fist down onto the table, making everyone jump in their seats.

"I said no!" he roared, his words resounding throughout the room.

Everyone waited in silence for Boss to continue. He attempted to regain his composure as he felt out of character.

As he reflected on his team, recollections of a subterranean chamber shrouded in smoke inundated his mind's eye.

Memories of the past engulfed Boss's mind, making his heart race with fear and anguish. Caught between the weight of duty and the tumult of his personal life, he was roughly thrust to his knees by a callous hand. The sound of his daughter's innocent voice echoed in his mind as a phone was forcefully placed at his ear. Tears rushed down his cheeks and he was overwhelmed by a sense of desperation as the phone was taken away, leaving him coughing in the dense smoke of the flames. His attempts at standing up were futile as a cold pistol pressed against his temple.

The World of the Triads sought to rebuild humanity and assert its dominance over the New World by following the sacred commandments that placed supremacy above all else.

Boss shook his head, trying to come back to the present. The weight of his past mistakes and the fear of losing everything he had ever known threatened to consume him once again. Fei watched him with concern.

"So, we're talking about the Triads, right?" Leo cautiously asked.

Boss took a deep breath, managing to hold back tears as he looked away.

"We will infiltrate them without fail,' Eddy repeated with confidence, mirroring the same assurance their boss held two decades ago.

"There has to be a way to take them down," Leo added.

Li Li listened attentively.

"Picture this," Boss clasped his hands as he looked at the young agents, "A chain of electric bulbs. Each one shining bright, illuminating the path ahead. But when one burns out, the others light up even brighter, refusing to be dimmed by adversity." He paused for a moment, letting his words sink in before continuing. "These bulbs, they're like a puzzle. The harder you try to unravel them, the more they entangle you. It's a tricky business, but the only way to succeed is to set your sights on becoming like them." He looked around the room, his focus pausing on each of the young agents before concluding with a warning, "There's a fine line between becoming like them and losing yourself entirely. We shouldn't get tangled up in their web and become just another bulb in the chain."

"We'll unravel them! We'll return, no matter what happens," Eddy declared with conviction, his words carrying a resounding sense of determination as he nodded in approval.

Boss turned around and unbuttoned his shirt, revealing a magnificent dragon-shaped tattoo that spanned across his entire back and left shoulder. Leo and Li Li were left speechless, in awe of the sight before them. Fei couldn't help but let out a worried sigh.

As Eddy fixated on the tattoo, a bizarre hallucination like a distant memory resurfaced, causing him to shake his head in disbelief. He heard a faint echo from the depths of his mind, "*General Lai Ji!*" Startled, he placed a hand on his temple and felt a strange sensation wash over him as if he were experiencing a vivid dream. "*Your Majesty, we will defend the princess's life at the cost of our own!*" The unfamiliar sequences lingered in his mind, causing him to close his eyes and feel overwhelmed with dizziness.

With a swift motion, Boss buttoned up his shirt and turned to face the group of four with a gentle demeanour.

"Just like my own children, I couldn't bring myself to let you go, leaving you stranded in a sea of uncertainty," Boss whispered, his gaze shifting from Eddy, who had now regained his composure, to Leo, then to Li Li, and finally to Fei, whom he regarded with a small smile, attempting to conceal his anxieties and regrets. "If you give me your word, I'll embark on this mission with unwavering dedication. But all of you promise me, to come back unharmed, whatever it takes."

The three agents, Li Li included, offered a brief nod of agreement, signifying the finality of their decision. With their course of action now set in stone, there was no room for hesitation or retreat.

Chapter VI

The young agents immersed themselves in their mission week after week, tirelessly toiling day and night in relentless preparation.

The ticking clock fuelled their adrenaline as they braced themselves for the impending operation. Time had become their ally, rekindling Boss's conviction and reigniting the inner strength that flickered in moments of vulnerability. His years of experience and hardened wisdom set him apart from the rest of the force. His focus was now fixed solely on the safety and well-being of his promising protégés.

With steely determination, Boss was ready to confront the ghosts of his past. As Eddy so aptly put it, wavering in the face of this critical juncture would be the epitome of cowardice.

Prior to his temporary departure, Leo skilfully orchestrated an abundant feast for his family. As he stood in the hallway clutching his luggage, he affectionately watched his family, brimming with both fondness and a hint of longing.

"Why are you standing there? Come and join us," his mother urged him, offering him a piece of her fried chicken.

His older sister took a seat at the kitchen table with a critical look on her face.

"Since when do you cook?"

Leo smiled without saying a word.

"Hey, what's with that sulky face?" his older brother laughed with a hint of irony in his voice.

Leo let out a sigh, but his lips curled up into a smile as he looked at his mother, father, sister and brother eagerly devouring their meal, only occasionally glancing in his direction. They almost seemed like an illusion, lifted right out of a fairy tale. A sense of tranquillity and affection embraced his heart.

Leo cleared his throat before speaking up. "We've got ourselves a couple of tiny hiccups. You know... We got this stubborn detainee acting all crazy, causing a whole lot of trouble. And on top of that, we got some unexpected legal stuff popping up."

His father nodded while chewing his food. His mother reached for another slice of meat and shared it with her daughter. The older brother offered a brief acknowledgement by raising his hand.

Leo couldn't help but smile, content in the knowledge that he could leave with a clear conscience.

"When I make my grand comeback I'm gonna produce some serious culinary magic for you guys!" he declared as he threw his luggage to the floor. "Hold up, hold up! I got an even better plan brewing. Brace yourselves, 'cause when I return, I'm gonna go all out! I'm talking top-notch, prime cuts of expensive meat that'll make your taste buds dance with joy."

With this promise, Leo vowed to survive no matter the cost. Hands in his pockets, he leaned against the door frame and smiled.

Alone in his empty apartment, Eddy watered a small cactus. Placing it in a shaded spot, he bid farewell, as if speaking to a dear friend. Grabbing his bag, he switched off all the lights before leaving.

Li Li was allowed to spend time at the police station, though she wouldn't be directly involved in the case. The remaining agents kept busy with certain tasks. Fei waited nervously, but her anxiety dissipated as soon as Eddy entered the room. Leo arrived five minutes late, placing his suitcase by the wall. He greeted them with a goofy laugh, but everyone overlooked it as they could tell he was overcome with emotions.

Boss approached Eddy and gripped his shoulders with both hands, trying to instil the courage he himself also needed. Looking into Eddy's eyes, he saw a reflection of himself from two decades past. Boss smiled, his eyes filled with tears of emotion. It wasn't just the smile of a superior; it was the one of a parent. His nod was slow and deliberate, expressing more than just gratitude, trust, or sadness. He shook Leo's hand showing him support and giving him courage. He finally turned to Fei and smiled hesitantly. The young woman smiled back, showing that she was ready, both physically and mentally.

A long moment of silence followed.

"Let's get going. Eddy's voice pierced through the silence as he took the reins as the team leader.

A muffled sound of a chair being pushed aside caught everyone's attention as the youngest of the agents stood up from his computer, saluting with military precision. The room fell silent once more as each agent and Li Li stood up, placing a hand to their temple in a show of utmost respect.

Eddy, Leo, and Fei glanced around, seeing all the agents standing at attention. Boss slowly raised his right hand to his temple, leading by example as each agent followed suit. Leo struggled to hold back tears.

"At the cost of our own lives, we will return unharmed!" Eddy's words echoed throughout the room as he saluted, his hand still at his temple.

Leo and Fei mirrored the gesture, aware that this could be their last interaction. The emotional weight of the moment was palpable as the show of unity and dedication moved every agent.

"We're starting the mission," Boss uttered with a heavy heart, his words were almost a whisper.

"We'll survive at any cost," exclaimed the three young agents before slowly lowering their hands and taking one last look around.

As Eddy, Leo and Fei made their way towards the exit, Boss remained still, his hand trembling as he struggled to contain his emotions.

"We'll survive at any cost!" Two long decades had passed since Boss and his comrades had made this same solemn oath, yet not a single one of them survived to see the pledge come to fruition. He had indeed returned unharmed, at the price of his team's and his wife's life.

The weight of being the sole survivor bore down on him like an unrelenting and cruel sentence. The loss of his team, along with the death of his beloved wife on the same day, was a punishment too severe for him to bear and he had never fully confronted the magnitude of his grief. Eddy and the team's words were a painful reminder of that day.

As the rush of memories came flooding back, Boss felt his stability falter and he instinctively grasped the corner of the table, struggling to stay upright. Despite the two young agents who quickly came to his aid, he kept saluting, resolute in his determination to stand independently.

Downstairs, the car engine was off and the three agents sat in absolute stillness. Eddy gripped the steering wheel with both hands, while Fei sighed, uncertain if it was appropriate to break the silence. Leo flashed a grin, pivoting in his seat to face Fei, propping himself up with his right hand against the backrest.

"Let's nab those scumbags and bounce outta here without a scratch, aight?"

"Let's do this," Eddy concurred, his energy surged back as he spoke.

"I have faith in you two, Agent Leo—" Fei chimed in, then turned to Eddy with a self-assuring smile. "Agent Eddy."

Chapter VII

The trio leapt out of their car parked right in front of the lavish villa, alongside several other high-end vehicles that were meticulously aligned along the street.

Donning a leather jacket, Leo wrapped a bandanna around his head, attempting to channel his inner rebel. He pulled out a pair of sunglasses, only to stash them away when he realised that the tint was too dark for the occasion. Eddy flexed his muscles and tested the durability of his vest, ensuring it could withstand any sudden movements. Jealous of his friend's biceps and comparing them to his own, Leo smirked, satisfied that his leather jacket covered most of his skin.

Fei hit the intercom, returning in the same posture as before, but this time with another new identity. She zipped up her jacket almost to the top and let her hair down only to tie it back up tighter.

The colossal gate opened surprisingly fast. The young agents scurried along the winding path towards the entrance, looking like a group of smugglers who had come to take back what was rightfully theirs.

As the double doors swung open, the guard in his fancy suit nearly jumped out of his skin. Upon closer inspection, he recognised the couple with the foreign language-speaking husband. However, seeing their demeanour, he reached for his jacket to call for reinforcements. Before he could even utter a word, Eddy launched a right hook into the side of his head. Dazed and disoriented, the guard stumbled. Eddy leaned past him to grab the door and slammed it into the side of his face. The guard fell unconscious, with a nosebleed and a partially bruised eye.

Hearing the commotion, a group of guards rushed downstairs. They stopped just before the door, seeing Eddy's confident smirk that taunted them to hurry up. They kept a cautious distance from one another, never taking their eyes off the three agents. The first guard charged forward after a battle cry. He fell to the ground, clutching his shoulder and jaw in agony. Eddy flexed his wrist, gesturing to the other guards not to hesitate.

Without a moment's delay, the remaining guards rushed forward, determined to capture the three young agents. The next two guards fell one after the other and Eddy became even more enthusiastic to fight when Fei joined in. As the group of thundering twits—as Leo liked to call them—hit the ground and groaned or limped back up to attack once again, Leo seized the opportunity to whip out his sunglasses, signalling that he meant business.

Leaning over the unconscious guard still slumped against the door frame, Leo studied his face with apparent concern, sighing audibly. He then gave the guard his sunglasses, smiling as if he were dressing up a mannequin.

"Swag!" Leo added in a self-satisfied tone, pleased with the outcome. Straightening his back, he followed Eddy and Fei to the end of the corridor.

Eddy patted his vest. "I should buy more of these cheap things," he muttered to himself.

Fei signalled him to follow and the two quickly made their way to the office of the self-proclaimed President. Eddy strode confidently towards the door, his attention fixed on the guard who reached for a knife. With lightning-fast reflexes, Eddy dodged the guard's initial slash and countered with a powerful punch to his jaw. As the guard staggered back, Eddy brushed aside his disorientated attempt to counter-attack and landed an uppercut. The guard was slammed back against the doorframe and slid into a pile on the floor. Dismissing him as insignificant, Eddy flung the door open and boldly entered the room.

The Mobster-President jolted in surprise, quickly removing his feet from the desk as the pipe he was smoking slipped from his lips. A pungent cloud of smoke pervaded the room, so thick that it seemed to choke the air out of it. In the background, the melodious notes of "The Blue Danube" wafted softly.

As his eyes fell on the unexpected visitors, the President rose to his feet, but his initial recognition turned to fear as he took in their dishevelled appearance. He stumbled backwards, hitting his back against the closed windows in a moment of panic.

Eddy advanced with intense fury, his eyes blazing as he closed in on the mobster. In one swift motion, he seized the collar of the man's brown jacket with both hands.

Meanwhile, Leo strolled through the room, hands clasped behind his back. His gaze landed on the sinister portrait that had unsettled him since their first encounter, so he shuddered. With a shake of his head, he attempted to avoid the portraits that remained incomprehensible to him.

Eddy tightened his grip on the now vulnerable mobster, radiating a menacing presence that caused the latter to break out in a cold sweat.

"Where's my money?!" Eddy bellowed, delivering a performance so convincing that even he believed his own words.

With a sardonic chuckle, Eddy relaxed his grip, prompting an involuntary docile smile from the mobster, who was unsure of how to respond. Seeking to defuse the tension, the man forced out a loud laugh, but Eddy's menacing presence caused him to tense up again.

"The transfer won't happen tomorrow unless I receive my 50% now!"

"50%...?" stammered the Mobster-President. "Which 50%...?"

Eddy's grin grew wider as he observed the dawning realisation reflected in the mobster's eyes. He now knew that Eddy knew. Although the extent of Eddy's knowledge remained a mystery.

"Let's come up with a 50% right here and right now." Eddy spoke with an air of seriousness, a sly smile tugging at the corner of his mouth as he gestured for the mobster to take a seat at the desk.

“Snitch…” the man dared to whisper under his breath.

“What was that?” Eddy laughed. “Listen up. You see, folks in your position? They tend to end up swimming with the fishes. So how about you start spilling some names? We'll take care of our cut without any help from you.

“I’m not in charge.”

"Let's call it a deal,” Fei interfered while settling into the couch in a relaxed manner. “50% and we'll be out of here in no time.”

The atmosphere shifted as a group of guards in suits stormed into the room, sporting bloodied lips and swollen cheekbones.

"Yo, man, time to bounce, you losers!" Leo exclaimed with a flourish, raising his right hand with cool confidence.

The Mobster-President let out a resigned sigh, feeling utterly defenceless as he waved his hand urging the guards to withdraw and close the door behind them. To his relief, they obediently complied with his request.

"We'll sign the contract," he replied, projecting confidence as he directed his assured attention at the trio. “You have your 50% share.”

Eddy flashed a charming smile.

In a matter of minutes, the contract was meticulously drafted and signed with fingerprint signatures from both parties. Eddy held up the document with a sense of pride.

"May I ask… Mister Eddy," the President interjected, adopting a tone that was both amicable and deferential. "May I ask as to which organisation you represent?"

With a self-assured smile, Eddy reached into his pocket and pulled out his phone. He tapped away at the screen for a moment before presenting it to Leo. With a gesture that spoke volumes, he indicated that he had said all he needed to and that his subordinate would take it from there. As Fei rose to approach the phone, Leo stared at it with interest, eager to understand what Eddy had written. On the screen, an infinity symbol had been sketched out, leaving Leo wondering.

The room fell silent.

"Zero… Zero…" Leo said aloud. "Organisation... Zero Zero!" he exclaimed, enunciating each syllable with precision as he raised his head.

Fei let out an exasperated sigh as she brought her fingers up to her forehead. With his hand on the door handle, Eddy took a deep breath and wondered why he had allowed Leo to speak up in the first place.

"Ah, Organisation 00," confirmed the gangster with a nod of recognition. "I haven't heard of you people, but it seems like we're already closely connected."

With a shared sense of relief, Fei and Eddy let out a collective sigh.

Leo waved goodbye with a smile, biting his lower lip in style as he headed towards the door. Eddy and Fei followed suit, exiting the room behind him.

Chapter VIII

As midnight drew near, the team's GPS pinpointed a bar at the very end of a dimly lit narrow alleyway. It was flanked by a motley assortment of bars, clubs and restaurants exuding an air of seediness and uncertainty.

The entrance sign glowed with brilliant light and challenged them with its bold declaration of no admission fee, almost goading them to come in. Eddy couldn't help but laugh wryly as he recognised the irony. After all, it was apparent to him that the price of admission was nothing less than the currency of life itself. Leo fidgeted by shifting his weight from one foot to the other, trying to get used to the crammed street and the flashy lights beaming out of the different joints around them. Fei unfurled her locks, gracefully sweeping her fingers through each strand.

Eddy took one last look over his shoulder before slipping behind the half curtains and walking down the steps of the Harmony Dungeon. The other two followed Eddy without uttering a word.

As they made their way down the poorly-lit hallway, a guard materialised before them. His imposing figure causing the trio to come to an abrupt stop. With an outstretched palm, the guard simply waited. Eddy reached into his pocket and produced the contract he had received earlier, only to have it deftly snatched from his grasp. Without a word, the guard motioned towards the right side of the hallway, indicating the direction Eddy was to take.

Silently, they advanced down the hallway. Their steps were muffled by the sound-absorbing carpet. As they neared the end of the corridor, they noticed a partially-open door; a tantalising glimpse of the continuation of the same pathway beyond.

With a subtle hand gesture, a second guard communicated to the trio that they were required to leave behind any objects in their possession. It was a clear indication of the strict protocols in place. Eddy, Fei and Leo were quick to pull out whatever they had in their pockets and hand it over, following the request without any fuss.

As they stood in the semi-darkness, a third guard emerged holding three black blindfolds. With a nod from the guard, the three agents wordlessly blindfolded themselves.

They trudged down a straight corridor, navigating solely by sound and touch. Suddenly, a jolt beneath their feet signalled that they were in a lift. Judging by the sensation in their stomachs, they were most likely descending. Eddy's hand stretched out to graze Fei's elbow. Leo attempted to keep his emotions in check, but his adrenaline was already off the charts.

"You can take the blindfolds off now," one of the guards said as soon as the lift stopped.

All three removed their blindfolds and looked ahead in anticipation as the elevator doors opened.

"Holy shit, we actually made it here! This place really exists," Leo whispered under his breath, barely containing his excitement. "How far underground are we now? This is insane!"

The atmosphere was heavy with a musty smell of metal and concrete. The only sound that accompanied them was the resonance of their footsteps as they cautiously made their way forward.

Massive iron stairs loomed before them, leading to different sectors of the underground space. The stairs had seen better days, with rusted metal and chipped paint giving them an aged and weathered appearance.

The ceiling disappeared into the darkness above them, creating an overwhelming sense of height and space. The iron ceiling that must have served as the floor for the bar above stood like a weighty burden that was pressing down on them.

Despite the immense size of the hall, there was a sense of claustrophobia that surrounded them. The low light cast eerie shadows along the concrete walls and the occasional drip of water echoed through the space. The agents couldn't help but feel like they were descending into a dark and dangerous world, isolated from the rest of civilisation. Stillness in the vast hall had reached a suffocating level, creating a prison-like atmosphere where escape seemed impossible.

The sound of a gunshot shattered the eerie silence, causing Leo to whip his head towards Eddy.

Eddy gasped for air, clutching his left shoulder in the same instant. The searing pain left him unable to exhale. Fei's eyes widened in horror as she watched Eddy’s arm covered in blood.

“Eddy!” Leo's impatient call filled the room as he leaned towards him, desperate to help.

Fei searched for any signs of an attacker in the now empty hall. The two guards had meanwhile retreated and the vast space began to feel like a deadly trap for the trio.

Sinister laughter bounced of the walls of the hall, causing Leo to jump in alarm. Fei frantically looked around, but there was no one to be seen. The laughter grew louder, reverberating off the walls and making it impossible to determine its source.

As Leo hastily tore off his bandanna, his eyes widened at the sight of Eddy's wound. With a mix of dread and relief, he realised that the bullet had barely scraped Eddy's arm, leaving behind a shallow, crimson trail. Leo draped his bandanna over Eddy's shoulder, the fabric serving as a makeshift shield against the pain. Eddy directed his attention upward, his breathing laboured as he started struggling to remain upright. The male voice echoed seemingly from above, but it was most likely just the sound bouncing around the impressive room.

"Who are you?!" Leo shouted, turning around with trembling hands covered in his friend's blood.

The diabolical laughter filled the surroundings without pause. Fei balled her fists in anger.

"Who are you?!" Leo yelled again, losing his temper.

The voice consumed them, a deafening assault that left them reeling. The team struggled to regain their bearings amidst the relentless barrage of sound. In a desperate attempt to cope, Leo pressed his hands against his ears, squeezing his eyes shut in a futile effort to block out the sound. But the onslaught only intensified, pushing him to the brink of his sanity.

The pungent metallic tang of warm blood filled Leo's nostrils and he stared at his trembling hand in horror. A flood of confusion washed over him and as he glanced at Eddy, a wave of guilt threatened to consume him entirely. Slowly, the echoes of manic laughter subsided and the voice spoke for the first time, sending shivers down their spines:

"So, it finally dawned on you that you're the one to blame?"

The sudden outburst made all three of them jump, their heads snapping upward as they searched for the source. It didn't take long for Leo to realise that the words were directed at him.

"That's right, how does it feel?" the gruff voice sneered. "How could you do something like that?" the voice dripped with irony and criticism, directed squarely at Leo.

Leo raised both hands, looking impatiently at his palms.

"No way! You shot him!" Leo exclaimed, indignant but still disoriented.

"Are you absolutely sure?" the voice inquired, its repetition bouncing off the walls three times.

As Leo gasped for air, he turned to his friend in desperation for comfort, but Fei was at a loss for words to ease his distress. Leo's sense of guilt began to weigh heavily on him, despite not having done anything wrong. The voice snorted once more.

"Stop it, you know you did it!" Leo brought both hands to his temples as he couldn't bear it any more.

The echoes persisted from all directions, as though a chorus of voices were uniting in their amusement.

"Stop it!"

Fei tried to locate the source of the voice.

"You're not so sure yourself," the voice laughed, enjoying Leo's reaction.

Eddy concealed his agony but soldiered on, stepping closer to Leo.

"Calm down, he's playing with our minds."

Gradually, Leo's trembles ceased and he locked gazes with his friend, coming to the stark realisation of the veracity behind his words.

In an instant, one after the other, the colossal spotlights flickered and died, plunging the entire hall into uncanny darkness. The three agents held their breath, straining their ears for any hint of danger.

A loud noise shattered the stillness. The entire row of spotlights ignited in a dazzling column, making the sudden transition from pitch-black to blinding light almost unbearable.

As their vision gradually adjusted, they realised with a sinking feeling that they were completely surrounded. Triad members wielding deadly knives loomed over them from every direction, their faces twisted with amusement as they enjoyed the trio's terror. A tall man descended the metal stairs, casually tossing aside his pistol.

"Bravo! Bravo!" he exclaimed, clapping with a sardonic smirk.

Leo couldn't help but shudder at the sight of the foreboding tattoos adorning his assailant's arms and the untamed, disquieting gleam in his eyes. Desperately, he fought to conceal his rising fear.

"What if we showed a little hospitality and extended a warm welcome to our new guests?" the man suggested, gesturing towards his subordinates.

A second figure emerged from behind the trio, brandishing a knife and holding it directly at Eddy's throat.

The three young agents stood defenceless and immobile, their only hope for respite from the harassment of the mobsters was a swift end to it. Fei's body tensed as the mobster pressed his knife against Eddy's throat. He maintained his composure, clenching his left arm without so much as a flinch.

A hard nudge in the back signalled that they were to begin walking. Eddy moved without argument while Leo briefly entertained the idea of rebellion. But the two armed men lurking behind Fei caught him off guard, leaving him no choice but to follow Eddy's lead and abandoning any further attempts to resist.

"Bravo! Bravo!" the man exclaimed again, now moving along the platform.

As they approached, one of the metal doors slid open and invited them in. From the moment they entered, the mood shifted dramatically. The artificial light was dim and carried an oppressive, brown hue. The hall was sectioned off by towering grilles, revealing glimpses of movement within. The surroundings were filled with the sound of clattering machinery and frenzied voices coming from various rooms. As they looked around, it was clear that the people on either side of the hall were preoccupied with their tasks, but there was little indication that they were working together as a cohesive team.

As they were ushered forward, Eddy found himself leading the way, but it wasn't until some time had passed that he realised Leo and Fei had vanished. It dawned on him that they must've slipped away through one of the side doors that he had been instructed to avoid at all costs.

Upon entering, Eddy was forced to take a seat on the only chair next to a small table in a cramped, dimly lit room. The man he had encountered earlier materialised before him, now more than just a voice. Eddy took note of the tattoos on his arms, depicting ferocious animals and black roses dipped in blood. Seeing all of this, Eddy couldn't help but blink several times as the present image overlapped with the memory of the day his boss had revealed his back tattoo depicting a dragon. Eddy shook his head and closed his eyes. One of the members in the corner still had a gun pointed at him. The man laughed maniacally and leaned towards Eddy, resting his palms on his knees. With one hand still covering his wound, Eddy locked eyes with the man.

"Superb! Excellent!" he exclaimed theatrically. "I'm starting to like you!"

Eddy remained silent, his gaze fixed ahead.

In a nearby room, another member pushed Leo from behind. Leo's steps faltered, but he quickly pivoted around in anger. He placed his hand on his hip and lifted his index finger with purpose. Fei let out a sigh, hoping that the chaos wouldn't start all over again.

"Hey, you wanna know what the real problem is?!" Leo exclaimed, somewhat teasing the Triad member. "I mean, I don't know you and you don't know me, but the way you strut around here, it's all kinds of wrong. You think it's cool to wave a knife around and shove folks from behind just 'cause you got a couple extra inches in height?" Leo continued his lecture, gesticulating wildly. "Seriously, take a good look at yourself, man!"

The Triad member's expression turned puzzled as he glanced down at his chest before raising his head again.

"Is that how you like it? Do you really like the way you are now?" Leo pressed on.

The Triad member mulled over the question for a moment before childishly shrugging his shoulders.

Leo nodded in agreement with himself. "See, that's exactly what I'm talking about! You need to grow up and toughen up, man! This world's cruel!" Leo then paused, scanning the room with a careful eye. "I gotta ask, where's your other partner in crime, man? You know, the one who's been rolling with us until about a second ago. What happened to that dude?" He noticing that only the three of them remained in the cramped room.

Meanwhile, Eddy sat in the dimly lit room with his hands bound behind his chair. He straightened his back and flashed a confident smile, hoping to speedily win over their trust.

"Your every move screams 'coward'," Eddy muttered through clenched teeth, his wild gaze fixed in a manic stare as a trickle of blood ran down his face.

The Triad leader relished their conversation but was at a loss for words. "I don't even know what to say to you," he finally admitted.

Stepping back, he grabbed a knife from his subordinate's pocket after which he returned to Eddy.

Rather than brandishing the knife to intimidate him, he viciously struck him across the face. Eddy's head jerked sharply to the right. As he lifted his head again, blood seeped from his lip.

With a triumphant grin, the mobster leaned closer and stared into Eddy's face.

"Here it is." He savoured the sight before him as he clenched his teeth. He struck Eddy once more, causing the young man to wince and lower his head in a daze.

The man awaited a response from Eddy, but the resilient agent merely searched for the mobster's gaze, meeting his eyes without uttering a sound, despite spitting out blood.

With an air of overconfidence, the mobster wore a wide grin on his face. Keenly aware of the situation, Eddy made a subtle adjustment to his body positioning, ensuring that his movements remained inconspicuous. His gaze never wavered as he flexed his fingers, testing the tightness of the rope. His acute senses allowed him to gauge the exact tension required for success. Eddy deftly rotated his wrists in a clockwise motion, using the friction between the rope and his skin to his advantage. Slowly but surely, the coarse fibres began to give way, their grip loosening. He concealed any signs of discomfort or exertion, gritting his teeth as pain surged through his body.

"Ha!" scoffed the man, relishing in his power. "Let's see how much longer you can keep up."

He gripped his knife in one hand and seized Eddy's wounded arm with the other, tightening his grasp on the young agent's shoulder. Eddy balled his hands into fists and shut his eyes, the wound oozing blood. With a sudden release of his grip, the man then clasped his hand around Eddy's neck, curiously examining the young man's facial expression.

In the adjacent room, Leo stood with hands on his hips, emitting a forlorn sigh while slowly shaking his head. Fei watched with curious fascination as the dramatic scene unfolded.

"Wait, I've got a tale to tell," Leo proclaimed, assuming the air of an intellectual as he gestured with his hand and narrowed his eyes.

The mobster was now captivated by Leo's words, eagerly awaiting the information to come.

"I once had a friend just like you… you know… I think you might actually know him. And to him, well… I once said something..."

The mobster's pupils expanded in anticipation of the climax of his speech.

"*Hitler, mein Freund, carpe diem*!" Leo's face lit up as he leapt forward, catching the mobster off guard and delivering a swift kick to his wrist, causing the knife to clatter to the ground.

In one fluid motion, Leo scooped up the knife. A broad smile spread across his face. The mobster, now staring at his own blade, raised both hands in surrender. Fei's expression shifted from a smirk to one of astonishment and satisfaction, impressed with Leo's quick thinking and skilful execution.

In the other room, Eddy was finally released from the mobster's grasp. Gasping for air, he coughed and spluttered. The man laughed, seeing the blood marks he had left on the young man's neck.

Eddy heard the malicious laughter once more and a troubled expression clouded his face as he was weighed down by the heavy loss of blood. Despite his weakened state, he persevered in a long and gruelling struggle until he finally managed to free one hand from the tight grip of the rope that bound him. Though he remained silent, he closely tracked the man's movements.

With the man looming over him, Eddy's mind raced with a desperate plan of action. Despite one of his wrists still being bound, he managed to grab the end of the thick rope with his free hand. In one swift motion, he looped the rope around the mobster's neck, feeling the tension building in his muscles.

Surprised by Eddy's sudden movement, the mobster's laughter turned into a startled gasp. Eddy capitalised on the element of surprise, springing to his feet and briskly manoeuvring behind the mobster. With his captive now within his control, Eddy turned him sideways so that the mobster could also see his subordinate stationed at the door.

Realising the tables had turned, uncertainty flashed in the man's eyes as he struggled against the constricting rope around his neck. The subordinate guarding them reacted agilely and aimed his pistol at Eddy.

Undeterred, Eddy tightened his grip on the rope, applying pressure to the mobster's windpipe. The man gasped and choked, his face turning a deep shade of crimson.

To Eddy's surprise, he then began to laugh maniacally. The gurgled chuckles implied that he was deriving pleasure from the spectacle of his own impending demise. With a faint wave of his hand, he signalled the subordinate to lower his pistol and step back. He was eager to savour every moment of his grisly fate.

As his face became fully flushed and the veins on his forehead threatened to burst, the man's laughter gradually subsided. His lips were still curved into a smile.

Realising that he had accomplished his goal, Eddy released the man who plummeted onto his knees, gasping desperately for air. The subordinate readied his pistol once more. The leader slowly regained his composure and straightened his back. Eddy held his ground, studying both men intently.

"Marvelous!" the leader exclaimed, applauding in admiration. He gestured for his subordinate to exit the room.

With the door shut behind him, only the two adversaries remained locked in a tense stand-off. The man rolled his shoulders and neck, signalling his readiness for a fight. He stretched his arms and rotated his wrists in a way that suggested that this was not his first rodeo.

Meanwhile, Eddy winced in pain as he touched his wound. After a brief display of fancy footwork, the man extended both palms, indicating that he was prepared to begin. Eddy remained undaunted, grinning confidently as he clenched his fists. Fuelled by adrenaline, he embraced the rush of energy coursing through his veins. The heightened sense of awareness sharpened his focus, amplifying his determination to succeed.

Without further hesitation, they launched simultaneous attacks.

Amidst the chaotic sounds of fists connecting and bodies slamming against walls coming from the next room, Leo and Fei had managed to overpower their opponent and emerge victorious. As they burst out of the cramped room and onto the hallway, they held the once-feared mobster captive between them.

"Come on! Let's see some action, man!" Leo prodded, pressing the blade of his knife into the mobster's back.

The two agents surveyed their surroundings with cautious eyes, trying to acclimatise themselves to the unfamiliar environment.

"What the hell are you doing, Eddy?" Leo's voice took on a tone of both indignation and curiosity.

In the secluded room nearby, the leader wiped the blood from his mouth. He leaned against the wall trying to take a quick break. Eddy fought to keep his bearings, shaking his head and blinking repeatedly to keep the room in focus.

Fuelled by determination to win, his opponent leapt back into the fight with renewed vigour. The man's fists flew in a flurry of punches, aiming for Eddy's face and body. Eddy managed to evade some of the blows, but others landed with brutal force. As he absorbed a particularly powerful blow to his jaw, Eddy stumbled backwards with blurred vision. Gritting his teeth, he pushed through the pain and found his balance. He charged back into the fray, his fist colliding with raw power. Eddy's right hook landed square on the mobster's cheek, the impact causing both fighters to lose their footing. They crashed to the floor in a tangle of limbs with the air knocked out of their lungs.

Gasping for breath, Eddy fought through the exhaustion. Struggling to regain his senses, the man propped himself up on one elbow, blood trickling from a split lip. His face was contorted in pain, but the fire in his eyes remained. Eddy fought against the spinning room. He knelt down and tried to steady himself, so he grabbed hold of the mobster's shirt. The room appeared to dissolve into the background as Eddy launched a flurry of punches. With each strike, the mobster's consciousness waned. Eddy's knuckles burned with pain, the numbing ache creeping up his arm, but he refused to stop. He knew that if he let up for even a moment, his opponent might have a chance to recover. The violence of the punches caused the man's face to swell and contort. His breathing became shallow. Eddy shook the man's body, aware that he needed to keep him conscious. The sound of his exertion filled the room.

Eddy released his grip and the man collapsed on his back. His body was bloodied and battered, yet an insidious grin was still etched on his face, hinting at a twisted satisfaction. The room fell into a heavy silence. Eddy stood up, his hair matted with blood. In the midst of this eerie stillness, the leader's laughter pierced through. A chilling sound that sent shivers down Eddy's spine, serving as a grim reminder that the battle was far from over.

The sound echoed all the way outside, causing Leo to flinch and turn his head towards the source.

Eddy let out a tired sigh, while the man rose to his feet, shaking off the dust from his clothes.

"Excellent!" the man exclaimed, his guffaw ringing out as he theatrically raised both fists to head level.

Eddy stood still as the man limped towards him. Instinctively, his hands clenched into taut fists as the man's face broke into a seemingly affable smile. Eddy braced himself for the possibility of another fight. Much to his astonishment though, the man surged forward, wrapping him in an unexpected embrace while affectionately patting him on the back with an encouraging gesture. Caught off guard, Eddy's mind raced, unsure of how to react. He ultimately surrendering to the warmth of the unexpected embrace.

Leo forcefully pushed the mobster he was holding hostage aside and stormed into the room, accompanied by a focused Fei. Eddy was instantly freed from the man's unexpected grasp, acknowledging the sudden shift in his behaviour. With a quick adjustment of his focus, Eddy turned his attention towards Leo and Fei, signalling that the situation was now fully under control.

"I'm Tiger," said the leader, raising his right hand in a friendly salute.

Eddy winced in pain but clenched his teeth and took a step forward.

"I'm Eddy." He extended his arm and firmly shook Tiger's hand.

The man's attention shifted to one of admiration, his expression almost devoid of suspicion. Observing the exchange, Leo lowered his knife and moved closer. Tiger turned his head towards the two, releasing Eddy's hand.

"I'm the Left-Hander-With-The-Right-Fist!" Leo confidently introduced himself.

“Fei.” She strode forward, presenting herself with a graceful nod of her head.

Tiger greeted them with warmth, his jaw clenched and his lips taut with respect.

Chapter IX

Despite Tiger's admiration, the trio had little to show for the night besides a dimly lit room, a meagre pile of blankets and a basic first aid kit.

The cramped and dank chamber resembled a prison cell, its walls crafted from frigid stone and metal. Submerged deep underground, the scant illumination did little to lift the shroud of darkness. Only the steady rhythm of dripping water broke the eerie silence, the sound reverberating off the walls. The pervasive dampness caused moisture to cling to every surface. A sense of gloom and foreboding hung in the space, designed to invoke despair in those confined within. A thick and musty odour permeated the atmosphere.

Leo had already curled up in a corner, hugging himself tightly and occasionally shivering under his thin blanket.

Eddy struggled to locate a clean towel from inside the first aid kit, his knees trembling as he knelt. In a deft move, Fei seized the tools and held out a fresh towel, urging Eddy to take it.

"Hang in there. I'll do my best to make this as painless as possible," she whispered reassuringly, uncorking the bottle of disinfectant and promptly setting it down on the cold concrete.

Eddy nodded and clenched the towel tightly in his mouth. Fei took a deep breath and approached the wound. Tears welled up in her eyes as she watched Eddy suffer, his head against the wall and his body shivering.

Fei's touch was gentle as she cleansed Eddy's arm, her fingertips tracing the edges of the wound with utmost care. Wrapping a fresh bandage around his shoulder, she secured it with a tender touch, reassuring him of her presence. Overcome with fatigue, Eddy closed his eyelids.

Fei noticed he was still trembling. With a concerned expression, she set aside the kit and moved closer. She gently took his cold hands into her own and enclosed them between her palms, blowing warm air to try and ease his discomfort.

As a faint ray of light filtered through the grates on the wall above, it illuminated his damp strands of sweat, prompting Fei to reach out and tenderly wipe his forehead with her fingertips. Without hesitation, she pulled him into a warm embrace, resting her head on his chest. He remained trembling, his eyes shut tightly as she felt his heavy breath.

"*Please pardon my audacity, Princess, but the night may bring a chill!*" Fei was suddenly startled by the sound of Eddy's voice, though it felt as if it had come from another world.

Eddy had already drifted off to sleep. She closed her eyes and took a deep breath as she whispered softly:

"Eddy, forgive me, but it will get cold overnight!"

The next morning, Leo was squatting in silence in front of the pair.

The artificial light filtered through the grates above, spotlighting the dancing dust particles. Eddy slept soundly. Propped up against the cool wall, his breathing indicated a vast improvement. Meanwhile, Fei rested peacefully, her head nestled against his healthy shoulder. Leo couldn't help but stare in disbelief, extending his finger to briefly poke Eddy's forehead. Suppressing a chuckle, he watched on as the two slept obliviously.

After another nudge, Eddy flinched, hitting his head against the wall. The commotion roused Fei from her sleep, prompting her to withdraw her arm from beside Eddy.

Wearing a look of suspicion, Leo shifted his tongue between molars and observed the two. He then turned his attention to Eddy, raising an eyebrow.

"Well, good morning," Leo said, his voice tinged with sarcasm as he rested his palms on his knees and stood up. As Eddy eased away from the wall, Fei shot him a worried glance.

"Your dressing needs changing!" She sprang to her feet to rummage through the kit.

Eddy grabbed her wrist, stopping her next to him.

"It's fine, I can handle it myself."

"Let me help you." she insisted, taking out a clean bandage and searching for the disinfectant.

"It's okay, I can handle it." He reached out to take the bottle of disinfectant from her hand. Leo peered down at them, arching his other eyebrow in puzzlement.

Minutes later, Eddy swung open the colossal door that led to the seemingly endless hallway. The clamour of machinery carried through the corridor.

One of Tiger's subordinates revealed themselves from behind the door. He hesitated and then elected to remain silent.

The claustrophobic hallway stretched ahead, its narrowness amplifying the sense of confinement. A suffocating atmosphere pervaded, intensified by the dim lighting that cast elongated shadows on the walls. To the left, a tall iron wall stood ominously, its imposing structure obstructing the view beyond. Small perforations punctuated its surface, offering tantalising glimpses into a world of machinery and bustling activity. The distant hum of engines and the rhythmic clanking of gears filled the space, mingling with muffled voices that echoed through the holes. The trio's curiosity surged, their imaginations ignited by the enigma concealed behind the iron barrier.

Nestled beside the towering iron wall, the trio walked with a mixture of anticipation and trepidation. Their fingertips felt the chilling touch of the metal. Amidst the muffled hum of machinery, their attention fixated on a towering four-meter-high door, a jagged portal that beckoned them forward. Eddy nodded, acknowledging the subtle cue from the subordinate and they prepared to step through the enigmatic threshold.

Inside, Tiger was sprawled out on a plush leather sofa. Upon noticing their arrival, he took a drag of his cigarette and flashed a friendly wave, as if the bruises on his face were merely a whimsical accessory. Eddy reciprocated with a smile, closing in on the relaxed figure.

"Eddy, you made it! Take a seat," Tiger gestured, making room for him on the inviting sofa.

The trio settled in, though Leo remained slightly confused. He scanned the room for the source of the noise.

Tiger produced another cigarette, lighting it with a flick of his fingers before carelessly tossing the lighter onto the low table to sit among other trinkets. Leo couldn't resist a critical mutter under his breath, his words lost in the din.

"Care for a smoke, Eddy?" Tiger proffered his pack, its price tag commanding triple that of standard fare.

Eddy politely declined, prompting Tiger to turn his attention to Leo. However, he too declined with a shake of his head.

"Not a smoker either, I see. How about a drag?" Tiger shifted tactics, extending his lit cigarette towards Fei.

As she caught a glimpse of his piercing eagle-like stare, she snatched the cigarette from his grasp. She took a puff and handed it back to him with an air of indifference. Eddy jumped a little in surprise. Amused by the woman's beauty and her nonchalant act, Tiger flashed a grin and took the cigarette back between his fingers.

After a brief pause, Tiger shifted the topic. "Sorry for that wound," he said as he turned to face Eddy.

Eddy smiled in response, mimicking Leo's gesture and running his tongue over his teeth.

“I've caught wind of your little request there,” Tiger added. “The 50%, right? Listen up! When you're dealing with those pathetic losers, you gotta understand who's really in control here. Anything you desire, you name it, and I'll make sure it lands in your lap. You and me, we're like blood now, inseparable. From stacks of cash to the finest reputation and even the most alluring dames; everything you crave, I've got it at my fingertips. We're brothers now, you understand?"

Just then, one of Tiger's subordinates stepped in and interrupted their conversation with an urgent message.

"Brother, Kingpin needs to talk to you."

Tiger extinguished his cigarette with a sharp flick of his wrist and rose to his feet.

"I'll be right back," he announced, before disappearing behind the towering iron fence with his subordinates trailing behind him.

Eddy heaved a deep sigh, expelling all the air from his lungs in a single breath. Leo curiously leaned closer towards Fei.

"Do you smoke?"

Fei shook her head, a confident smile lighting up her face.

"No."

Leo's brows furrowed in confusion.

"Then...?"

"I'm Agent Fei. How about you?" she stated in a hushed tone, as though she were clarifying the most obvious thing in the world.

Leo looked down at his feet, still a little perplexed. Eddy chuckled, pleased with Fei's bold statement.

"I used to smoke back in high school," Leo admitted, his voice tinged with melancholy. "But then my mum caught me. Man! She wasn't happy about it at all, you know what I mean? She straight-up hit me with a frying pan, like bam! And to make it worse, she grounded me for three whole weeks! And get this, it was during freaking summer vacation! Like, what kinda timing is that? And on top of all that madness, she had me solve math problems all day long. Can you believe that? It was like torture." Leo's tone suggested that he still felt the sting of his punishment. "Anyway, that whole experience opened my eyes, you know? Made me realise that smoking isn't worth it, not at all. I don't need Tiger's weed or any of that stuff."

In the next instant, Tiger returned, beckoning the three forward with a wave of his hand.

As they walked, they were handed clothes to change into in order to be prepared for what was to come.

They arrived before a grand entrance that opened up to a vast hall. Leo couldn't help but be awed by his surroundings. Rows upon rows of people were seated before them, an army of hundreds. Upon closer inspection, Fei could make out the tattoos etched on the skin of each individual. The flickering candlelight cast enormous shadows on the cavernous walls, lending the place an eerie ambiance.

At the centre of the room, an altar exuded an irresistible allure, captivating all who beheld it. Fashioned from ancient stone, it showcased carvings depicting long-forgotten gods and mysterious ceremonies. Enhanced by the soft glow of flickering candles, its very essence echoed with the whispers of age-old secrets and profound wisdom, as if it guarded the gateway to eternal truths.

A commanding figure emerged from behind the sacred sanctuary. As he stepped forward, the flickering light revealed the haunting remnants of a fiery past etched upon his visage. Half of his face bore the scars of severe burns. Despite the disfigurement, his piercing eyes held an intensity that demanded attention. He wore a long, thick cloth that covered his arms and neck. However, he couldn't hide the scars on his face. They stood as a constant, tangible reminder of a truth he couldn't escape.

As he focused intently on the three young newcomers, Leo experienced a shiver running down his spine. Eddy couldn't help but make a connection between this man and his own boss, both of similar age and stature. Yet, where Boss exuded warmth, this man emanated a chilling aura that left no doubt as to his authority.

As the trio watched the seconds tick by, Boss, back at the police department, leaned heavily against his sturdy desk. His deep contemplation gave rise to a swirling realm where thoughts and reality intertwined, creating a vivid fusion. The agent who was stationed beside him at the computer, stood up with a worried expression. Though he longed to inquire about Boss's well-being, the weight of the moment made him hesitate.

Two decades ago, Boss found himself face-to-face with the formidable figure known as KB for the first time. The encounter took place amidst the chaotic atmosphere of an exuberant acceptance ceremony. KB, whose initials represented the chilling moniker "King and Blood," boldly showcased his inked masterpieces sprawled across his chest, arms and back. Each tattoo encapsulated his ruthless reputation and power. It was a striking sight, as KB's body art depicted a menacing narrative. Back then, the absence of scars on KB's body painted an invincible image.

Little did KB and his devoted followers know, Boss had an agenda of his own. In a subtle yet powerful gesture, Boss revealed his own tattoo. A silent proclamation that marked the establishment of a clandestine organisation operating covertly under the watchful eye of the Triads. While KB revelled in his grand display of dominance, oblivious to the hidden intentions surrounding him, Boss and his team assumed their roles.

Back to present times, Eddy, Leo and Fei knelt before the altar, their every move scrutinised. Unable to endure the earlier demands any longer, Leo stood up in protest. His voice thundered so fiercely that it filled the room.

"Hey, I don't know what name you go by, KB or whatever, but I hope you weren't serious about what you just said!"

Startled, Eddy and Fei turned their gaze towards Leo. From behind the altar, KB descended, casting an immense shadow in the flickering candlelight. As he approached Leo, a sinister expression settled on his face.

Tiger's ears perked up, taking in every word as the crowd of thousands was silent as the grave.

Leo threw up his hands in protest.

"Come on, man!" he whined. "You want me to cut my hand, mix my own blood with this stagnant water and drink it? That's gross! What's next, a tattoo of your face on here?" He turned around and smacked his own rear end. "Sorry, pal, but that's a hard no from me."

Eddie weighed up his friends' apprehension against the urgency of the mission. Arriving at his conclusion, he grabbed the knife and swiftly sliced his left palm. He collected the flowing blood in his fist. Leo gasped in disbelief, his words of caution now rendered pointless by his friend's sudden action. KB observed the scene with utmost seriousness. Fei also took the knife, joining Eddie in pouring their drops of blood into the bowls of water.

"Guys, what are you doing?" Leo whispered, still trying to dissuade them, his eyes darting nervously between his team and the intimidating Triad members.

He then attempted to smile at KB, hoping to avoid the unspeakable horrors he had already witnessed. Sensing Leo's reluctance and agitation, KB motioned to Tiger, who promptly marched over and shoved Leo towards the altar. Trembling, Leo knelt and felt the cold steel of the knife pressed into his hand.

"Hey, you know what this is? I feel like we can solve this whole thing without all the drama. Let's think about it together, do we really need to spill blood for a little agreement?" Leo blurted out, his anxiety mounting.

Leo was surrounded by a group of people devoid of any compassion. Instead of support, he received a shove from behind by Tiger, urging him to hurry up and stop speaking. Leo's shoulders slumped and his hands began to quiver as he set his gaze on the bowl of water. Hoping for a way out of trouble, he forced a laugh and desperately sought eye contact with someone. However, Tiger shoved him again, causing Leo to brandish his knife with a shaking hand.

"What an exquisite knife!" Leo tried to lighten the mood while holding up the blade. "What a charming piece, ha-ha!"

Tiger's demeanour intensified as he firmly grasped Leo's right wrist, compelling him to slice his palm. As the sharp blade inched closer to Leo's hand, he began to frantically shake.

"Please, just a little more time! There's so much left for me to consider! What if my muscles aren't relaxed enough and the blood clots? I haven't even approved of this yet!"

KB and the other mobsters looked on, bored and exasperated by Leo's ramblings.

"What if I get tetanus? Will you cover my hospital bills? They sure won't be cheap!"

Tiger drew the knife closer to his palm.

"A-ha-ha-ouch... mummy!" Leo complained when Tiger nicked his palm, leaving a shallow cut.

Eddy and Fei let out a collective sigh of relief. Prompted by Tiger, Leo pricked his palm, letting a few droplets of blood fall into the water. With a signal from KB, they were all compelled to drink to the very last drop. Leo gagged in disgust, while Eddy and Fei clenched their eyes shut. In the meantime, the crowd of men had prostrated themselves on the floor, their voices raised in an unintelligible chant.

"Let this be a tribute to the Organisation—" proclaimed KB, his hands raised high in the air as he struggled to find the right words to express his devotion.

"The Organisation 00!" Eddy completed his sentence, bowing his head towards the altar. The crowd's synchronised chant was so loud that Leo winced in response.

With this ritual, the trio of young agents had officially become members of the secret fraternity. Carefully setting the bowl down on the altar, Eddy maintained his attention fixed on the spot, a self-satisfied smile playing on his lips as he realised their plan had worked perfectly. Emboldened, Leo lifted his eyes and scanned the crowd. His face lit up with recognition as he caught sight of someone in the distance.

"Kevin Lee!" Leo shrieked in a hushed whisper. "It's little Kevin Lee!" he added with a beaming smile directed towards the individual who remained oblivious to his gaze.

As Leo delved into the memories of the IDs they had examined together in their office some time ago, a smile formed on his face. It felt like Li Li's presence magically materialised in that very moment. Amidst the surge of emotions that washed over him, Leo couldn't help but shake his head in disbelief. But these bittersweet feelings only grew stronger as he closed his eyes. In that nostalgic reverie, Leo acknowledged that those times weren't so bad after all. He came to realise that, compared to his current circumstances, those days held a certain charm. The weight of melancholy lifted momentarily, replaced by a renewed appreciation for the moments he shared with his wider team. The camaraderie, the inside jokes and the humorous banter now held a special place in his heart.

KB had disappeared without warning, leaving the team bewildered. Tiger came along and nudged Eddy to his feet. The three agents turned towards the crowd, ready to respond with a bow to their unintelligible chants.

With a warm smile, Tiger urged Eddy and the team to follow him. With the crowd still chanting behind them, they fell in step behind Tiger as he led the way.

The rusty metal walls loomed over them, with occasional patches of peeling paint revealing the underlying decay. Drops of water from leaking pipes echoed throughout the narrow corridor. Their progress was slow, but steady, as they wound their way deeper into the labyrinthine maze. Finally, after what felt like an eternity, they surfaced from the dingy corridor into the refreshing light of day.

Chapter X

Tiger had adroitly covered his arm tattoos with a fashionable, lightweight long-sleeved shirt. The trio swapped their attire for casual clothing.

Tasked by none other than KB himself, Tiger felt compelled to form a bond with his new team members. Determined to facilitate this process, he ruminated on ways to loosen up and get to know each other in a relaxed setting. Pushed by Leo's insistence, he agreed on a carefree destination that promised equal parts fun and adventure. Although feeling awkward about the idea, he led them to an amusement park.

As they sauntered through the entrance of the park, Eddy recognised the significance of the moment and resolved to play his part and fully immerse himself in the experience. With an air of enthusiasm, he retrieved the camera he took from one of the subordinates and began capturing the vivacious surroundings. However, his attempts were quickly halted as Tiger covered his lens.

“Come on.” Leo attempted to persuade Tiger to relax, gesturing emphatically before soothingly massaging his shoulders. “Loosen up.”

Undeterred, Leo then took the lead and guided Fei through the vibrant ambiance, acquainting her with the attractions.

Eddy and Tiger followed at a distance. Fei shifted her gaze towards Eddy and he responded with a warm smile. Their brief moment was interrupted as Leo hurriedly approached, diverting Fei's attention back to him. As he neared Eddy, a growing sense of unease enveloped Tiger, making him feel out of place with the young crew.

After a short while, Leo came back brimming with enthusiasm and excitement. He tightly held four ice creams in his hand.

"Why this one? You know I don't like vanilla," Eddy protested, upset with his friend's carelessness. "I thought we knew each other."

"Here, let's exchange," Fei suggested, smiling and offering her chocolate ice cream to Eddy.

Leo extended the third ice cream to Tiger, urging him to take it.

"I'm allergic to strawberries," Tiger muttered, looking away and feigning disinterest.

"Then let's trade!" Leo suggested and shoved his ice cream in front of his face.

Tiger snatched the ice cream from Leo's hand as if he had forced him to, tasting it as if he was obligated to do so. Leo grinned foolishly, then turned to Eddy and Fei, who were already walking ahead. Feeling guilty for holding the chocolate ice cream that was undoubtedly much tastier than Fei's, Eddy offered her his cone, encouraging her to try it.

Instead, she lifted her vanilla ice cream, the rich aroma of the frozen treat tempting him. Eddy shook his head, refusing to indulge, but her insistent gesture made him lean in. In a sudden move, she playfully smeared the sweet cream on his cheek, causing him to jump in surprise. Fei laughed, her finger pointing at him in amusement, delighted at how easily she had fooled him.

A few steps behind, Leo squinted in suspicion. He then sighed, nodding his head at Tiger.

"Hey, over here. Let's toast to loneliness!" he exclaimed, touching his ice cream cone to Tiger's before hurrying to catch up with the others.

Tiger savoured his ice cream in blissful silence, no longer pretending he didn't enjoy it. Eddy gestured towards the ominous tunnels where trains whizzed by, but Fei shook her head in fear. Despite her reluctance, Eddy persisted, already making his way to purchase tickets.

Leo tugged Tiger along, eagerly following the others.

On days like this, even the most sour treats seemed to taste sweeter. Fei glowed with excitement as she gazed at the jewellery on display. Eddy focused his camera and snapped a secret photo, smiling at the screen as he enlarged the successful shots.

Leo fed Tiger cotton candy from a small plastic box and Eddy playfully placed a cowboy hat on Fei's head, eager to capture the moment in a photo. Tiger followed along in quiet contentment, seemingly unaccustomed to enjoying such simple pleasures in the daylight. Fei pointed to the water-filled balloons hanging on either side of an interactive game.

Eddy paused in his role as group photographer and trailed after his companion. Discovering a comical wig, Leo tossed it in Tiger's direction, hinting that it might enhance his appearance, given his unappealing, almost brush-like haircut. Amused by Tiger's puzzled expression, Leo chortled briefly before sprinting in the direction of Eddy, as a precaution, in case Tiger considered resuming his former role as an assassin. Left to his own devices, Tiger stood alone, bewildered, gazing at the wig before returning it to its original place, questioning why he had allowed himself to be involved in such affairs.

The group made their way through the bustling theme park, their eyes wide with wonder and their voices filled with laughter. They immersed themselves in the atmosphere, where the sounds of cheerful music and the aroma of popcorn filled the air. A hand suddenly tapped Eddy's shoulder as they weaved through the lively crowds. It was Li Li.

The trio whirled around in astonishment. Li Li's gaze flitted briefly towards Tiger before nonchalantly pivoting away, as if unaware of the situation at hand. The agents took her cue and followed suit. Despite her apparent relaxed demeanour, Li Li was immediately troubled by the scrapes on Eddy's face.

"Your uncle visited today. He told me to give you his regards," she said. "He asked if you were doing fine."

Eddy nodded.

"Tell him I'm fine," Eddy declared, careful to avoid any hint of suspicion. "And let him know that... I'll honour my word." Eddy's voice trailed off wistfully before he regained his composure. "Yes, I'll make good on my promise and visit him at the earliest convenience."

Li Li wasted no time in joining the group as soon as Eddy took the lead. Leo noticed Tiger's subtly raised eyebrow and narrowed gaze, perceiving his underlying suspicion. He couldn't dismiss the doubt emanating from Tiger. With a meaningful glance, Leo acknowledged Li Li's presence and conveyed that Li Li was nothing more than an innocent old friend.

Eddy's face lit up with happiness as he reached for his camera, eager to capture the moment. With an excited gesture, he pointed towards the vibrant trees in full bloom, just across the road. Li Li hastened her steps, keeping pace with Leo as she joyfully called out Eddy's name.

She then came to an abrupt halt when she saw Fei gently holding onto Eddy's arm and giggling as she pointed to the flower park. Sensing trouble, Leo reached out and took Li Li's hand, shaking his head ever so slightly to dissuade her from coming between Eddy and Fei. As he held Li Li's hand, Leo couldn't help but wonder if he had acted in his friend's best interest or if he had let jealousy cloud his judgement.

Standing under the cherry tree, Eddy waved to Leo, Li Li and Tiger, pointing at his camera.

"Hurry up, let's take a photo."

Tiger lingered off to the side, observing the scene. Noticing his reticence, Eddy passed him the camera, taking care to show him how to operate it. The quartet huddled closely together, forming a tight-knit group. When the moment was right, Tiger lifted the camera and the four of them beamed with smiles. The first shot was a success, prompting Eddy to beckon for Tiger to join in the fun. Despite the invitation,

Tiger remained solemn and hesitant, shaking his head in consternation.

With a sudden move, Eddy pulled Tiger from behind and brought him closer to the group. He raised the camera, determined to take the perfect group photo. After a moment of hesitation, even Tiger cracked a smile, just enough to capture the moment in a photograph.

The camera clicked, freezing the group's smiling faces. The vivid hues of the blossoming trees and flowers encircling them only added to the cheerful ambience. Nevertheless, they were all aware that this instance of joy would soon be eclipsed by the gravity of their clandestine affairs.

The photograph immortalised their happy faces, but it also captured the final vestiges of their innocence before everything was about to change. Blood would be spilt and the group's accountability would be questioned. The happiness in their eyes would give way to apprehension and regret and the park's vibrant colours would soon give way to the obscurity of their secrets.

However, for that fleeting moment, they experienced true happiness.

As the sun set, Eddy pulled up near a row of restaurants and stepped out of the car with a sense of urgency, announcing that he needed to dash across the street to grab some take-out. As Tiger prepared to follow suit, Leo waved him off and joined his friend instead, already bounding towards the traffic light. By confiding one of his precious cars to Eddy, Tiger demonstrated his deep trust in the capable driver.

Meanwhile, Tiger reclined in his seat and shut the door, making himself comfortable. Now barefoot, Li Li propped up her legs on the front passenger seat and retrieved her phone, tapping away aimlessly as she fought boredom.

She flicked through an album of the most striking Hollywood actors, breaking the silence with intermittent giggles that piqued Fei's curiosity. With an infectious grin, she turned her screen towards Fei, proudly showcasing her favourite pictures and biting her tongue with delight.

"Do you know him?"

Fei shrugged.

"Since his debut in that film back in 2014, he's become a household name! You can't possibly tell me you haven't heard of him!"

Fei shook her head, waiting to see the next photo.

"How about him?"

"I like him. I've seen him on TV a couple of times," Fei said, touching the screen with a finger.

"Isn't he gorgeous?" Li Li exclaimed, zooming in on the image.

As the conversation carried on, Tiger leaned in, his curiosity piqued by the subject at hand. Li Li playfully covered her screen with her left hand and flashed a mischievous smile. Despite the attention, Tiger remained stoic and silently returned to his previous position.

"Brad Pretty!" Li Li presented with enthusiasm. "Do you like Brad Pretty?"

"I don’t know, is he still around?" Fei asked, scratching her forehead.

"For God's sake! Of course he is!" Li Li clasped her hands together while holding her phone between her palms. "He's exactly my type!" she sighed. "I wish I was Angela Juliana…"

Fei offered a reassuring smile and chimed in, "You're beautiful too! And you're destined for a great life yourself, you'll see."

Li Li blushed at the compliment and looked away, shyly avoiding a response. She then flipped through yet another photo album, eagerly presenting the screen to Fei.

"What about him?!" Her eyes widened in excitement. "Ho… Hoo…" she stumbled over his name, the syllables falling from her lips as she tilted her head to the side, admiring the image in her mind's eye. "Anyway, this is him." She pointed to the photo with a grin. "He's everything I've ever dreamed of!"

As Fei struggled to recall the unfamiliar names that continued to be mentioned, Li Li leaned in as if to divulge a secret. With a curious expression, she extended a finger towards the phone in her hand.

"Tell me, would you kiss a guy like this? You know, like in Hollywood!" Li Li's question was posed with utmost seriousness, as she waited with bated breath for Fei's response.

Fei chuckled and flashed a warm smile while at a loss for words. Tiger listened intently, but couldn't make sense of the conversation.

Li Li gestured towards her lips and clarified, "I'm not referring to a brief peck, but that kind of kiss, you know..." Her words trailed off as Fei leaned in, intrigued.

Li Li scanned the bustling street as she spoke her mind.

"To be honest, I've thought about it a few times. But I wouldn't just kiss anyone like that… no way!" She shook her head in disbelief at the thought. "I mean, just look around us… definitely not!" She cast a disapproving gaze at the pedestrians waiting at the traffic lights.

Li Li's tone softened as she continued, "Maybe a quick kiss, but definitely not that kind of kiss. I would reserve that for someone special." Her face lit up with the thought of a loving partner who cherished her. "Someone who truly cares about me and shows it. Someone who calls every night to check up on me and says 'Have you eaten? Are you okay?... Sleep well!'" Li Li punctuated her words with a theatrical flourish, raising her phone to mimic the action. "Yes, I would definitely do it with someone like that."

Fei chuckled in response but remained silent, leaving the conversation hanging. Finally, Tiger's face brightened with comprehension as he realised the topic of discussion.

Their conversation was abruptly cut short by the sound of the car door swinging open. Leo strode closer, holding bags of steaming hot food in his hand. He chucked one of them into Li Li's arms.

"Eat up, I don't want you starving in my presence," he added with a lack of facial expression.

"You see what I mean?" Li Li's disappointment was clearly evident as she muttered to Fei, yet her satisfaction was equally tangible as she surveyed her meal. The sight of her favourite side dish and the perfectly fried chicken brought her immense contentment.

Eddy placed the drinks on the sleek car hood before handing the packaged food to Fei and Tiger.

Meanwhile, Leo settled into his cherished spot next to the driver and began rummaging through the bag to unearth his meal. As Tiger calmly chewed his food while watching the passing cars, Eddy leaned back against the seat and smiled at the team.

"Enjoy," he said to his comrades, then looked at Fei, encouraging her not to hesitate to help herself.

With a gloomy look on her face, Li Li took out a chicken wing and squinted her eyes as she began to sing:

"I've been here for so long, but I still feel empty and alone... Our story..." Li Li's sombre words lingered, causing Leo to abruptly lean forward and raise both hands in surprise. Just as he was about to respond, he realised his mouth was full and quickly searched for his can of Coke.

"Stop her, please!" Leo implored, still chewing and struggling to swallow. "She's not only ugly, but she also can't carry a tune to save her life."

Li Li persisted in singing, determined to rise above the negativity that often befalls artists due to envy and criticism.

Leo's plea for relief was met with high-pitched notes that made him cover his ears. Fei and Tiger found amusement in the situation, while Eddy humorously suggested an alternative solution by pointing towards the radio and asking if turning it on would be a better option. Leo frantically shook his head, determined to avoid another unpleasant situation and raised a hand to signal for Eddy to stop.

Eddy, Tiger and Fei casually diverted their attention and resumed eating, as though unfazed by the disturbance. Leo scanned his surroundings in a state of desperation, seeking a way out. Li Li managed to remain composed by clenching both fists, all the while continuing to sing out loud. Just like in Hollywood.

Chapter XI

Precisely at the stroke of midnight, a surge of tension swept through the brotherhood.

Through the dimly lit corridors of the Harmony Dungeon, Tiger strode alone, his fists clenched like coiled springs and his eyes ablaze with anticipation. Disregarding Leo's presence as he brushed past, Tiger abruptly veered left and vanished behind the imposing wall of cold iron. Leo stood frozen, his outstretched hand suspended, the remnants of his greeting swallowed by the oppressive silence. Leo's face twisted in confusion. But just as quickly, the uncertainty gave way to a casual shrug. He then set off on a determined quest to track down Eddy in the nearby rooms.

Tiger burst into an illuminated sanctum. His forceful movement effortlessly displaced subordinate figures in his path, until he confronted one of his comrades leaning nonchalantly against a rack laden with jet-black crates.

"What do you mean you lost them?!" Tiger bellowed with a ferocity that reverberated through the room. His fingers dug into the collar of his colleague's shirt.

"They slipped away before I could seal the deal. They betrayed us, plain and simple," Tony shot back, struggling to break free from Tiger's clasp. He found no respite as Tiger's grip tightened like a vice.

"You should have fought tooth and nail, made them yield. This stuff doesn't just gather dust for no reason." Tiger thundered, jabbing an accusatory finger towards the meticulously packed bags lining the room's left flank.

Eddy arrived at the doorstep, scanning the area with a sense of anticipation. Tony forcefully shoved Tiger aside.

"They've been whispering about the goods being tainted. If you're really that sharp, then it's your job to handle it," he sneered, making his way towards the exit.

Tiger kept his attention on Tony's retreating back until he caught sight of Eddy stationed at the entrance. With a confident stride, Tony sauntered out. He grazed Eddy's shoulder, momentarily diverting Eddy's attention from the meticulously bundled bags.

"Cocaine? I'll do it," Eddy declared without a moment's hesitation. "Count on me. I'll make sure it gets sold." His conviction surged, recognising the opportunity that had presented itself.

Tiger paused for a moment, then nodded in approval. Eddy's confident smile grew wider.

As Eddy, Leo, and Fei prepared for their mission, Tony and his comrades supplied them with the required equipment. This included duffel bags containing smaller, carefully wrapped bags of cocaine. Additionally, they were each armed with a pistol.

"Keep it subtle. Last time I used one down-town, it went south real quick," Tony underlined, his tone laced with caution.

"Guns are guns, my friend." Leo's shrug oozed an air of nonchalance.

"Yeah, but these ones are really loud. Save them for a last-ditch effort," Tony insisted, his voice firm.

Leo's eyes sparkled with mischief as he snatched the pistol from Tony's hand. "We'll see!"

Meanwhile, Tiger seized the valuable opportunity to arrange a meeting with the Distant Coalition—the alias given to a secretive smuggling network that specialised in the illicit trade of large quantities of illegal goods across borders. Tiger emphasised the unforgiving nature of their dealings with the Distant Coalition to the team. Negotiation was typically non-existent in such transactions, leaving them with a stark choice: money or life.

Clutching the sleek black duffel bags on their shoulders, the trio arrived at the abandoned factory. Their footsteps resounded on the crumbling concrete as they advanced towards partitioned chambers delineated solely by shattered walls. The weathered façade of the structure displayed scattered remnants of windows that had been transformed into mere cut-outs embellishing its exterior.

"Now I don't know why... but I feel like I need the toilet," Leo mumbled, tilting his head towards Eddy before going back to a straight position.

"Save it for later," Eddy replied in a lower voice, looking ahead cautiously.

"Okay," Leo whispered back, tilting his head once again.

Stepping forth with a faint squeak, a slick looking mobster emerged from the concealment of the wall. His attire exuded refined elegance. As he removed his stylish sunglasses, a mischievous grin played on his lips while his eyes sparkled with an undeniable sense of intrigue.

"I'm hating this already…" Leo muttered as he looked at the sunglasses.

In one swift motion, Leo and Fei reached for their concealed pistols, their instincts primed for action. Unperturbed, the man's laughter erupted as two of his loyal cohorts materialised behind him, armed and ready.

"I'm Johnny," the man said as he then pointed behind himself. "That's Frankie "Dragon Claw" and "Mickey "The Cobra". Where's Tiger?"

An old, dirty fan spun above them. The ceiling was coated in layers of grime and dust that obscured the original colour beneath. Leo analysed the three men in front of him, waiting for more insight.

"Is that it? Don't you have any nickname?"

"No, I'm just Johnny."

"Ah." Leo nodded at Johnny as the two men behind him pointed their pistols at the group.

In a silent gesture, Eddy asked his team to maintain their composure. With an air of nonchalance, Johnny slipped his hands into the depths of his pockets and revelled in being in control of the situation. A subtle tilt of his head to the left revealed a knowing smirk, a dance of confidence as he savoured his awareness of the reinforcements standing steadfastly behind him.

"We were told that there was a problem with our goods," Fei exclaimed to make herself heard, a strange shiver running down her spine.

Johnny sighed and shook his head.

"You've seriously got a knack for selling your garbage, kid!"

He pulled out a small bag from his jacket pocket and chucked it with all his might. The bag smacked against the hard concrete and a fine powder of drugs burst into the air like a flour explosion. Leo's face twisted in annoyance, showing his clear displeasure with what was going on.

"So, are the rest of them messed up too?" Johnny questioned, giving the merchandise a sceptical look as if he could spot a serious issue with it.

Quirks, according to Tiger's words.

"What's the problem with you guys?!" Leo exclaimed with anger, dropping the duffel bag from his left hand and unzipping it. He took out one of the small plastic bags.

Johnny, Frankie and Mickey remained patient. Leo tore the bag open with his nails and some of the powder scattered onto his trousers. Johnny flinched noticing the waste of expensive goods. Leo moistened a few fingers, then put them back in his mouth, tasting the cocaine with a smack.

"Why the hell are people buying this crap? It's straight-up terrible!" Leo mumbled to himself pulling a face. "But hey, from where I'm standing, it looks like some damn fine merchandise!"

Johnny paused for effect.

"What about the herbicide?"

"Herbicide? They put freaking herbicide in this?! Are you kidding me?!" Leo desperately attempting to spit out the remnants from his tongue. "Dude, why the hell didn't you mention that right off the bat?! Aw, damn it! If my mum finds out I got stoned *and* swallowed herbicide, she'll whoop my ass twice as hard!" he muttered under his breath, his tone laced with a mix of frustration and anxiety.

Tiger's words echoed in Eddy's memory, a reminder of their willingness to resort to any accusation in order to drive down the price.

"How about we overlook everything for a cool 80 million?" Johnny proposed, edging a step closer, a sly grin spreading across his face.

"We agreed on 100 million," Eddy emphasised.

"100 million?!" Leo blurted out, his eyes popping wide open in disbelief. "Who in the world would cough up 80 million, let alone 100 mil, for two damn bags packed with drugs and freaking herbicide?!"

Fei nudged him.

"Now, if those bags really had herbicide in them, you wouldn't even consider buying them at half the damn price, am I right?" she chimed in, a confident smile spreading across her face.

Johnny pondered for a moment, his mind scrambling to conjure up a fitting response. Without waiting any longer, Leo grabbed one of the already open plastic bags and scattered its contents all over the floor.

"Alright, I guess you don't need these any more."

Frankie and Mickey stood frozen in place, their muscles tensed. Sensing the urgency, Fei signalled the henchmen to put down their weapons. Without hesitation, they complied and kicked their firearms against the adjacent wall. Leo cleaned the powder off his hands.

"Now we're talking."

Taking advantage of the moment, Fei drew her pistol and aimed it with intent. Leo proceeded to open a few more plastic bags and spill the powder.

"Straight-up terrible, this stuff. You guys gotta get us a discount."

Eddy nudged him.

"Enough, now. You're not helping."

As Fei took a deep breath, a sense of unease settled within her. Something felt off. Instinctively, she swallowed hard, a gulp of air catching in her throat.

"Are you okay?" Eddy whispered.

She inspected her pistol in two quick moves. Her heart sank—the magazine was empty, leaving her with nothing but an empty shell in her hands. Eddy checked his own weapon coming to the same conclusion.

"Damn Tiger is testing us. We're idiots."

Grasping the opportunity, Johnny, Frankie and Mickey shot a quick glance at their pistols on the floor. Eddy, Leo and Fei's focus shifted onto those very same weapons.

This wasn't a matter of negotiation any more. This was a matter of speed.

The trio of mobsters sprang forward, keen on arming themselves.

Eddy removed the duffel bag from his shoulder and forcefully threw it ahead, striking Frankie in the face with precision. Meanwhile, Leo took advantage of the advancing opponents and tossed an open bag of powder directly into Mickey's eyes.

As Johnny approached his gun, Leo grabbed a handful of powder bags and skilfully launched them towards the ceiling fan. The bags exploded upon impact, creating a chaotic whirlwind of white dust that engulfed the entire hall. Despite the chaos, Johnny successfully reached his weapon. As he looked up, Eddy appeared before him, emerging through the floating powder.

Eddy's hands closed around Johnny's wrist. With a twist, Eddy executed a wrist lock to disarm him of the weapon. The pistol clattered a few feet away from them.

Eddy followed up with an elbow strike to the head, but Johnny ducked it with surprising speed. Their next strikes hit each other simultaneously and they stumbled back. Both froze, eyes locked on each other before flickering over to the fallen weapon.

Eddy feinted as if he wanted to go for the pistol. As Johnny dived towards it in order to try to catch up, Eddy delivered a brutal side kick to Johnny's gut, causing him to double over in pain. Eddy's shoulder ached from the recoil, but he pressed on.

Meanwhile, Leo's movements were fluid and precise as he unleashed a series of well-practiced kicks. Frankie was forced to retreat under the unrelenting assault, struggling to defend himself against Leo's onslaught.

Across the hall, Mickey's eyes darted between his comrades. Seeing her opening, Fei took advantage of Mickey's momentary distraction and went for a double leg take-down. With a dull thud, she tackled him to the floor and rolled away immediately to avoid a counter attack.

With every move, white powder danced around them like malevolent spirits. Bodies twisted and clashed, blows landing with bone-crushing impacts.

The room was filled with grunts of pain and determination.

Amidst the chaotic fight, the scattered pistols on the floor taunted the mobsters, their power just out of reach. Johnny's eyes were darting between his adversaries and the coveted firearms. Frankie decided to make a daring dash towards the nearest pistol. But before his fingers could close around the grip, Fei's boot sent it spinning away, skidding across the cold floor. Mickey attempted to grab another pistol, only to have it kicked from his grasp by Leo. Johnny manoeuvred gracefully towards one of the pistols, but Fei planted herself in front of it at the last moment and stood her ground.

The fight raged on. The agents and their opponents were locked in a frenzied dance, desperately attempting to gain control of the firearms. Amidst the chaotic brawl, the pistols were constantly kicked and redirected with astonishing accuracy. Despite the mobster's determination to gain an advantage, the weapons remained just out of reach, taunting them with their unattainable promise.

As everyone was tiring, the trio of agents managed one last burst of adrenaline-fuelled energy. Eddy parried a fierce blow and countered with a swift elbow strike, knocking Johnny out. Leo executed a spinning kick to the chest, flooring Mickey. Fei tightened the crook of her elbow around Frankie's neck until he gradually stopped resisting and passed out.

The agents now stood victorious in the midst of the swirling cocaine. Their bodies glistened with sweat. The room fell silent as the powder settled, a testament to their hard-won victory. Eddy secured their arms and legs by binding them together, securing them in a kneeling line.

“If this was captured and posted online, it's highly likely that it would’ve garnered a staggering 80 million views. What do you think about this?” Eddy playfully quipped, giving one of them a friendly nudge. Johnny angrily struggled to catch his breath, inhaling cocaine. “Anyway, let's be forgiving today and choose to turn a blind eye to it.”

Leo rummaged through Mickey’s jacket pocket, retrieving his sleek smartphone and promptly calling the police.

"Good day," Leo said, his voice infused with gravity. “I’d like to speak to the police.” His gaze shifted towards the trio of kneeling mobsters, their expressions giving him a sense of satisfaction. “*You're* the police? You’re the damn police! Of course you are.” his attention snapped back to the call. “Ain't that just typical? Look, fellas, I'm just trying to file a complaint over here, you feel me?"

Fei exchanged a relieved smile with Eddy, a weight lifting off their shoulders.

"You're handing us over?!" Johnny uttered, his confusion seeping through. "Who exactly are you? We've never met before."

Eddy crouched down to the mobster's eye level, his voice laced with a mischievous grin.

"Agent 00," he whispered.

Johnny furrowed his brows, struggling to grasp the meaning behind the enigmatic phrase. However, Eddy then retrieved an unfinished check and a pen from his jacket, assuring him of his honest intentions. With a sense of integrity, he vowed to only claim the predetermined amount from the initial agreement.

"What?! You want me to break it down for you, step by step?" Leo exclaimed, wildly gesticulating as he spoke into the phone. "I just told you someone was transporting cocaine... What? You think I'm into drugs?... Man, you better believe I stay clean!... Listen up, lady! Just 'cause I discovered the coke and later found out about the herbicide doesn't mean I'm suicidal!... No, I ain't got no behavioural disorders!" Leo's voice grew more agitated, his frustration seeping through. "So, are you coming to haul these dudes away or what?... Yeah, I'm dead serious!... Fine, I'll wait then!... You want to see my damn ID? Hold on a sec, who's the real target here?... Legislation? I know the law like the back of my hand!... No, I already told you I ain't into drugs!... How the hell am I supposed to know the quantity of... What?!"

In the distance, the wailing of police sirens reached their ears.

"We need to leave," Eddy said to Fei and she nodded in agreement.

"Blood type?!" Leo bellowed in frustration. "Why the hell do you need my blood type?... I ain't about to give blood! But I'll be damned if I ever decided to donate blood, I'd do it right this second, 'cause, hell no, I'm not into drugs!"

Eddy seized the phone from Leo's grasp, interrupting him before the next sentence could escape.

In a final gesture, Leo glanced back at the mobsters and shook his head in disapproval.

"You better quit messing with these drugs, man. They're not doing you any good!"

Back at the hidden underground den, an eerie calm engulfed the area. It was rarely quiet there. The continuous hum of machinery which typically saturated the air, now lingered faintly.

The trio of agents pressed forward until they reached an expansive room. They halted just shy of the corner leading to the entrance, as two voices could be heard exchanging dialogue. Eddy motioned for his comrades to remain in place. He ventured forth alone, hugging the wall closely and peering around the corner.

KB produced a wad of currency, flinging it disdainfully at Tiger's feet. From Eddy's vantage point, only the left contour of KB's cheek and shoulder were visible, concealed beneath a lengthy, formidable coat.

Not far away, a police car arrived at the scene where Johnny, Frankie and Mickey were abandoned. The police officers were accompanied by two young agents and Boss. With a confident wave, Boss presented the diligent policemen with his warrant. Without delay, the police car departed, leaving the stage to Boss and his team.

"Cocaine, huh?" one of the young agents affirmed, standing up from next to the broken bags.

"Who called the police?" the other agent asked Johnny. Wearing a sly grin, Johnny betrayed an undercurrent of resentment hidden within his eyes.

"Agent 00."

“Agent 00?”

“Three bastards. Two guys, one hot chick.” Frankie confirmed.

Boss looked at the half-empty bags.

"Alright, let's get you guys out of here."

Back in the underground, Eddy inched closer to the entrance of the room. A fleeting glance revealed Tiger's countenance in its entirety. It was an amalgamation of tension and unyielding pride, refusing to concede any guilt, should it even be warranted. KB crossed his arms and fixated on Tiger, exuding an enigmatic blend of impassiveness and discernment.

Elsewhere, Boss marched with purpose towards the parked car. His eyes were fixed ahead, yet his mind was transported to a realm of bitter memories. Lost in a mix of nostalgia and regret, he felt a ghostly connection, as if he were seeing through Eddy's own eyes. Through this mystical lens, he plunged into the depths of his own past, reliving long-gone memories.

Deep in his thoughts, Boss found himself reminiscing about KB. He was once a figure who resembled him in both manners and loyalty. But unlike Boss, KB had been tainted by the corrosive forces of hate. As he journeyed into the past, Boss could almost visualise the world as Eddy was doing so right now, reliving the mystery of KB's authoritative presence.

Life had its way of cruelly revealing who would endure the harshest suffering and who would bear a lighter burden. There were no winners in this dark tale.

The fateful day of change came to pass two decades ago. In a hidden, shadowy chamber, a young Boss sat surrounded by his loyal undercover team.

They had endured a gruelling six months as members of the ruthless Triads. They all knew that tonight was the night when the final verdict would be delivered, sealing their fate.

The tension in the room was palpable. Dim lighting cast eerie shadows on their determined faces. At the appointed hour, a special unit was preparing to converge on the target location, their mission to encircle the building and cut off any escape routes. At the same time, Boss and his crew geared up to set the ultimate snare for their prime suspect, KB. Even though they had amassed a significant pile of evidence, the true identities and exact count of the shadowy co-conspirators remained elusive. The haunting prospect of being so close to completing their mission gnawed at the hearts of the rookie agents, injecting an eerie sense of trepidation into their veins.

Boss kept his composure, offering a reassuring smile to his three trusted comrades.

"In a few short hours, we'll have our guy in cuffs," Boss announced to his team. "Tonight's our night to make a clean getaway. I gotta say, I've got total faith in all of you. We're going to pull off this mission like pros. We'll survive at any cost," Boss' voice dropped to a low whisper.

Grins spread across the faces of the young agents as they started brainstorming their plans for the future.

"Great!" exclaimed one of them with suppressed excitement. "You won't believe it, but I've been holding onto that ring for ages. I'll finally get to slip it onto her finger tomorrow evening."

“Congrats, buddy! I bet she’s really missing you.” a fellow agent whispered, nudging the one in the centre with a playful smile.

“My wife's due next month. I’ll be back just in time.” The agent on the right next to Boss beamed with pride, sticking out his tongue before bursting into contagious laughter of pure joy.

“My younger sister is waiting for me back home.”

“How old did you say she is?”

“She's turning nineteen. How old is your future fiancée?”

“Twenty-three.”

“Idiot! You're only twenty-two! Are you sure you want to get married?”

“Are you laughing at me? You!” shouted the young man back, pretending to be ready to strangle his comrade.

"Hey, I bet you've really been missing your family all this time," commented the soon-to-be-dad, casually glancing at Boss. He received a nostalgic smile in response. "You've got a daughter, right?"

"You got that right!" affirmed Boss, letting out a sigh while sporting a confident smile. "My lovely wife and little Fei have been waiting for me forever. Can't keep them waiting any longer!"

“Just a few more hours,” whispered one of them, nodding in approval.

The four agents extended their hands, stacking their palms in unity.

"We'll survive at any cost!" the team affirmed in a hushed chant, their unwavering loyalty pulsating through every word.

The resounding echoes of triumphant laughter reverberated through Boss's mind, intertwining the fabric of distant recollections with the vivid reality of the present. It was a transcendent thread that wove together memories and the urgency of the moment, igniting a fire within.

Pinching the bridge of his nose, Boss looked up to see Johnny, Mickey and Frankie being escorted into the waiting vehicle. With practised ease, the two accompanying agents flung the bags into the trunk to conceal the incriminating evidence. Boss's internal struggle remained unnoticed amidst their nonchalant banter and casual chatter.

Boss retrieved his wallet, savouring each deliberate motion. With meticulous precision, he unveiled the cherished photograph of his beloved wife. His thumb glided tenderly, tracing the delicate lines of her visage with a loving caress. A bittersweet smile played upon his lips, a silent tribute to the depths of his emotions.

"I'm sorry for allowing our dear Fei to go to such a place, my love. Please keep a vigilant eye on her until the day I can warmly welcome her back home," he whispered, taking a deep breath to compose himself.

The room fell silent back in the underground chambers. KB's eyes unexpectedly locked onto Eddy. Reluctantly, Eddy, Fei, and Leo obeyed the unspoken signal and entered the room, positioning themselves side-by-side, unsure of what awaited them. Meanwhile, Tiger stood in stoic silence.

Eddy made a conscious effort to appear at ease, loosening the tension in his shoulders and subtly clearing his throat. With a smile on his face, he greeted the others with a wave of his hand. KB's expression remained unreadable, adding an air of mystery to the encounter. Sensing the uneasy atmosphere, Leo let out a forced chuckle and took a step closer, attempting to alleviate the tension.

"Well...! We're back, my friend," Leo greeted, but his words fell flat. "Those individuals..." he started formulating, but then stopped, intimidated by KB's penetrating gaze. "Those individuals, you know, those drug addicts..." Leo stuttered. KB showed no reaction. "Come on, man! You know, those guys with the cocaine...! Yeah! I don't know how to say this, but they're damn lucky. I mean, out of all the possible places, they could only choose one where the police have quick access? I didn't think they were such idiots! Anyway, they're gone now, disappeared into thin air!" Leo joked, laughing foolishly, but his smile gradually faded. "But don't you worry, my friend! They didn't catch a glimpse of us. We slipped away like ghosts, leaving no trace behind, obviously!" he affirmed while holding his hands on his hips.

The silence hung heavily.

"Alright, alright, I hear you loud and clear!" Leo continued. "Today it's my time to do the talking and you do the listening, got it. But hey, my friend, you've been looking way too serious lately! Is it 'cause of those dudes with the cocaine and the herbicides? Well, guess what? We took their cash and kicked 'em to the curb! Ain't that right, Eddy? Show 'em the proof, my friend! Whip out that cheque!"

Eddy and Fei listened with caution. KB's expression twisted into a horrifying contortion as he moved the corner of his mouth.

"What? Did I say something wrong?... Cocaine?... Or maybe... herbicides?" Leo added, subsequently revising his words while scrutinising KB with a tinge of curiosity.

KB flinched once again.

"Ha! Herbicides! Yeah, that was the word! You moved! I made you move!" Leo's voice erupted with exhilaration as he observed a glimmer of emotion flicker across KB's face.

A grin erupted from KB's mouth, cutting through the tense atmosphere. He abruptly turned and launched himself towards the shelves positioned behind him. With a surge of energy, he propelled his body forward, causing an avalanche of boxes and doses to cascade downwards in a seamless sequence. The once orderly display transformed into a scene of chaos as the containers crashed onto the floor. Their contents became victims of a frenzied airborne ballet scattering in every direction. Tiger recoiled, his attention locked onto KB.

"Did you say herbicide, you bastard?" KB shouted.

Leo widened his eyes. But he quickly realised that KB was in fact addressing Tiger.

"There were a couple of goddamn unfinished business deals," Tiger admitted in a gritty tone.

"Personal affairs, huh?" KB hissed through his teeth, growing increasingly furious. "Your personal matters are ruining *my* business."

KB extracted a concealed pistol from beneath his coat, promptly aiming it at Tiger. Eddy flinched, taking an involuntary step forward. Sensing Eddy's inclination to intervene, Fei grabbed his shoulder.

Leo exhaled a gulp of air and summoned his courage to interrupt the conversation.

"What kind of herbicide nonsense are we all squabbling about here, huh?"

Unfazed, KB advanced towards Tiger. He was resolute in his intent.

"Hold up, hold up, hold up! Are you seriously trying to tell me that those damn bags of cocaine were actually filled with herbicide?!" Leo blurted out abruptly, his disbelief and astonishment evident.

KB brought the pistol closer to Tiger's forehead, who seemed unapologetic for his actions.

"Guys, what the hell are you playing at?" Leo revolted, his face contorting in disgust as he stuck out his tongue and dramatically spat out imaginary remnants, expressing his utter disdain.

Tiger's grin remained unabated, devoid of any trace of remorse. KB once again assumed his expressionless countenance, exuding an air of unyielding dread.

"Come on now, friends, you ain't seriously gonna take this all the way, are you?" Leo attempted to defuse the situation, stepping forward in an effort to bring about some semblance of calm. "All right, listen up, people! Everything's smooth sailing until two good buddies start going at each other's throats."

KB turned his focus towards Leo, seemingly drawn in by his words.

"Yeah, that's what I'm talking about!" Leo exclaimed with a big grin, knowing full well that he had grabbed KB's attention. "Friends shouldn't be going at each other like that! I mean, seriously, what's the point of friendship if you're just gonna fight all the time? Look at me and Eddy here, we're like the dynamic duo of friendship!" Leo yanked Eddy closer by the collar. "It's me, Eddy, Eddy, me. Friends. Best damn friends you'll ever meet! So how about you two follow our lead? Put that damn gun down and let's sort this out!"

KB looked convinced, slowly lowering his gun. Tiger couldn't help but let out a sigh of relief, although he made an effort to conceal it from plain sight.

"That's what I'm talking about! You see? Peace! Love! They're heaven-sent, my friends!" Leo affirmed with a triumphant tone.

KB emitted an almost disinterested sigh, closing in on Leo with an inscrutable expression. Interpreting KB's approach as a gesture of embrace, Leo raised his arms. But KB rapidly and nearly imperceptibly delivered a sharp strike to the back of Leo's neck, instantly causing him to lose consciousness. Leo hit the floor.

"Clean up this mess," KB muttered, his voice dripping with authority as he vanished into the shadowy corridor.

Chapter XII

Some days flew by in the blink of an eye, while others dragged on like never-ending Mondays. The three agents, always on the move, found themselves on countless missions negotiating shady deals with a web of traffickers. Surprisingly, they managed to fly under the radar, skilfully avoiding suspicion despite Li Li's occasional flashy presence. Meanwhile, Eddy had taken a daring step and gained approval to oversee the production of fake currency. It brought him an exhilarating sense of accomplishment, as he knew each counterfeit bill was solid evidence in their pursuit of justice.

Within the department, the agents worked tirelessly, collaborating to craft foolproof plans. They understood the dire consequences that awaited any infiltrator unmasked in the treacherous world of the Triads. Exposed identities meant certain death, leaving no room for escape. No matter how many secret agents were deployed, they couldn't match the sheer number of devoted fraternity members scattered across various domains. The chances of capturing them were slim to none, like trying to catch smoke with their bare hands.

The team found themselves atop a relic that appeared to have materialised directly from the 80s—a weathered warehouse rooftop. Bathed in the sun's golden rays, the city sprawled below, its towering skyscrapers reaching for the heavens. The view from up high was a mesmerising blend of organised chaos, capturing the essence of the urban jungle. But amidst the spectacle, something else grabbed their attention.

Eddy tucked away the polaroids of the three women they had been patiently waiting for. Each photograph bore their head-shots and code names underneath. Ivory, Shadow and Lady Silk were integral members of the notorious Distant Coalition. With a quick glance, Eddy verified that the women walking before him were an exact match to the photographs.

Leo sprang off his perch and pushed away his plastic chair, landing deftly on his feet. He wiped away the drool from his mouth as his eyes widened. Smacking his lips twice, he sported a foolish grin, tilting his head with curiosity.

Ivory, Shadow and Lady Silk walked with purpose, their attire leaving little to the imagination. Their smiles carried a playful suggestion. Eddy found himself spellbound, his attention locked on their enchanting presence. Fei nudged him, snapping him back to reality.

The wind danced across the rooftop, a force to be reckoned with. Leo brushed aside his unruly bangs, discreetly spitting out any strands that dared to cling to the corners of his mouth. With a radiant smile of unadulterated joy, he revelled in the moment, basking in the thrill that coursed through his veins.

"Yo, who brought these little cuties here?" he hollered, strutting over confidently.

He zeroed in on Lady Silk, entrancing her with his piercing gaze. Frozen in place, she felt his gentle touch as his fingers grazed her neck, their cheeks brushing in a tender embrace. The scent of her lip gloss filled his senses as he closed his eyes, raising his hand like a conductor.

Eddy scratched his own neck, trying to divert his attention from Leo's nonsense.

Meanwhile, the young woman responded with a smirk, her grip tightening on Leo's shirt as their gazes locked, yet not a word was spoken. Leo suppressed a triumphant chuckle.

As soon as he opened his mouth to speak, a collective gasp rippled through the space. In a flash of movement, she struck Leo with a powerful knee below the belt, causing him to double over in pain. Leo extended his trembling right hand, signalling for everyone to pause for a moment. Despite his efforts to speak, his voice failed him. Fighting to maintain his balance, he wavered as he tried to take a step forward. His right hand shook while sporadic sounds escaped his lips, a desperate attempt to communicate.

Ivory, Shadow and Lady Silk paid him no mind, now advancing towards Eddy and Fei. Eddy sighed, placing both hands on his hips in exasperation.

"Couldn't you have just given us the USB?"

"I didn't say a single word. Looks like your buddy over there holds a contrasting viewpoint." She shrugged nonchalantly as she gestured with her thumb towards Leo, who was presently on all fours and struggling to rise, audibly expressing his agony.

Fei reached into her pocket and pulled out an envelope, revealing the cheques contained inside.

"Here you go. Now hand over the USB."

"Seems like Tiger no longer makes personal appearances. He prefers to send his minions instead," Shadow spoke with a hint of irony. She chuckled and tilted her head as the wind swept strands of hair across her face.

As a storm was approaching, a few thunderclaps echoed in the distance. The air carried a refreshing scent, indicating the arrival of rain.

"I must say, Tiger has sent quite an interesting group: a pretty chick, a handsome dude... And someone who seems rather frail," Lady Silk remarked as her gaze shifted behind her, where Leo struggled to regain his composure.

Fei held up the cheques, signalling their readiness to proceed.

"Let's not waste any more time. We should get this over with."

Eddy nodded in agreement, pressing his lips together as he let Fei handle the matter.

Leo erupted into the midst of the gathering, his body language demanding attention. His left hand rested on his hip, while his right index finger gestured at Lady Silk, emphasising his desire to make his presence known.

"Okay, what the hell was that?!"

Eddy sighed. Leo took a deep breath.

"So let me get this straight! Just because you're rocking those skyscraper heels and are suddenly matching my height, don't go thinking you got some kinda special privilege! There's no exemptions just because you're a lady either, 'cause trust me, you got a knee that's been through some serious conditioning!"

"I want to see the cheques," Lady Silk stated, stretching her hand to Fei, ignoring the noise around her.

"The USB first," Fei insisted.

"Hello? You think you can just ignore me?" Leo squeezed himself between the two to catch Lady Silk's attention.

As rain clouds loomed overhead and the wind picked up, the atmosphere grew tense. Lady Silk extended her hand, aiming to grab the cheques. Fei pulled her arm back.

"The USB first."

"If there's no other choice," Lady Silk muttered, retrieving a silver flash drive from her pocket. "Now hand over the cheques."

"No, the USB!"

"The cheques!"

"The USB!"

Caught in the middle, Eddy's eyes darted back and forth, waiting to see the responses on both sides.

"Man, are you really gonna keep going back and forth like this 'til the break of dawn?" Leo snapped, snatching the cheques out of Fei's hand. Not wasting any time, he handed them to Lady Silk. He then took the flash drive, plopping it into Fei's hand. "Boom! Problem solved, plain and simple."

Lady Silk stowed the cheques away, her hands moving with practised precision. Herself, Ivory and Shadow gracefully executed a synchronised retreat, their steps calculated and precise. Fei attempted to open the USB lid, only to realise that it was fake.

"Stop them!" Fei exclaimed, causing Eddy and Leo to turn their alarmed focus towards the three young women. Realising that their cover was blown, Lady Silk began running towards the stairs.

With no place to hide, they found themselves surrounded. Leo shook his head in disappointment and let out a sigh.

"Now I believe it's time for you to hand over the real USB," Fei demanded.

"You know how life is... Come rain or sunshine..." Leo tried to sound philosophical while looking up at the dark clouds gathering in the sky and contemplating the mysteries of weather and existence.

"The USB," Fei repeated in a commanding tone, emphasising it as a final warning.

Lady Silk's eyes locked onto Leo as he approached, deep in thought and ready to contribute to his existential musings. Eddy ensured he didn't lose sight of Shadow and Ivory.

Leo occasionally fluttered his eyelashes to project an air of intelligence. As he readied himself to begin a new sentence, he was met with a forceful punch causing his head to jerk back. As he straightened his spine, blood ran down his nostril. Lady Silk let out a loud laugh.

Ivory and Shadow seized the opportunity, making their ways towards the metallic stairs at the rooftop's edge. While Leo blinked in bewilderment, Eddy chased after them.

Fei lunged forward, her hand shooting out to grab Lady Silk's elbow, determined to restrain her. However, Lady Silk's body possessed uncanny flexibility as she twisted and turned, evading Fei with ease. Lady Silk flashed a mischievous smile at Fei, taunting her with a lift of her chin.

"Sorry, but I've got better things to do this evening," Lady Silk exclaimed, her voice dripping with playful defiance.

Her fist swung towards Fei, aiming straight for her jaw with pinpoint accuracy. Fei's instincts kicked in just in time, allowing her to dodge the incoming blow.

"Yeah? Like what?"

Fei countered with a barrage of punches aimed at Lady Silk's midsection.

"Like knitting socks for my goldfish!"

Lady Silk's attacks became even more ferocious, coming at Fei from all directions. Bursting into laughter, Fei skilfully parried and evaded her blows.

"Don't you dare mock my goldfish!" Lady Silk's voice rang out, her anger fuelling each strike.

Eddy lunged forward, his hands shooting out to grab both Ivory and Shadow firmly by their shoulders. In the rush of the moment, his grip tightened unintentionally, pulling them back towards him in a sudden embrace. Their bodies collided and for a brief moment, Eddy found himself wrapped around them. Feeling the constriction against his chest, Ivory and Shadow reacted, their minds racing to break free from Eddy's hold. They wriggled and twisted, their muscles straining against the unexpected restraint.

Ivory twisted her torso like a contortionist, determined to escape Eddy's clutches. With a grace that would make a yoga instructor jealous, she wriggled free, surprising Eddy with her escape skills. As soon as she found her balance, she launched a spinning hook kick. Her foot spun faster than a ceiling fan, aiming straight for Eddy's cheek. The impact sent him stumbling backwards, releasing Shadow from his grip.

Shaking off the disorientation, Eddy retaliated with a roundhouse kick. Ivory sidestepped, leaving Eddy kicking at thin air. Shadow leapt into action, delivering a flurry of strikes faster than a hummingbird on espresso. Each punch and kick was a work of art, carefully calculated to create maximum impact. Meanwhile, Ivory continued her dazzling display of combat prowess, unleashing a storm of kicks. Her legs moved so fast they blurred.

The two girls attacked with impeccable coordination, their fists slicing through space with venomous hooks aimed at Eddy. Ivory struck, but Eddy's block was swift. Shadow followed suit, only to be met with an impenetrable defence. Ivory struck again, met by another resolute block. Shadow lunged forward, but Eddy parried the attack.

Their pace quickened, as Eddy transformed into a nimble maestro of deflection. The girls' fury escalated, their fists filled with aggression. Eddy intercepted each assault with determination, but he couldn't hold out forever.

In that crucial instant, he saw his chance. Lowering his stance, he unleashed a sweeping kick, striking both girls' legs with surgical precision. The impact sent them crashing to the ground. Eddy's heart raced as he used the moment to catch his breath.

Ignoring the pain, Ivory stood up and leapt forward after a battle cry.

In the midst of the chaos, Eddy caught hold of her shirt, tugging at it unintentionally. Caught off guard by the unexpected contact, Ivory jerked herself away, but Eddy's grip remained firm. In the struggle, Eddy inadvertently ripped her shirt open, exposing a glimpse of her bare skin. Realising his mistake, Eddy raised both hands in apology. Seizing the opportunity, Shadow saw her chance to strike. She executed a powerful kick, aiming to divert Eddy's attention. Eddy parried Shadow's attack, deflecting the blow with a skilful block. Not content with mere defence, Eddy seized the advantage. Grabbing Shadow's extended leg, he utilised his opponent's momentum against her. With a sudden twist, he brought Shadow crashing to the ground. With Shadow temporarily neutralised, Ivory returned to the fray. She launched herself at Eddy, her attacks coming from all angles. Eddy, however, remained calm under pressure, his mind calculating the best course of action. As Ivory's strikes rained down upon him, Eddy showcased his ingenuity. He sidestepped and weaved through her assaults, anticipating her movements with uncanny precision. With a final, sweeping motion, Eddy delivered a decisive blow that sent Ivory sprawling to the ground.

Fei and Lady Silk grappled fiercely on the dusty floor, their bodies locked in a desperate struggle. Thunder rumbled above them, mirroring the intensity of their clash. Fei fought against Lady Silk's suffocating hold, straining for freedom. In a burst of adrenaline, she broke free. Gasping for air, she rose to her feet, ready to continue the fight. Lady Silk chose not to get up.

"Yo! That's what I'm talking about!" Leo clapped with excitement.

Eddy walked away from Ivory and Shadow, lifting his empty hands while the two didn't dare to move away from the spot.

"Nothing on my end."

Fei squatted and looked through Lady Silk's pockets. Eddy brushed the dust off his clothes and looked up at the approaching storm. With satisfaction, Fei found what she was looking for and stood up. Large raindrops began to fall.

"Well, nice try!" exclaimed Leo while pointing at Lady Silk and wiping the blood from his nose. "Imagine if you weren't born a woman, I would've beaten you to a pulp! Come on, let's go!" He took the initiative signalling Eddy and Fei to follow him.

The trio retreated under the nearby shelter of the roof. Lady Silk, Ivory and Shadow were nowhere to be seen.

They stood there in complete silence for several minutes. Their gaze remained locked on the sky above, as drifting rain clouds caused the sunlight to flicker inconsistently. The surrounding air embraced them with suffocating warmth.

"Ha! Here you are!" Li Li burst onto the scene, her voice filled with excitement and mischief. With a triumphant gleam in her eyes, she brandished two umbrellas, one tightly shut and the other open, ready to conquer the rain.

"What're *you* doing here?" Leo asked in astonishment and sceptically looked around.

Li Li evaded the question, "Well," she handed her umbrella to Eddy and gave the already-opened one to Leo. "I'm just checking on you guys. To make sure all's good, everyone's still alive, you know."

As Leo reached for the umbrella, his hand briefly brushed against Li Li's and an inexplicable magnetism coursed through him. He heard a voice, Li Li's voice, even though he was certain she hadn't spoken. Her face, filled with laughter as she enjoyed one of Eddy's jokes captivated him and sent a shiver of thrilling anticipation down his spine. The voice echoed in his mind again, "*Allow me to join you,*" It sounded vibrant and clear, yet distant as if originating from another realm.

Under the shelter of the roof, the four stood motionless for a while, their focus absorbed by the raindrops dancing on the pavement and forming delicate bubbles.

Eddy pulled Fei into his side and together they forged ahead, gripping the umbrella in their hands.

Leo approached Li Li, feeling the warmth of her hand. He closed his eyes. In that moment, a cascade of fleeting images from a past encounter flashed through his mind, an experience he was certain he had lived before. Startled, he opened his eyes and gazed at Li Li. "*My name is Lu Lu!*" her voice resounded, despite his firm belief that she hadn't even contemplated such words. Confused, Leo then heard his own voice playing in his mind, "*We don't care!*" as a sense of bewilderment overcame him, unsure of the unfolding mysteries within.

The two of them locked eyes in profound silence, their breaths held. They were convinced that this was a sort of deeply personal encounter. Li Li shook her head, searching for Eddy with her gaze. "*I knew it, General Lai Ji, I knew it!*" Li Li recalled her own excitement, picturing herself standing before Eddy. Yet, he appeared somewhat different.

Eddy shifted his attention towards Fei. Raindrops collided with the umbrella. Fei smiled and he glimpsed through her eyes. Princess Fei Yan stood under the ethereal moonlight, as it accentuated her flawless complexion, enhancing the soft curve of her lips and the genuine warmth in her presence. Eddy remained transfixed, studying Fei, unsure of why he was experiencing hallucinations. Perplexed, Fei brought a hand to her mouth, lightly grazing her lips with her fingertips. "*Thank you! Thank you for trying to save my life.*"

Time stood still. Past sequences intertwined repeatedly with the present. The Princess slowly extended a few fingers, delicately touching the general's palm. General Lai Ji, holding the reins in his right hand, embraced the Princess, pledging to protect her ceaselessly through this gesture. Stunned, Eddy stared at Fei, struggling to believe the authenticity of his vivid reliving. Remembering the same sequences, Fei couldn't tear her eyes away from Eddy.

Leo gradually distanced himself from Li Li, fearing that another touch might evoke further peculiar hallucinations. Li Li reached out her hand, desiring to touch him, yearning to unravel more from what hinted at being a past life.

Leaving the umbrella in Fei's grasp, Eddy retreated a few steps, examining Fei's expression to ensure he wasn't alone in these illusions. The pouring rain drenched his hair and clothes, lending him an appearance akin to his former self. Intrigued, Fei watched the youthful general from the past right before her. "*Princess, you cannot leave.*" Fei allowed the umbrella to fall and slowly parted her lips, attempting to utter a word. Instead, she closed her eyes. "*I won't let you leave, Princess!*" Fei shook her head, uncertain of the origin of these memories. She smiled and raised her hand. "*I'll wait for you for a year, ten, a hundred, a thousand… I'll wait for you for eternity! I hope to meet again in our next lives!*" Eddy was startled. Wiping his wet forehead with the back of his hand, he hastened towards her. Embracing her with sincerity, he held her close to his chest.

"Thank you," he whispered, resting his chin on her shoulder.

Fei raised her arms, embracing him in return. The thunder ceased, but the rain continued. Leo cautiously observed Li Li, hesitant to move. Li Li smiled, letting out a short laugh. She felt happy, regardless of the purpose or reason behind these memories. Instinctively taking Leo's hand, she rejoiced, experiencing a true euphoric sense of reunion after an eternity. A mere coincidence.

Passing through the heavy rain clouds, leaving behind these times and searching for the past in a distant universe, a parallel world came back to life.

The spilt potion vial rolled on its own through the tender grass, reaching the edge of the road. From there, the last drop trickled down and penetrated deep into the earth.

Through the dense curtain of rain, Lai Ji's wandering silhouette could be seen desperately searching around.

The once-frozen landscape came alive with a breathtaking resurgence of life. Delicate buds unfurled, painting the branches with vibrant colours. Flowers emerged from the ground, their petals dancing in the rejuvenating showers. The majestic mountains stood tall, shedding their icy chains and embracing the awakening world.

A desperate cry echoed from the mountain slopes, repeating over and over again.

"Princess Fei Yan, I've always been here. Please come back!"

Jumping back into the present Universe, Eddy shook his head making sure he was recovering. He picked up the umbrella, feeling light-headed.

Huddled together under the shared umbrella, Eddy and Fei darted towards the stairs, the persistent rain refusing to let up. Li Li quickly joined them, the umbrella's handle tightly grasped in her hands. With an exasperated curse, Leo trailed behind and shielded his eyes with his arm.

Tiger stood in front of the car, awaiting their arrival. Eddy greeted him with a cheerful wave, while Fei nodded her head. Leo caught up with Li Li, playfully protesting against her prank. A burst of laughter escaped Li Li's lips as she pushed him back into the rain. Seeking shelter under the umbrella, Leo tried to wrestle the handle from her grasp, but his attention was soon diverted when he noticed the focus on Li Li's visage.

Leo abruptly ceased his playful antics and looked up. It was then that he noticed the weightiness etched onto Tiger's face. Li Li's disposition shifted dramatically, her eyes brimming with unexpected resentment. Eddy scanned their faces. Realising that Tiger's suspicion may have been aroused by Li Li's presence, Eddy let out a brief chuckle.

"Tiger!"

Tiger shook off his tense demeanour, a smile materialising on his face. Li Li nudged Leo.

"Ah. You know what, my friend? The three of us have been keeping something from you all this time." Leo declared.

Eddy and Fei were taken aback, turning their full attention to Leo.

"So, let's reintroduce ourselves," Leo continued while placing his hand on Li Li's shoulder. "She's not just our friend. Our organisation got another person in the mix."

Eddy and Fei let out a collective sigh of relief, feeling foolish for entertaining any alternative notions. But what drove Leo to utter such a statement? The question lingered in the minds of both agents simultaneously. Even Leo himself found it astonishing that he could articulate such words, comprehending Li Li's intention with a single nudge.

Tiger stepped closer to Eddy's ear. "How much does she know?"

"Don't worry." Eddy patted him on the shoulder.

"Oh, come on!" Leo grinned. "Seriously, I bet you have spies too, right? Huh? Huh?" he began to move his head from side to side with each word. "All right, listen up! I gotta be on point, you know what I'm saying? Don't you have spies? That's right, man! You never know who's creeping and peeping on me, even when I'm taking care of business in the bathroom. It's a crazy world out there and I got no clue who's secretly keeping tabs on me either. No way of knowing, my friend." After a brief pause, the idea seemed in fact strangely plausible and irritating at the same time. "But I hope that's not the case... Right?"

It was only then that Eddy noticed Tiger's wet clothes and realised that he must have been standing in the rain without an umbrella for quite some time.

Tiger didn't seem to feel the water trickling down from the top of his head.

"Let's hurry up."

Tiger nodded in agreement, casting a quick glance at Li Li. His expression conveyed acceptance.

The five of them ventured into the dim depths of the Harmony Dungeon. Li Li's eyes eagerly explored every nook and cranny, absorbing each detail. To Eddy's astonishment, she seemed both exhilarated and daring in the face of such potential danger.

In the past few weeks, Li Li had been praying with great intensity to Boss, every single day, fuelled by a strong desire to become an agent. Her pleas for permission were persistent, driven by her strong determination to train and learn. However, Boss had learned from the regrettable situation with his own daughter and consistently turned down Li Li's requests. He was firm in his decision to avoid making the same mistake twice.

However, the dynamic shifted when Li Li stormed into his office one day. Her fists were clenched tightly, her jaw set, and tears were welling up in her eyes.

"Please, let me join," she implored, her voice barely a whisper.

"What happened to you?"

"I have to join. Please. I need to know Tiger. I want to see his true face, who he really is!" Li Li begged, grabbing Boss by the hand.

"What do you mean, my dear?" Boss tried to soothe her. "It's nothing more but a cruel place."

"I saw his kind face at the park, but that's not who he truly is."

"That's an undeniable truth. But what exactly are you getting at?"

"That Tiger... He's the one responsible for taking away my parents' lives!" Tears streamed down Li Li's cheeks, falling from eyes filled with a burning hatred. "Because of Tiger, my life turned out this way. Because of him, my uncle had to raise me all on his own!" She held her breath as she lifted an open pendant.

The old photos of her parents dangled in front of Boss's eyes, causing a tightness in his chest. He stared at the girl's face. His hands gripped her shoulders as a fleeting memory flashed through his mind. *"You won't believe it, but I've been holding onto that ring for ages. I'll finally get to slip it onto her finger tomorrow evening!", "Congrats, buddy! I bet she's really missing you."... 'My wife's due next month! I'll be back just in time."* As Boss finally regained his composure, disbelief washed over him. *'My wife's due next month! I'll be back just in time."*

"Weeks after the incident, all of their families were listed as dead," Boss whispered to himself. "That child... That child somehow made it out alive."

"Please, I'm begging you." Li Li clasped her hands together.

Boss shut his eyes, a sudden realisation striking him. This wasn't merely about Tiger any more—it was about KB. KB, the one who had instilled unfathomable fear in him, ceaselessly haunting his very being. KB had the power to dismantle his sanity and trap him within an eternal labyrinth of regret.

"You're not here by accident, are you?"

Li Li shook her head and tightened her grip.

"Please."

Boss lifted his head with a gentle smile. He understood that denying her request would condemn this young woman to a life consumed by hatred and vengeance. Even worse, she might take matters into her own hands. The weight of guilt became unbearable, forcing him to make a choice.

He would liberate her. Granting her permission to exact her revenge meant offering her the chance to pursue justice, even if it endangered her life. As long as she remained with his team, he could find solace in that.

Strolling through the Harmony Dungeon, Li Li couldn't help but revel in her surroundings. She savoured the faint hum of machinery. Eddy couldn't help but smile, admiring how effortlessly she acclimated to the environment.

The sound of shattering glass jolted Tiger into action. He raced ahead, his senses honed to the source of the sound.

KB hurled several glasses against the wall, unleashing an explosive symphony of crashing fragments. Tiger hesitated at the threshold of the room, torn between caution and the urgency of the situation.

The team stopped behind Tiger. Li Li's eyes darted between KB and the bewildering scene, her mind racing to assimilate the unfolding chaos. Unfazed by their presence, KB's clenched fist closed around Tony's coat. He raised him from the ground with a single, commanding arm. Veins pulsed on his forehead, a physical manifestation of his fury.

KB propelled Tony towards the adjacent wall, his body colliding with bone-shattering impact. The room fell into a chilling silence as KB fixed his ice-cold gaze upon the fallen figure, his anger stoking the flames within him once more. Leo flinched.

KB pivoted towards the shelves, snatching a box and emptying its contents to reveal a pistol. Without sparing a glance at the firearm, he surged forward, closing in on Tony. The wounded man writhed on the ground, his hand clutching his chest, struggling to rise as the weight of the situation sank in.

KB's grip on the pistol tightened, his eyes unyielding as he levelled it mercilessly at his target. Quivering with terror, the bloodied subordinate opened his mouth, desperate words teetering on his lips.

The sound of a solitary bullet ended his existence, forever silencing him. As if by cruel design, the walls transformed into a chilling tapestry of scarlet splatters. Leo instinctively shielded Li Li's innocent eyes, her grip on his coat growing tighter. Fei turned her gaze away, unable to witness the gruesome scene, while Eddy firmly clasped her arm. Tiger's breath hitched, his mind spinning as he grappled with the gravity of KB's swift and decisive actions.

Discarding the weapon, KB pivoted away without a backward glance, fixating on the exit. Li Li flinched, her senses jolted. With an air of indifference, KB strode past the bewildered group of five. Engulfed in his own contemplations, Tiger retreated in silence.

In a flurry of movement, three subordinates rushed to the scene. They lifted Tony's lifeless body and got to work meticulously erasing any trace of the macabre event.

Chapter XIII

A new day brought a new mission. The Harmony Dungeon basement door swung open wide, revealing Leo standing in the doorway like a surprise package from the 80s. Leaning against the door frame with both palms, he grinned as if he had just discovered a secret stash of disco moves.

Rolling up the sleeves of his leather jacket, he was ready to unleash his rebellious alter ego. But not before wetting his fingers and giving his eyebrows a meticulous makeover—clearly, the real stars of the show. With a swift blow of air, he elegantly brushed away a strand of hair, as if he were auditioning for a shampoo commercial. His narrowed eyes showcased a playful charm. Snapping his fingers, he smoothly detached himself from the door, executing a spin that even the most seasoned salsa dancer would envy.

And there stood Eddy, mouth agape, staring at his friend's overnight transformation into the long-lost sibling of Michael Jackson. Unable to resist, Leo ran a hand through his hair. Fei remained motionless and expressionless. Leo twirled around himself like a wobbly spinning top, attempting to replicate moves that he believed suited him. The end result was more akin to a toddler doing interpretive dance.

Li Li couldn't hold it in any more and burst into a fit of giggles. Sensing an opportunity for more madness, she dramatically pulled out a bandanna from her own bag and joined Leo in his outrageous performance. With a shoulder-shaking dance, she tied the bandanna around her head, transforming into Leo's partner-in-crazy-crime. Eddy struggled to close his gaping mouth, blinking like a confused owl at a magic show. By this point, it was Fei's turn to laugh out loud.

Side by side, Leo and Li Li were fully immersed in their own little spectacle, as if they were the stars of a basement extravaganza.

Eddy's eyes widened as he noticed Leo approaching as if he had suddenly become a wild, uncontrollable mime. Leo began mimicking invisible words and rhythmically tapped his fingers, like a conductor gone mad. Trailing behind him, Li Li struggled to keep up but enjoyed the process. Eddy sidestepped out of the way, wondering what on earth was happening.

As the performance reached its climax, Leo dramatically blew a lock of hair off his forehead, flashing a triumphant and ridiculously provocative grin at Eddy. It was as if he was trying to make Eddy feel pathetically inferior.

"What...?" Eddy murmured, his face scrunching up in confusion like a puzzled pug. He stared at Leo, whose sly smile and mischievous eyes made Eddy feel like he was caught in a comedy-drama soap opera.

"What?" he exclaimed, hoping his outburst would break the spell of Leo's intense stare.

Fei tried to stifle her laughter with a hand over her mouth. Catching Fei's reaction, Eddy started to adopt a playful demeanour. His confusion melted away, revealing a smirk forming at the corner of his mouth. He clapped his hands once, mimicking a secret melody only he knew. He playfully bumped into Leo's shoulder, unintentionally sending him teetering off balance.

Eddy suddenly broke into a spontaneous dance routine, twirling and shimmying with exaggerated moves that made everyone's jaws drop, including Li Li, who paused her own antics to watch in awe. In a surprising twist, Eddy showcased yet another hidden talent. He pretended to flick imaginary dust off his forehead, only to stop abruptly and give Leo a menacing glare. With both hands planted on his hips, Eddy sauntered past Leo, threatening him with a slight nod and a quick lift of his chin. Leo stood there, dumbfounded, as the imaginary dust fell onto his forehead, annoyingly tickling his sensitive eyes. It was like a bad hair day and a practical joke rolled into one.

As Eddy approached the briefcases, he extracted a handful of cash stacks, transferring them into a different briefcase. With an air of finesse, he suddenly whipped out a knife, playfully executing a series of stabbing motions. Catching Leo off guard, Eddy approached him and sneakily placed the knife in Leo's unsuspecting hand. Leo stood frozen, utterly clueless about what was happening. Seizing the opportunity for mischief, Eddy expertly disarmed Leo, effortlessly twirling the blade between his fingers. And just like that, he continued his impromptu dance, completely absorbed in his own amusing spectacle.

Feeling like a failure once again, Leo tried to salvage his wounded pride by rolling down his jacket sleeves and pretending to be busy, avoiding any mention of his latest blunder.

As they stepped into the hallway, Eddy clutched the meticulously prepared briefcase tightly in his left hand. Right on his heels, Fei trailed closely, her hair tied up in a determined ponytail. Leo and Li Li marched with purpose, their bandannas and leather jackets making a striking statement.

As they ventured into Tiger's domain, he gracefully rose from his couch with his arms extended in a welcoming gesture. The room was saturated with the lingering odour of cigarette smoke.

Resting on the low table was a small bamboo box. Tiger's voice carried a hint of intrigue as he pointed at it.

"Can you bring this with you? A small gift for our Distant friends."

Eddy leaned in closer. His eyes narrowed with scepticism as he whispered into Tiger's ear. The room fell into a hushed silence.

"What is it? An empty box? Tiger, I need my weapons ready and my goods clean. No empty promises."

Tiger reached out, offering his hand in a gesture of loyalty.

"We're brothers, Eddy. No empty promises."

After a moment's hesitation, Eddy clasped Tiger's hand, their bond reaffirmed in an unspoken understanding.

Leo let out a deep sigh. After a firm nod, Tiger excused himself.

Intrigued by the contents of the small box, Leo seized it, only to have Eddy slapping the back of his hand.

"We deliver; we don't care about the specifics. Have you forgotten?"

"Sir, yes, sir," Leo straightened his posture.

The door flung wide open again, revealing the unexpected entrance of two men. Leo's face erupted in pure delight as he noticed the two newcomers.

His mind wandered, conjuring up vibrant memories from the early days of the mission. Like faded snapshots in an old album, he could see Li Li's agile hands retrieving wallets from these two unsuspecting individuals. In a smooth transition, Leo imagined himself inside the police station, arranging the pilfered IDs with his fingertips. His mental image of the stolen identities coalesced into reality as the two faces stood before him. Arnold's fair complexion strikingly contrasted with Kevin's tan, reminiscent of the vivid photographs.

"Arnold von Weißenberger! Little Kevin Lee!" Leo whispered, his voice infused with a mix of astonishment and joy.

Yet, the two figures remained oblivious, completely failing to recognise him. Kevin remained impassive behind his sunglasses, while Arnold, deliberately averted his gaze.

As Eddy's eyes met Arnold's, he couldn't help but make a comparison of their heights. The realisation of his own inferiority gnawed at him.

"Let's get going," Kevin finally spoke, immediately turning his back.

Leo's eager anticipation dissipated as he bore witness to Kevin's arrogant response. The situation left him visibly disappointed, causing an involuntary grimace to cross his face. Arnold extended his hand towards the briefcase and Eddy handed it over.

The six of them emerged from the Harmony Dungeon. Arnold flashed the keys to a parked grey van, signifying his intent to take the wheel. Leo's grimace deepened as he realised he had no say in where he would sit. With a nod, Kevin claimed the coveted spot beside the driver, leaving Leo no option but to squeeze into the overcrowded back-seat. Despite the van's spaciousness capable of accommodating a few more, Leo felt suffocated.

Kevin and Arnold led the team as they stepped through the heavy double doors of Eclipse. The rhythmic pulse of the nightclub music ignited their senses. Flickering neon lights illuminated the dance floor. Bodies moved in a synchronised frenzy, surrendering themselves to the intoxicating melodies that spilled from the DJ's booth. The pulsating beats reverberated through their bodies, matching the adrenaline coursing through their veins.

"What's the deal with these nightclubs, man?" Leo leaned closer to Eddy's ear. "Seriously, what is it with nightclubs that they always choose this place for their business nonsense? Pisses me off."

As they manoeuvred through the crowd, Arnold's eyes darted across the diverse array of patrons. The eclectic mix of club-goers was a tapestry of human emotions—joy, desire and hidden agendas. The sea of faces blurred together, their features distorted by the strobe lights that danced across the room.

The group ascended the metal stairs cocooned by glass. The sound of their footsteps was drowned out by the blaring music. They walked along a narrow corridor that looked like it was designed by a mad architect on a tight budget. The walls were covered in an eclectic mix of colourful wallpaper and the flickering fluorescent lights added a touch of surrealism to the scene.

They reached the end of the corridor and Arnold opened a door. Before them lay a room filled with ten elderly individuals engrossed in a game of mah-jong.

The heavy door closed behind the team, muffling the aggressive beats from below. The elderly players glanced up, their faces devoid of any emotion at the sight of the newcomers.

Arnold and Kevin proceeded to make their way to the door on the opposite side of the room, hugging the wall on their right. Eddy, Leo, Fei and Li Li awkwardly tailed the two, while everyone else in the room watched.

"Gentlemen," Leo acknowledged their presence with an exaggerated nod.

One of the men spat out his dentures, holding them in his palm as if ready to start a fight.

"Alright, hurry up my friends!" Leo pushed himself into Eddy to speed up the process.

As they left the room, Arnold guided them up another round of stairs and out on a rooftop. Reaching the platform, the wind grew stronger and resembled the approach of a helicopter landing. Leo threw his hands up.

"Oh, come on! Another rooftop, are you serious?"

Li Li brushed past him.

"Just shut up, will you?"

Eddy shielded his forehead with his hand. Fei and Li Li proceeded cautiously. Arnold forcefully placed the briefcase on the cold concrete and promptly sat on it. Little Kevin started energetically shifting his weight from one foot to another, as if preparing for a confrontation. Despite his vigorous movements, his sunglasses remained immobile. Leo rolled his eyes.

In the midst of Kevin's warm-up, two men strolled towards the group.

Leo retreated, positioning himself next to Eddy. Li Li became curious, but Fei touched her shoulder, urging her not to attract attention as a precautionary measure.

The two mobsters scrutinised each person with dark, penetrating eyes. While maintaining eye contact, one of them opened a diamond-filled briefcase.

"Wow!" Li Li whispered in amazement, hoping she could at least touch some of them.

"Let's see the money," one of the men inquired, gazing insistently at Arnold's black briefcase.

"Throw the diamonds our way then," Kevin asserted and assumed a firm stance.

Eddy sighed, feeling like an extra brought in to witness the predictable exchange of dialogue. Leo flinched as he got a clearer view of the mobsters' faces. He then raised a finger as if wanting to say something. Examining the features of the mobster more intently, Leo inhaled abruptly.

"Eddy," he whispered to his friend, tilting his head discreetly so no one else could hear.

Eddy didn't respond, his attention fixed on the customary exchange of glances between the opposing teams.

"Eddy!" Leo insisted in a hushed voice.

"What is it, Leo?" he kept his attention locked on the mobsters on the other side.

"That's not Zayon, or is it?" Leo rushed to whisper back, even placing a hand over his mouth in case they possessed the ability to read lips from a distance.

"Who...?" Eddy murmured, only partially focused on his friend's words.

"You know! That Zayon... Zoyan!" Leo whispered again. "He's on TV all the time. He's in the movies."

Eddy snorted, after which he rapidly adopted a serious expression. He covered his mouth before speaking.

"Stop speculating, this is serious."

Offended by Eddy's indifference, Leo pouted and crossed his arms. He lifted his gaze once more, carefully examining the features of the mobster who was still engaged in the argument with Little Kevin. Convinced of his correctness and his instinctive inability to be mistaken, Leo took a confident step forward while wearing a smile on his face.

"The money," said the mobster.

"Diamonds first," insisted Kevin.

Just as Eddy considered intervening, Leo raised his hand capturing everyone's attention.

"I'm a huge fan!" he exclaimed enthusiastically, bursting into high-pitched laughter while gesturing towards the intimidating figure of the mobster gentleman in front of him.

Fei and Li Li sighed.

"What are you doing?" Eddy protested in a whisper.

"I'm proving you that I'm right," Leo whispered back, still holding his arm up. "Hey Zayon, my friend, I'm a big fan of yours!"

Eddy let out a disappointed sigh. Arnold and Kevin shifted their attention to Leo, then cast curious glances at the mobster, silently questioning whether there was a connection between them. The mobster's frown deepened, conveying a clear message of his stern reluctance to entertain any further jests.

"Zayon...?" Leo inquired, sounding more like a statement, desperately hoping he had nailed the pronunciation. Yet, his smile slowly faded away. "Ain't it Zayon...? Zoyan? Zayun? Zoyon? Nah...? Nah," he realised, the corners of his mouth gradually drooping, fully comprehending that he had gotten himself into one hell of a predicament.

Fei touched her forehead with two fingers. Eddy scratched his head to express a hint of desperate confusion. Li Li nervously swallowed, her anxiety palpable.

"Ah... ha-ha!" Leo attempted to brush it off as a simple incident. "Ha-ha... ha... ha," his voice faded when the mobster left the diamond briefcase behind and started approaching him with determination.

Leo widened his eyes and took two steps back. Arnold pulled out a pistol and pointed it at the man, prompting him to freeze.

"The diamonds!" Kevin stated decisively.

Leo then erupted into laughter once more, thrusting both hands into the back pockets of his jeans. In an attempt to be amusing, he took a few nonchalant steps forward, donning the same amicable expression while still chuckling. With the intention of brushing off the earlier incident, Leo was ready to come up with a different topic. As he came face-to-face with the man though, his demeanour quickly shifted back.

"Holy shit! Y'all really look alike, no lie!" His eyes widened again in astonishment. "You sure you ain't twins? Wait a minute!" he confidently interjected, pointing his index finger. "Doppelganger!" he added, accompanied by a slightly awkward grin, bursting into a clumsy yet wholehearted laughter.

The mobster's face contorted into a fierce scowl and with a sudden motion, he retrieved a concealed gun and pointing it at Arnold. Little Kevin flinched, acutely aware of being caught in the crossfire between two pistols. Regaining his caution Leo raised both hands in a defensive gesture.

"Yo, paws up! This ain't no joke!" he commanded Kevin, his tone completely serious and void of any irony.

The mobster mumbled something unintelligible, conveying a few disapproving words regarding Leo's presence.

Eddy pulled out his own pistol and aimed it at the mobster duo, strafing to one side to take the flank. He urged the man to drop his weapon.

"Ha, we got you!" Leo exclaimed, placing a hand on his hip.

Discarding his gun, the alleged lookalike clenched his fists. With a quick head tilt, Arnold's eyes locked onto Kevin, silently conveying the urgent message to release the briefcase. Kevin unleashed a swift kick that propelled the briefcase forward. It skidded along the concrete floor, leaving a faint trail of anticipation in its wake.

The lookalike mobster snatched a glance at the contents before shooting a significant look back at his partner. Without uttering a word, the other man dropped down to one knee. He drew closer to the open briefcase.

“Come on, hurry up,” Arnold ordered. “We don’t need a showcase, just hand them over.”

The man shuffled behind the briefcase. Sealing it shut with his left hand, he looked up at Arnold and grinned. Arnold’s eyes narrowed. The mobster’s right hand swung forward from behind his back and lobbed a small sphere towards him.

There was no time to react.

The grenade exploded with a deafening roar, lighting up the rooftop in a chaotic ball of fire. The forceful blast tore through the surroundings, shattering windows and sending shock waves of destruction rippling through the space.

Eddy, Fei, Leo, and Li Li were hurled mercilessly, their bodies tossed like rag dolls. Their ears rang and the pain of their collisions with the concrete around them was numbed by adrenaline.

As the smoke and dust began to settle, the aftermath revealed a scene of devastation. The two masterminds behind the lethal gambit had vanished, as had both briefcases.

Leo struggled to prop himself up on one arm and scanned the desolate scene.

"What did they say about guns being too loud?"

Eddy checked his inner pockets. The small bamboo box was intact.

The lifeless bodies of Arnold and Kevin lay motionless on the charred concrete. Arnold, the Nordic from Disneyland and Kevin, the little man hiding behind sunglasses—both extinguished in the blink of an eye.

As Leo remembered the moment when the two ID cards overlapped, his vision became blurred. It was even more disorienting to have never known anything beyond a name and a photo. Once again, it reaffirmed to him that the course of their lives was shaped by anonymous appearances and brutal disappearances. These events would ultimately carry no significance in the history of the Triads.

"Man, such a waste of a handsome face!" Leo cast a regretful gaze towards the direction the two mobsters had likely vanished. "But he's no Zayon, that's for sure."

Eddy helped Fei up, extending a hand to lift her from the ground. Fei's clothes were tattered and smudged with dirt. She had to put a hand on a nearby railing to steady herself. Leo and Li Li managed to help each other up, their faces similarly covered in a thin layer of grime and dismay.

As the four survivors gathered their bearings, their attention turned to Arnold and Kevin, who lay motionless on the floor. The blast had torn through their clothing, leaving tattered shreds clinging to their charred forms. Burns and deep lacerations marred their flesh.

Arnold's lifeless eyes stared vacantly at the sky, his once imposing spirit extinguished forever. His body lay twisted and contorted, a haunting reminder of the destructive forces at play. Kevin, too, bore heavy marks of the explosion. His limbs were mangled, broken beyond recognition and his body was sprawled at an unnatural angle.

Amidst the wreckage, a gust of wind swept through the scene, carrying with it a fluttering wad of money. The bills danced and twirled in the breeze, caught in a whimsical ballet as if mocking the tragedy that had unfolded. It was a stark juxtaposition—the beauty of the violet-hued sky against the grim reality of the fallen.

The team's attention lingered on the swirling currency, a sombre reminder of the motives that had led them to this treacherous precipice. They knew, however, that they couldn't dwell on it for long. Time was of the essence and with their fallen comrades in mind, they steeled themselves to carry on with their mission.

Rumours swirled about the Triads' ironclad dominion over souls, even in the realm of death. Eddy picked up the wad of money. As the radiant sunset unfurled its enchanting hues, a contrasting narrative emerged. It whispered of absolution, suggesting that these enigmatic beings had, in truth, achieved emancipation, a liberation beyond mortal constraints.

Darkness blanketed the city. What was left of the team nestled on a secluded set of steps, within a tranquil corner of a park overlooking the shimmering lake.

Eddy withdrew a crumpled banknote from his pocket and took out a lighter. He set the edge of the bill ablaze. The mesmerising dance of flickering flames brought an eerie charm to the scene.

"What are you doing?" Leo clutched Eddy's shoulder.

"For the afterlife."

"Man, that's a whole lotta cash! They better be throwing the wildest party up there, 'cause it's gonna be one heavenly celebration!"

"Don't worry, Tiger can and will print more," Eddy cautioned, his voice reassuring and confident.

As Eddy's words sank in, Leo loosened his grip on his shoulder. Eventually, he nodded in acknowledgement.

"Let's do it then," Leo declared with a decisive tone. He stretched his hand and Eddy released the rest of the money.

Eddy ignited another banknote and then passed the lighter to Leo. He placed the money on the curb and watched with gleaming eyes as it burned. Leo followed suit, mimicking the action. Without uttering a word, Li Li and Fei each took a banknote and ignited the corners of the bills.

The flames danced in the darkness.

As they stacked the bills one upon another, the smoke emitted a distinctive scent of smouldering wood. Eddy used the sole of his foot to push the remaining fragments into the water, causing the ashes to disintegrate and vanish.

Leo raised the lighter and locked eyes with his friend. Eddy nodded, encouraging Leo to burn the remaining money. As it caught fire, Eddy observed the gradual disintegration of the banknote. Leo narrowed his eyes.

"Eddy?"

Eddy turned his head and looked at his friend.

"Eddy, you have a lighter in your pocket."

He glanced down at the front pocket of his trousers.

"No, I mean *this* lighter," Leo rephrased, pointing to the lighter they used to burn the money. "Eddy, do you smoke?!"

"No."

"Eddy, my friend, you're keeping something from me!" Leo was fired up, trailing Eddy as he stood up. "Look, listen up, why are you acting like I'm invisible? Huh?"

Eddy rubbed his palms to remove residue from his hands.

"Eddy, are you smoking?!"

Eddy pointed towards the far end of the park, drawing Fei's attention.

"You're smoking!"

"Nah."

Fei shook her head as she observed the childish argument.

"Yes, you are," Leo insisted and swiftly moved past Eddy and Fei, positioning himself in front of both. He raised a finger, signalling his eagerness to contribute further to the conversation.

“I'm of legal age,” Eddy added, giving Leo a gentle shove before joining Fei in stride.

Leo froze in place, mouth agape and a finger pointing at Eddy. He let out a sigh that could power a wind turbine, bracing himself for a comeback. While Eddy and Fei gradually moved away, Leo lingered in a state of disappointment.

Suddenly, Li Li raised her phone.

“Now, if I don’t die naked!”

The three agents turned their gaze back towards her.

"Die, how?" Leo hollered, strutting towards her with a few quick steps. "Is that some new lingo you younger folks are throwing around, or are you genuinely hoping for that to go down?" he quizzed, narrowing one eye on purpose.

Li Li pointed at her phone, drawing Eddy's attention.

"I don't care if the devil comes after me, but I can't count all these zeros," she murmured as she stared thoughtfully at her phone.

"What?!" Leo snatched the phone from her hands. "Damn! How the heck do you read this number, huh?! Eddy, get over here! These decimals are seriously driving me nuts, man!"

His curiosity piqued, Eddy approached and peered at the phone. He read the staggering sum displayed in the message and his eyes widened. He turned to Li Li, his expression filled with questions. Fei joined them, curious as well.

"Where did you get this message from?"

"It's the amount Tiger just transferred from his account," she replied, taking her phone back.

"And how did you—?"

"I've been monitoring it for a while now." Li Li replied nonchalantly.

Leo clapped his hands in excitement.

"Girl, who are you?!"

"It's not a big deal. Tech is doing me a huge favour. I'm not putting in much effort myself."

"It *is* a big deal! Can I see?"

"Sure," she placed the phone in Eddy's hands.

Eddy meticulously read through the messages, while Leo struggled to comprehend the numbers he was seeing. The phone began to ring, showing an unfamiliar number. Eddy swivelled the screen towards Li Li, signalling that she had an incoming call.

She snatched the phone and answered, attentively listening for a few seconds.

"Apologies, but you've dialled the wrong number. I'll call you back," she said briskly, promptly ending the call.

Leo raised an eyebrow

"Huh?"

"He had the wrong number."

"Then why the hell did you tell *him* you would call *him* back?" Leo made sure to call her out.

"That's the polite thing to do."

"It's not! You can't just be nice to every creep trying to hit on you!"

"You're crazy." Li Li nodded to emphasise her words. "Has anyone ever told you that? Because if not, I'm here all day."

"By the way, just to clarify, you're making sure to keep worms away from your phone, yeah?" Eddy intervened, trying to steer the conversation away from trivial matters.

Confused, Li Li frowned, not fully understanding the question.

"I mean viruses, hackers."

"Do you think they're after me already?"

"They might as well be."

"Don't worry, I got this." Li Li showed her thumbs up.

With a delayed reaction, Leo took a deep breath

"The polite thing to do? Am I the one going crazy here? Picture this: what if it's a full-on psychopath? What would you do then, huh?! Nobody around to bail you out when you find yourself in trouble again!"

Li Li crossed her arms and took a firm stance.

"Leo, stop this shit, okay?"

Leo remained focused on her, his eyes locked onto her presence. A mix of joy and surprise formed across his face. With deliberate intention, he turned away. He purposefully avoided direct eye contact, ensuring that his anger had the necessary room to dissipate and fade away. As he moved, his fingertips grazed his flushed cheek. It was a rare moment, perhaps the only one, when she had addressed him by his name. Yet, he couldn't comprehend why this simple gesture had such a profound effect on him.

Eddy walked alongside Fei, with Li Li quickening her pace to catch up.

Leo found himself falling behind. He raised two fingers to his mouth, moistening them on his tongue and meticulously adjusted his eyebrows with the tips of his fingers. Running a hand through his dusty hair, he attempted to mimic a rehearsed dance move, but a sudden twinge in his shoulder reminded him of his wounds. He executed a smooth twist on the balls of his feet and gracefully followed his friends. His steps resembled a dance while he simultaneously mouthed a song known only to him.

Chapter XIV

"The two of them managed to get away with the money." Eddy's words were acknowledged by Tiger without questioning him further. "And we've suffered the loss of two lives."

The insignificance of life became apparent when compared to a briefcase containing counterfeit money. However, even the value of the money diminished significantly due to the excessive production occurring daily, rendering it ultimately inconsequential.

Eddy, Leo, Fei and Li Li found themselves in a small room within the Harmony Dungeon, surrounded by chaotic clutter. Computers stood atop stacks of old DVDs and tangled cables. The disarray of random paperwork filled the room with documents strewn haphazardly across the worn-out desks. Among the dishevelled mess, stacks of cash mingled with fake passports, forged documents and unregistered firearms and ammunition. Stolen jewellery and hidden safes containing large sums of undeclared cash all crowded the room.

"Man, where the heck did you learn how to do this?!" Leo exclaimed, leaning in close to Li Li as she meticulously worked on unlocking Tiger's small bamboo box. "I mean, I only knew the paper-clip method, but you're on a whole different level!"

"Hmm, there's also the safety pin technique," she murmured in a low and determined voice, her attention fully absorbed by the task at hand. "Eddy, could you pass me that glove?"

Slipping the glove onto her right hand, she turned her attention back towards the box. Eddy observed her with a mix of curiosity and intrigue.

"Do you need a hand?"

"Nope," she whispered with a smile as she popped the lid open.

"Wow! You're quick! Even faster than Eddy!" Leo was more than impressed. Eddy blinked a few times and tried to look away as if pretending to be unaware of Leo's statement.

The team then glared inside the box. It was empty.

"Why did Tiger give this to us?" Li Li questioned.

"He *is* playing with us. I still don't understand why." Fei picked up the box.

She proceeded to retrieve a small stack of cards containing the transaction records from the previous week and neatly packed them away in a bag under the table. Additionally, she went on to obtain a sample of the materials employed in the printing process of the banknotes.

"But wait a minute!" Leo asserted, standing up and sceptically looking at Li Li.

"What?" she muttered while putting all the items back in their place.

"Who taught you all this?"

"My uncle. That was already a few years ago. I learnt the thing with the needle and some other cool stuff from him."

Leo listened without saying a word.

"Look, you're not the only agents your boss has, you know?" she added in a whisper, proudly standing up.

"From a mere pickpocket…" Leo grimaced, scratching his head and tousling his hair.

A subordinate of Tiger's appeared from the dimly lit hallway, his eyes fixed on the four individuals in the room as he approached with curiosity. With composure, Li Li smoothly slid the cards behind her onto the metallic table.

Leo rapidly turned around. He ran over to the mobster and snapped his fingers to distract his attention, then effortlessly delivered a punch. The thug staggered backwards clutching his nose as blood streamed down his face.

Fei hurriedly gathered the remaining materials, while Eddy positioned himself defensively in front of her. In a quick scan of the room, Li Li verified that all of the evidence was hidden out of sight.

"Whoa, whoa, hold up! My bad, my friend! Leo here, expressing his sincerest apologies!" Leo stressed, trying to help the subordinate while also obstructing his vision. "I mean, damn, I caught a glimpse of your face and, uh, I thought you had a nervous tick or something. Wanted to give you a little scare, you know? Thought it might help. Totally misread the situation, my bad, really sorry!"

The subordinate signalled that everything was fine and turned his head to wipe the blood from his nose.

"What an idiot," Leo muttered as he turned back to his team.

Two days later, one of Tiger's subordinates intercepted Eddy in the hallway and informed him that they needed to have a discussion regarding certain matters. Once again, the topic centred around the ongoing conflict between them and the Distant Coalition.

Eddy and the team were summoned into a meeting room.

Once there, they discovered five other subordinates awaiting their arrival. The room buzzed with anticipation as each subordinate scrutinised them closely.

The briefing unveiled. The stage was set for a dramatic montage, a symphony of commitment and steadfast focus.

But Leo was having none of it.

"Wait a minute, you mean to tell me those dudes want our stuff, but they ain't willing to cough up the dough?"

"Yeah, man. They want the memory cards real bad, but they ain't about to drop a dime for 'em," one of the men shot back, lounging in the chair next to the wall.

"Oh, so they're trying to play us for fools now!" Leo exclaimed, hands planted firmly on his hips, his words dripping with frustration.

"You need these," one of them clarified, producing a few tiny microphones.

Leo frowned while looking at the small device in his palm. He grimaced as he pinched it between two fingers.

"Are you trying to tell me to shove this damn earplug up my ear?!" His face twisted in disgust. "Man, it's all waxed up!"

The mobsters looked at him with dumbfounded indifference.

"Listen up, folks! Personal hygiene is a must!" Leo shot back in an intellectual tone. "Whose nasty ear gunk is on this damn earplug? I wanna know, right now!"

The mobsters glanced at each other. They didn't provide any answer. Leo sighed, shaking his head in exasperation.

"Yo, yo, yo, we ain't about to sport these duds, what the hell! But also, come on, this mess can't just stay as it is, my friends. We need to sit down and have a serious talk."

After meticulously clarifying all the details and reviewing the guidelines for personal hygiene to ensure the well-being of the mobsters, the four agents set out on their mission to deliver the cards. The information stored on those cards appeared to hold significant value for the Distant Coalition, lending an intriguing element to the entire endeavour right from the outset.

As the four raced along the highway, a gentle warm breeze caressed their faces. Leo leaned his arm on the door and rested his chin on his left wrist, fixating his gaze ahead while stray strands of hair danced across his forehead. The meandering road stretched out before them, leading them to the meeting point. Amidst the journey, Li Li reached into Eddy's backpack and retrieved his camera. Skilfully, she aimed the lens at Leo and discreetly captured a photo of him. Satisfied with the result, she shifted her focus to the right, capturing the sunny surroundings.

As Eddy checked his rear-view mirror, he noticed a sleek black car trailing closely behind them. The car managed to effortlessly glide along, maintaining firm proximity to their own vehicle. A blend of curiosity and apprehension stirred within Eddy as he pondered the potential dangers that lurked behind the tinted windows.

"They've been tailing us for the past fifteen minutes."

Leo jolted and theatrically turned his head, noticing the car as well.

"Could you be any more obvious?!" Eddy snapped.

"What's your problem? I didn't even say anything!" Leo sulked and leaned back against his seat.

The navigation system announced the approach of a gas station.

"If there are a maximum of five people in the car and we're expecting three guys on the other side, do you think we can handle it?" Fei asked and Eddy quickly turned his head.

"Of course! I'm the Left-Hander-With-The-Right-Fist!" Leo flexed his muscles.

Li Li rolled her eyes.

"Shut up..."

The car followed them closely as they turned towards the gas station.

"The meeting place isn't far from here. We have to shake them off before we get there," Eddy said as he looked ahead and counted the seven cars waiting in line. "It won't take long here; we just need an open space in front of us."

Leo attentively scanned the area, taking in his surroundings. The sleek black car came to a halt a short distance behind their convertible. The vehicles ahead were moving at a steady pace. Just as the car in front of the young agents made a left turn, Leo acted promptly. Before Eddy could react, Leo reached down and unzipped one of the black bags at his feet. From within, he retrieved a handful of balloons, originally meant to be inflated with helium.

"Where the hell did you get those from?" Li Li was stunned by whatever was happening.

Leo grinned and jumped out of the car without opening the door.

“Let’s give them a reason to say hello.”

Approaching one of the employees at the gas station, Leo politely asked if they could inflate a few balloons for him. He explained that he desperately needed them for a special birthday party. Eddy watched the dialogue with curiosity. The black car wasn’t moving. Leo handed each balloon one by one to the employee, glancing mischievously at his friend while raising an eyebrow. Eddy laughed. Two more cars pulled up behind them. Li Li watched them out of the corner of her eye. As the employee filled the last two balloons, Leo returned to the car, pulling out another stack of colourful balloons.

"What on earth is he doing?" Li Li whispered, sensing the mounting tension.

"He's provoking them." Fei watched the rear-view mirror

Seeing Leo approaching him again, the employee gestured that he wasn't in fact allowed to do this.

“It's for the anniversary of my first love," Leo insisted with puppy eyes.

Yielding to Leo's persistence, the employee reluctantly took another balloon. Leo reciprocated with a smile before shifting his focus towards Eddy, conveying a serious nod.

A civilian car impatiently blared its horn, oblivious to the hold-up ahead. This triggered the mobsters inside the black car, who promptly emerged onto the street, forcefully slamming their car doors with aggressive grunts.

One of the men adjusted his jacket to reveal a lavish knife hanging onto the belt embellishing his trousers. With deliberate slowness, he advanced forward. Noticing his approach, Leo rushed to hand the employee two balloons simultaneously, now completely focused on the mobster's every move. Eddy caught a glimpse of the approaching man through the rear-view mirror, his heart pounding with anticipation.

Eddy catapulted himself out of the car and grabbed a nearby water hose. He sprayed the jet of water directly at the mobster's face, momentarily blinding him and disrupting his balance. Five more figures emerged from the vehicle, charging towards Eddy.

Weariness seeped into Eddy's bones. A sigh escaped his lips as he placed a hand on his hip, realising he underestimated his count by one.

Eddy's eyes darted around, searching for an advantage. He noticed a row of small fuel canisters nearby and instantly grabbed one. He swung the canister, hitting one of the mobsters and sending him crashing into the hood of his car. Wincing, he hoped he hadn't damaged his beloved vehicle.

The second mobster lunged at Eddy with his knife raised. Eddy dodged to one side and seized a fuel pump nozzle. He twisted it, releasing a jet of fuel at the mobster in retaliation. The man slipped and fell, losing his knife in the process. As the man struggled to regain his footing, Eddy pulled out his cigarette lighter and wiggled it threateningly. Wide-eyed, the man hastily attempted to roll away to one side.

The commotion had captured the attention of the lone employee, who continued to inflate balloons as he watched the chaos unfold. The balloons started shaking in his hands.

Fei jumped out of the car, ready to back Eddy up. Li Li slid out of the car and grabbed the balloons from Leo's hands. She shoved him towards the fight.

"Stop being useless."

The remaining three assailants darted towards Eddy. Fei spotted a rack of motor oil. Without hesitation, she grabbed a bottle and twisted off the cap. She doused the floor, creating a slippery barrier between Eddy and their assailants. Discarding the bottle, she armed herself with a fire extinguisher.

As the first mobster lunged towards Eddy, Fei swung the extinguisher and knocked the mobster off balance. His foot slipped and he crashed hard onto the slick concrete. The force of the motion caused Fei to stumble and fall onto her knees.

Eddy evaded the punches and kicks of the second mobster. Fei seized the opportunity and manoeuvred around the distracted mobster. She deployed a canister of compressed air, spraying it towards the man's face, momentarily blinding him.

Eddy seized the advantage. He grabbed the nearby stack of metal shelves and tipped them over. The shelves crashed down, creating a formidable obstacle that impeded the progress of the third mobster.

Regaining his composure, the blinded mobster swung wildly in Eddy's direction, his aim off-kilter. Fei intercepted the attack, parrying the knife strike with a metal rod she had found on the ground. She countered, landing a series of precise blows that left the mobster disarmed.

Fei's quick thinking allowed Eddy to regroup and join the fight. Working in tandem, they cornered their final adversary. Eddy launched a side kick that folded his adversary in half. Fei snatched the discarded gasoline nozzle and aimed it at the mobster, threatening to douse him in fuel.

Realising the dire consequences of his actions, the man froze, his eyes widening in fear. With a flick of her wrist, Fei gestured towards the gasoline-soaked floor and held up a lighter. The danger of a potential fire compelled the mobster to submit, abandoning his knife in defeat.

Holding his hands on his hips, Leo strode up behind Fei. He stared down at the mobster and shook his head disapprovingly.

The employee's grip on the balloons tightened. With a deft manoeuvre, Li Li diverted his focus away from the escalating confrontation.

"Blow." she threatened her hostage while widening her eyes, not allowing him to be concerned about what he shouldn't be.

The employee's hands continued shaking but Li Li paid no attention to his uneasiness as handed him another balloon.

The floor was littered with groaning criminals. One managed to rise to his feet, having regained possession of his knife. He assessed the situation and charged at Eddy, as a couple of others struggled to a standing position.

Leo lunged forward and grabbed the wrist holding the knife. He used the mobster's own momentum against him, spinning him around in a dizzying circle. The disoriented assailant stumbled and his grip on the knife faltered. Leo delivered a powerful strike with the back of his hand, connecting squarely with the mobster's jaw. The mobster collapsed to the ground, unconscious and disarmed. Leo clenched his fist in satisfaction, admiring his own muscular prowess.

Meanwhile, Eddy's vision blurred from a direct punch to the head and he desperately tried to regain his bearings. Dazed from being kicked, Fei stumbled backward and inadvertently collided with the door of Eddy's car. She tipped over and landed in the passenger seat.

Leo's quick thinking and actions had bought Eddy a crucial moment of reprieve, but it hadn't quite been enough. Focusing through the pain, he spotted the mobster preparing to strike again. Eddy reached out and grasped a nearby broom-sized wind-shield squeegee.

Time seemed to slow as Eddy swung the squeegee with all his might, deflecting the incoming blow just in time. The improvised weapon struck the mobster's arm, causing him to drop his weapon in surprise and pain.

The honking cars behind them added to the chaotic scene, providing a cover of noise and confusion. Eddy sidestepped the mobster's desperate lunges, using his car as a makeshift obstacle.

Li Li attentively observed every movement while continuing to hand out balloons, ensuring they were inflated at the same pace.

Leo spotted another man reaching for his knife. He lunged forward. With a firm grip, Leo seized the mobster's arm, initiating a fierce battle of strength and willpower.

Leo and the mobster engaged in a wild struggle, their faces contorting with determination. Muscles strained and bulged, sweat dripping down their brows like a leaky facet. It was a fight to end all fights, the kind that makes you question the sanity of the universe.

Out of nowhere, Tiger leapt into the fray with impeccable timing. He unleashed a couple of blows, each one landing with a satisfying thud. The mobster staggered under the onslaught, taken aback by Tiger's unexpected ferocity.

"Tiger!" Eddy grabbed his attention, throwing a knife for him to catch.

Tiger thanked him with a quick nod and returned to the fight.

With a mighty roar, Leo finally toppled the mobster backward, leaving him sprawled on the ground, defeated and disoriented. Leo rose to his feet, a victorious glint in his eyes, though he couldn't help but glance at Tiger.

Breaking through the mobster's guard, Tiger's clenched fist swung down and plunged into his shoulder. The thug cried out in pain. Then stopped. Both adversaries looked at each other, and then at the knife embedded in his shoulder.

The retractable, plastic blade popped back out of the handle as Tiger withdrew it. The knife, once a symbol of imminent danger, proved to be nothing more than a prop.

Panic flashed across Tiger's face as he glanced at Eddy for an explanation, but there was no time to dwell on the absurdity. Refocused and undeterred, he ducked under the mobster's desperate left hook and countered with more brutal strikes to the body.

Eddy forcefully seized one of the mobsters by the collar, slamming him onto the unforgiving asphalt. The thug still resisted, so Eddy continued to slam his head into the floor. Behind him, Leo closely observed every move Eddy made. His gaze fixed and his body frozen in place, his head throbbed from a recent blow.

In that intense moment, a memory from the past intertwined with the present. Leo vividly recalled himself striking his forehead against the floor while Boss, in an odd posture, pleaded for him to stop. Dazed by these haunting memories, Leo instinctively placed a hand on his temple. With each merciless blow, Eddy pounded the mobster's head against the floor.

"Stop!" Leo shouted, reaching out a hand.

In an instant, Eddy jolted awake as if emerging from a deep trance. He released his grip on the mobster. The beleaguered mobster remained limp, his breathing laboured.

"What the hell is this?" Tiger questioned Eddy, showing him the prop knife.

"Well what's the deal with all these empty guns and fake-ass delivery items you've given us, huh?" Leo replied instead. "Like it when it happens to you?"

"Ask Kingpin." Tiger avoided further conversation and walked to his car.

"How did he find us here anyway?" Leo wondered.

"He's probably tracking those earplugs." Fei shrugged.

"Ew, gross! I should've known better."

Li Li handed the employee his final balloon, while festive balloons surrounded her, scattered in abundance. As the final balloon was inflated, the relieved employee dashed into the store.

"Come on, let's get moving!" Li Li urged the team as she was the first to hop into the car.

The team piled in into Eddy's convertible as he turned the car around, stepping on the gas pedal and merging onto the road with a surge of speed. Tiger tailed him in his own car.

While the car was speeding down the road, Leo grinned as he took out a bag of chocolate cookies.

"Ah, man, all this crazy stuff got me feeling real hungry."

Turning to the two girls in the back, he urged them to help themselves. Both of them declined, still recovering from the incident.

"More for me." He shrugged with a mouthful.

"We gotta make it to our destination before these guys go blabbing about their failure," Eddy said and stepped on the gas.

"What? Huh? What'd you say? Sorry... I was too busy chomping down to catch that," Leo mumbled with a mouthful of cookies, crumbs spilling out as he spoke.

"I said we need to hurry," Eddy repeated while paying attention to the road.

Leo nodded in agreement, pulling out another cookie.

"Pass me one too, you jerk," Eddy murmured while glancing at him out of the corner of his eye.

"What? Huh? What'd you say?" Leo repeated, this time fully understanding the statement but wanting to tease his friend.

Eddy signalled his desire for a cookie by tapping his bottom lip with his index finger. Grinning mischievously, Leo wasted no time and shoved two cookies into Eddy's mouth. As Eddy began to choke, Leo couldn't help but chuckle, his eyes gleaming with a devilish delight. Holding the bag of cookies tightly to his chest, he felt confident that he was in the clear, knowing Eddy had to concentrate on driving.

The two cars came to a stop at the designated spot, at the bottom of a large cliff. The vehicles were dwarfed by the majestic hills in the distance. The land ahead was filled with rolling hills, covered in vibrant leaves and lush greenery. The cityscape glimmered in the distance, illuminated by a soft, ethereal glow.

The team and Tiger cautiously stepped out of their cars, their clothes marked by stubborn dust and smudges of oil. Eddy found comfort in the pocket of his vest, his shaky fingers ensuring the safety of the memory cards hidden inside.

Two men and a woman walked out from the shadow of the cliff and stood next to Eddy's car. Rough, tattered attire clung to their weary frames.

Tiger took the lead in front of Eddy and nodded his head.

"Kaida, Pete, Max. It’s been a while."

The three nodded in reply.

Max stood tall with a strong, imposing build. His sharp jawline bore a faint stubble, accentuating his rugged charm. Dark eyes, framed by a few lines of experience, surveyed the surroundings with an intense focus. Pete possessed a leaner frame, yet his piercing eyes held a depth that hinted at hidden layers beneath his seemingly calm exterior. Kaida stood beside them, her fiery hair cascaded down her shoulders, framing a determined face.

With nonchalance, Kaida assessed the team's wounds. Expectantly, the trio looked towards the highway and awaited their reinforcements. Tiger grinned as Pete's eyes widened in realisation. The truth struck him—there would be no reinforcements coming to their aid.

Leo couldn't help but smirk, sensing an opportunity to stir up some mischief. He approached Pete, gesturing that he had a secret to share. Piquing Pete's curiosity, Leo placed a hand on his hip and leaned in close to his ear.

"I got a little secret for you, my friend, but keep it hush-hush, alright? It's some top-secret stuff, but I'm spilling it because I know you ain't gonna blab it to anyone else."

Pete adjusted his posture, his eyes shifting from puzzlement to curiosity.

"Listen up, my friend! You know what I ain't buying? This flat Earth nonsense. You know who's behind it? Them sneaky birds. They're tired of flying in circles, so now they're spreading rumours to keep us all grounded! It's a bird conspiracy, I'm telling you!"

The three mobsters synchronised their head tilts to the right, their expressions showcasing a blend of confusion and curiosity. They endeavoured to grasp the philosophical implications embedded within his statement. They then looked at Tiger for an explanation.

"You didn't bring any cash, did you?" Tiger pointed at Max, after which he rubbed his index finger against his thumb.

"You owe us that information, Tiger. You know it."

Tiger let out a deep sigh, hands in his pocket.

"I don't owe nobody nothing."

"Come on, my friend." Leo brushed past Tiger and faced Max. "We brought you your memory cards. Give us some dough."

Without uttering a single word, Max pulled a knife out of his sleeve. In one move, he sliced Leo's wrist and up his arm, tearing through his leather jacket. At that moment, Leo was reminded of his intense aversion towards knives.

Eddy jumped in, restraining the mobster by grabbing the hand that held the knife. Leo crouched down, squinting his eyes and clutching his arm with his other hand. The surroundings started spinning and his vision blurred as he envisioned the sight and smell of blood.

After Eddy struck Max, his knife clattered to the ground, temporarily neutralising the immediate threat. With a growl, Max threw himself towards Eddy, ready to take him down. The young agent caught the man's wrist and the back of his neck, redirecting his energy to one side and delivering him to the ground in a crumpled heap.

Leo blinked at his own arm, realising that he wasn't wounded. He straightened his back and wiped the sweat off his forehead.

As the vibrant hues of the setting sun painted the city skyline, Tiger's eyes reflected a chilling determination. With a graceful flick of his wrist, he revealed a gleaming butterfly knife, its slender blade glinting in the dying light. The weight of the weapon felt familiar and comforting in his hand, a deadly extension of his will.

Max, still fumbling to pick up his own blade, found himself frozen in fear as Tiger closed in without a hint of emotion. He plunged the knife deep into Max's abdomen, silencing any chance of resistance. As Tiger withdrew the knife, blood stained the ground beneath them.

Witnessing the brutal demise of his comrade, Pete retrieved a karambit knife of his own. Tiger's butterfly knife danced through the air with speed and fluidity. With two skilful strokes, Tiger brought Pete to a sudden and irreversible end.

The chaos of the moment brought Kaida running, her battle cry echoing through the night. Yet, Tiger was a formidable adversary. He parried Kaida's attack and riposted, ending her valiant charge with a cold finality that matched the steel of his blade.

As their struggles waned, a hushed stillness settled over the scene that was accompanied solely by the gentle murmurs of the wind. The air carried a strange aura, dominated by Tiger's unstoppable prowess. The sun had set, leaving behind a city consumed by shadows.

Tiger only needed one deep breath to reset. He turned to his team with a proud nod as he packed his knife away.

"I've got your backs."

Eddy refrained from looking at the lifeless bodies. Unable to find the right words, he comforted Tiger by patting him on the shoulder.

Li Li removed the bandanna from her head and hastily secured it around Leo's wrist, her actions filled with unexpected tenderness. As Leo observed her care, a curious smile formed on his face.

However, it didn't take long for her to realise that Leo was not actually injured. She withdrew her hands and let out a cough, feeling a touch embarrassed. Just then, Leo bent over, emitting a loud groan while clenching his eyes and gripping his wrist. Panic washed over Li Li, causing her to turn back towards him. Leo opened one eye and upon catching sight of her expression, playfully stuck out his tongue. She frowned and kicked his shin in a flash, providing him with a genuine reason to complain.

Tiger casually placed a cigarette between his lips and extended his pack to Eddy, who politely declined. Instead, Li Li happily accepted a cigarette, eagerly anticipating the moment to light it. Leo snatched it from her hands. Tiger shifted his attention towards the mesmerising cityscape that shimmered in the background.

"All of this belongs to you, Eddy." Tiger's arm draped over Eddy's shoulder as he exhaled smoke. "As long as we remain brothers, I assure you, the world is yours to conquer."

Chapter XV

Boss shuffled through his wilted flower garden, wearily treading the desolate path beneath the sombre sky.

As he shut the door behind him, he cast a forlorn glance upon the vacant living room. Unconsciously, his eyes drifted to the table beside the window. A haunting vision rendered him motionless, his gaze locked in emptiness.

At the table next to the window sat his cherished wife, her visage untouched by time, mirroring the same countenance she wore decades past. A bitter-sweet smile adorned her face, emanating an ethereal allure as her delicate hands wove threads with almost divine grace. With a gentle tilt of her head, her eyes locked with his as a radiant glow enveloped her. She momentarily captivated his trembling heart. Fearful of her imminent departure, he extended a hand. Yet, in a cruel twist, the light consumed her, engulfing the table beside the window in a shroud of darkness and chilling emptiness, leaving him bereft.

An overwhelming wave of dizziness washed over Boss, causing him to clutch the edge of the chair desperately. His knuckles turned white. With a heavy sigh, he closed his weary eyes and sought solace in the cold touch of the couch's fabric against his palms. A rush of poignant memories pierced through his fragile heart like a sharp stab of bitter-sweet nostalgia.

In the dimly lit basements of his mind, he witnessed a haunting reflection of himself from two decades prior. Beads of sweat trickled down his furrowed brow as KB walked across the expansive hall, methodically rolling up his sleeves. His eyes, wide and manic, mirrored the depths of his tormented soul, while veins pulsated on his strained neck. His clenched fists trembled, locking his jaw in a tight resolve.

Boss and his team stood frozen, statues of silence. No words escaped their motionless forms.

"Traitors!" was the only word KB managed to spew forth, tinged with a venomous mixture of rage and despair.

The four agents flinched, their bodies recoiling at the sheer force of his roar. Boss's heart sank as he comprehended the irreversible consequences of their betrayal. It was too late to act, too late to salvage their crumbling loyalty.

A maniacal laughter erupted from deep within KB. Its echoes permeated the air like the haunting reverberations of an organ in an abandoned cathedral. The team surveyed their surroundings, their faces pale with realisation—they were surrounded, trapped in a web of their own making. Boss clenched both fists, ready to confront the imminent doom that awaited them.

"And I trusted you," KB bellowed.

His youthful voice carried echoes of shattered hope and betrayed friendship. As he reminisced about days gone by, he realised it had all been a charade. The new-found friend in whom he had invested so much trust turned out to be nothing more than an undercover agent, ready to condemn him for the remainder of his existence. His demeanour visibly darkened and a malevolent hatred consumed his features.

"You're no better than them. You're all just the same." KB inched closer.

KB pressed his palms together in a desperate gesture.

"What, you thought you could just waltz in here and arrest me?"

Boss discreetly assessed his surroundings. The mobsters surrounding them were overwhelming in numbers. Without reinforcements, their chances were bleak.

"And so, our friendship meets its bitter demise," KB declared, his eyes collecting all of his hatred and releasing it through a solitary tear.

Jolted back to the present, Boss sank onto the sofa. His hand sought solace over his heart, weighed down by the gravity of each heavy breath. But as he surrendered to the closure of his eyelids, he found himself whisked away once again to that pivotal and fateful past.

The Harmony Dungeon was engulfed in raging flames. Their fiery tongues devoured the surroundings, casting eerie shadows that danced upon the cold floor stained with his comrade's blood.

Forced to kneel amidst the inferno, Boss found himself once again locking eyes with KB, while two of the mobsters pushed down on his shoulders.

KB approached slowly and pressed his phone against Boss's ear. A desperate voice surfaced from the other end of the line, piercing through the crackling, chaotic inferno. It was Fei's innocent voice, crying out for his father's presence, echoing with a plea that resounded deeply within her father's soul.

Overwhelmed by a deluge of tears, Boss fought against the scorching reality. His desperate attempts to rise met with an immovable force as if the weight of the moment had rendered him motionless. The next voice he heard over the receiver was his wife's.

"Please come back," she cried, her anguish piercing his soul. The call ended abruptly.

Boss lifted his head, straining against the subordinates holding him down. A fierce determination burned in his eyes as he longed to break free.

"You've just slain your very own wife and daughter," KB uttered in a diabolical tone as he discarded the phone.

Boss roared in frustration and collapsed to the ground, succumbing to the weight of his shattered soul.

An explosion behind them filled the space with smoke and the flames began to surge forward.

KB witnessed the fire dance before his eyes. Many of his subordinates were groaning in pain. Only a few had escaped the blast.

In an act of desperation, one of Boss' young agents leapt out from the ashes. With an anguished cry, he launched himself at KB and slammed both feet into his chest. Both of them hit the ground hard. As KB's clothing caught fire, he instinctively rolled to quell the flames that consumed him.

Struggling to catch their breath, the four agents fought their way through the smoke towards the exit. Boss swivelled his head back at KB, ready to jump and save him from the flames. Li Li's father saw this and propelled Boss forward, resolute in his decision to spare his life from further danger.

Boss now stood mere footsteps away from the dwindling trio, his eyes fixated back on them.

In a heart-stopping instant, a colossal section of the ceiling violently detached, crashing down with thunderous force. The impact formed an impenetrable wall, a formidable barrier that now separated them, casting a dire shadow upon their fate.

Boss cried out their names with an intensity born of desperation. Tears streamed down the cheeks of one of the young men. He bravely brushed them away, mustering the strength to signal Boss to proceed on his own.

Boss realised there was only a slender chance left for his own survival, accepting the bitter truth amidst the chaos and uncertainty surrounding them.

"No," Boss shook his head. "At any cost…"

The flames surged with alarming ferocity, mercilessly devouring any lingering traces of hope. Tears welled up in Boss's eyes as he surveyed the surroundings in frantic desperation. His heart sank at the realisation that he had lost sight of his comrades. Their voices would be swallowed by the ceaseless thunder of the fire-storm, rendering them unheard.

He pushed forward with a faltering gait.

At his residence, the curving footpath covered with scented blooms led towards the wide-open entrance door. In the depths of night, the piercing lights of the fleet of ambulances cast a haunting glow on Boss' home.

Hidden beneath the table near the window, a young Fei trembled. Her wide eyes peeked through the veil of the long tablecloth, capturing the unfolding tragedy.

As the distant wails of police sirens reached Boss's ears the sound faded away, leaving behind a profound silence as he stormed into the living room.

Boss's world shattered into a thousand pieces at the sight of his beloved wife's lifeless body sprawled on the carpet, drenched in a pool of crimson. He crumbled to his knees. His tear-streaked face mingled with trails of snot, washing away the remnants of ash mirroring the anguish within his soul.

He had failed. As a man, as an agent, as a husband, as a father.

In his agony, he wept silently, his sobs stifled and barely audible. The weight of his grief pressed upon him relentlessly, crushing his spirit. He collapsed into a fetal position, a mere shell of the once formidable figure he embodied. As his tears streamed ceaselessly, Boss succumbed to the depths of unconsciousness, his body coming to rest beside his wife's pallid cheek.

Chapter XVI

The atmosphere in the Harmony Dungeon was heavy with an otherworldly quietness, as if the very walls held their breath. No machinery hummed and no chatter filled the space any longer. The corridors stood as empty as forgotten tombs, an abandoned labyrinth frozen in time. Only a few fragments of shattered glass littered the floor. Silence draped every nook and cranny.

With each step Eddy took, the weight of the dungeon's secrets pressed upon him. As he walked, he felt a twinge of unease prompting him to fix his shoelace. While tying it, he pricked his finger on a shard of glass, staining his shoe with a few drops of blood.

Annoyed, he wiped the blood away. It wasn't a good sign though; Eddy was nothing if not a careful person. Catching himself like this was normally a bad omen for things to come.

Eddy ventured into Tiger's domain only to find him waiting. Tiger's enraged expression was unmistakable, his eyes gleaming and his cheeks trembling.

"Tiger," Eddy greeted, sensing trouble in an instant.

Tiger's devilish smile widened as he clenched his jaw. He dragged a black briefcase from behind his couch and forcefully threw it at Eddy's feet. Counterfeit money spilled on the floor. Tiger lifted a few more contraband goods and slammed them against the briefcase.

"Hey, where's everyone at?" Leo bounced on his heels as he joined the duo. "Am I the only one feeling like we're playing hide and seek or what?" But his expression turned serious as he noticed all of the items across the floor.

Tiger cocked his head, intensifying his wide-eyed stare as he pursed his lips. Eddy looked away, bracing for the impending talk. Leo cautiously joined his comrade, keeping a watchful eye on Tiger.

"You're a traitor!" Tiger clenched his fists.

Leo felt a knot of nervousness tighten in his throat. Just then, both Eddy and Leo realised that Fei and Li Li were nowhere to be seen. Sensing their shared concern, Tiger broke into a maniacal laughter. His lips trembled and tears of anger welled up in his eyes. Eddy gathered his courage, taking a deliberate step forward and inhaling deeply before finally speaking.

"Where is—"

"Agent Fei?" Tiger smoothly concluded Eddy's sentence. "Ah, a very astute inquiry indeed. But allow me to enlighten you with an answer that surpasses brilliance itself."

Seeing Tiger's diabolical grin, Leo was rendered speechless. Tiger approached the formidable metal wall and pressed a button.

"A skilled young lady. She hasn't given up without a fight. Impressive, I must admit."

The colossal wall before them parted with the fluidity of an immense sliding door, revealing the very same vast hall they had ventured into when descending into the depths of the dungeon for the first time.

Wide-eyed, Eddy surveyed the scene unfolding before him. Leo took a hesitant step alongside his friend. The blinding radiance of the spotlights and the towering expanse of the ceiling bore down on them, assaulting their senses.

With a resounding clap of his hands, Tiger's presence filled every corner of the hall. Beyond the giant staircase of metal was Fei, restrained to the robust chair that teetered perilously over the edge of the railing.

"Fei!" Eddy shouted, wanting to move forward.

Tiger examined their reaction with satisfaction. Fei passively turned her head and sighed with an empty gaze.

"Fei…" Eddy whispered once again, as he saw her wounded face.

Tiger advanced with deliberate, weighty steps.

"I don't believe she can hear you."

Eddy's head swivelled frantically to survey every shadowy recess of the hall, his eyes widening as he took in the presence of the numerous Triad members surrounding them.

Ensnared by the clutches of a debilitating drug, Fei found herself utterly incapacitated. Her arms, limp and lifeless, hung by her sides tightly bound to the chair by heavy ropes.

“Eddy, you're nothing but a treacherous backstabber.” Tiger continued. “No surprises there. Your criminal game is weak, my brother, just plain weak. Kingpin had it right—I should've blasted you with every damn bullet, shut you down early on. But you know what? Deep down, I almost didn't want to believe it. Yet every part of you screams "cop". Our so-called brotherhood? Turns out it was all smoke and mirrors, an empty promise that's now been exposed.”

Li Li stirred, her feet kicking in a desperate display of resistance. Suspended close to the railing, her hands were bound by a taut rope descending from the towering ceiling. She swung barefoot, an eternity above the unforgiving floor. She sought Tiger's attention, feigning a defiant kick in his direction.

“I’d spit in your eyes if I could!"

Tiger smirked, paying no attention to her. He revelled in delight as he admired his masterpiece.

"Once upon a time," Tiger exclaimed theatrically, hands held behind his back, "There was a beautiful girl, just like those in fairy tales. But alas, what a tragedy! Prince Eddy couldn't save the poor damsel in distress."

Tiger began to applaud once again, gracefully bowing his head, while Fei weakly mouthed words. Leo observed her from afar, contemplating how to liberate her. Li Li struggled again, causing the sturdy rope to shake.

"How about one last showdown?" Tiger proposed while turning fully towards Eddy, standing tall as he gazed into his eyes.

Eddy stared at Tiger in silence, refusing to give a response.

"I'm deadly serious," Tiger insisted, his tone unshakeable. "It will be just you and me."

Tiger signalled to the entire Triad entourage to vanish. One by one, they retreated. Only one subordinate remained behind to threaten Leo with a pistol, cautioning him to remain calm.

"There! Up there!" Tiger exclaimed, cautiously pointing towards the imposing iron platform.

Stretching out from the massive stairs, the iron platform stood firmly against the concrete wall. Steps on both the left and right sides ascended towards the platform to a series of shut doors. On the opposing side, a narrow space was occupied solely by a protective railing. A web of girder supported the entire structure. Fei and Li Li were each held captive at opposing ends of the platform.

Without uttering a word, Eddy boldly advanced towards the left staircase. Mirroring him, Tiger confidently headed for the right set of iron stairs. Upon reaching the metallic platform, the gravity of the situation became evident—falling from there meant certain death. They stood ten steps apart, their fates hanging in the balance. Li Li strained to turn her head and catch a glimpse of them.

"What the hell, I'm not an owl!"

Tiger unfastened his shirt, once again exposing his tattoos. Eddy glanced downward, choosing not to calculate the exact distance to the ground. Li Li hung suspended at nearly the same height. Leo clenched his fist, an expression of encouragement on his face. Eddy nodded in approval.

The subordinate forcefully nudged Leo, causing him to involuntarily step forward.

"Are you dumb?" Leo protested, looking back at the man, but then seeing the gun pointed at him, he smiled friendly, signalling with his hand that he had chosen the wrong tone and words.

After a battle shout, Tiger charged forwards. Eddy tightened his fists, advancing with determination to claim victory.

Each of Tiger's punches brimmed with anger. For once, he had trusted someone and considered them a close friend, only to discover that fate had played a cruel trick—it was a secret agent sent to arrest him. It served as a stark reminder that trust was a luxury he couldn't afford. Anyone who crossed his path was an enemy or a potential victim. Foolishly, he regretted ever getting involved with these kids.

Unwilling to accept his fate, Tiger was now prepared to turn his former brother into a victim. Eddy deflected every blow, offering a resolute response to the questions plaguing Tiger's mind.

With each dangerous slide towards the railing, Leo and Li Li tensed, their breath held. The spotlights that bathed the vast hall gained a sharper glow and the invigorating breeze from the fans filled the hall.

Tiger stumbled, hastily retreating four steps. He raised a hand, wiping his cheek with the back of his palm. As he stared at the blood staining his hand, his fist clenched and his contemptuous focus settled on Eddy. Tiger renewed his assault, driving Eddy closer to the edge of the railing against his will. Seizing an opportunity, Eddy struck Tiger's kneecap and caused him to kneel. Yet in an instant, Tiger rebounded, smashing Eddy's head against the iron railing.

Rising on his tiptoes for a clearer view, Leo grew increasingly concerned. But both men rose back to their feet.

Warm blood trickled down Eddy's forehead, staining his face. With a deep breath, Tiger tensed his muscles. Eddy unbuttoned his black jacket, casting it over the railing. It floated down slowly, taking its time to reach the ground. Adjusting his sweaty t-shirt, Eddy tightened both fists. Tiger smirked.

Li Li fluttered her feet, swinging barefoot through the air.

Eddy lunged forward, his fist driving towards Tiger's midsection with incredible force. The impact of his strike reverberated through Tiger's body as Eddy's knuckles collided with his ribs, unleashing a wave of pain.

Tiger's breath hitched, his chest constricting as the blow connected with his solar plexus. The sheer power behind Eddy's attack left him gasping for air. Tiger's body doubled over in response to the pain.

Eddy wasted no time and capitalised on his advantage. He followed up by seizing Tiger's arm. Twisting it behind his back, Eddy applied a joint lock that pressed Tiger to the wall.

Gritting his teeth, Tiger managed to catch Eddy with his free elbow, loosening the arm lock. Taking advantage of the momentary reprieve, Tiger pivoted on his heel and launched a sweeping roundhouse kick towards Eddy's head.

Eddy ducked, narrowly evading Tiger's deadly strike. As Tiger's foot whizzed past him, Eddy used the momentum of his dodge to launch a counter-attack. Springing up from his crouched position, he unleashed a barrage of fast punches aimed at Tiger's exposed flank.

Each blow struck Tiger's body like a thunderclap. Tiger grunted, feeling the sharp pain intensify with every strike, but he refused to succumb to defeat. He braced himself, channelling his remaining energy into a defensive stance.

The fight raged on, a furious ballet of punches, kicks and defensive manoeuvres. Flying knees were thrown, kicks were caught and punches were slipped. Their bodies bore the marks of their clash. Bruises bloomed like dark flowers on their skin and cuts painted crimson lines across their faces.

But neither combatant showed signs of surrender. They pressed on, locked in a fierce struggle, the determination to appear victorious fuelling their every move.

A front kick from Eddy sent Tiger flying across the iron podium, his back hitting the platform. The young agent then discreetly glanced towards the continuation of the railing, where Fei's chair was bound. Tiger recovered, goading Eddy to attack again. Eddy obliged.

Eddy lost his balance, teetering towards the edge, but managed to grip the railing, averting a fall. Tiger closed in, ruthlessly raining down a barrage of strikes. Momentarily blinded, Eddy tumbled, his palms desperately clinging to the cold iron.

A flood of memories, almost in chronological order, flashed through Eddy's mind—moments they had shared together. The images blurred his thoughts, hindering his ability to rise. Tiger delivered a brutal blow across Eddy's face, jolting him back to reality.

Eddy drew a deep breath, summoning every last ounce of strength to drag himself up.

Exhausted, Tiger slipped backwards, his back colliding with the massive iron structure. Eddy rose, his feet dragging as he approached Tiger.

Leo watched on, willing Eddy to keep going. Even the gunman holding him hostage seemed reluctantly captivated. Seizing his opportunity, Leo spun around and delivered a powerful kick to the subordinate's hand, forcing him to release the gun. With a pinpoint strike to the temple, Leo rendered him unconscious. The weapon tumbled beyond the threshold separating the vast hall from Tiger's office. The sensor-activated sliding door started closing, ensnaring the gun inside.

Leo's nose crinkled in displeasure.

"Shit…"

Turning abruptly, Leo glanced upward at the colossal staircase and caught a glimpse of Fei, her head tilting softly, eyelids blinking lethargically. Li Li observed them intently, radiating quiet hope.

Stealthily, Leo ascended the right side of the stairs, intent on reaching Fei undetected. Li Li remained vigilant, surveying both directions. Upon reaching the chair to which Fei was bound, Leo pondered the best method of untying her. He had to take care to ensure that the chair wouldn't dislodge completely and send her plummeting.

"Fei! Fei!" he called her as he repeatedly tapped her cheeks.

Fei stirred sluggishly, her movements unresponsive. Leo prepared to untie her. Before that, he stole a quick glance at Li Li.

"Be careful," she whispered before closing her eyes shut to pray that Leo would navigate this delicate task without mishap.

Meanwhile, the duel continued. Eddy attempted a clinched knee strike, but Tiger executed a leg sweep that sent him crashing to the ground. Tiger capitalised on the opportunity and locked Eddy's arm into an armbar submission, applying intense pressure.

Leo managed to unravel the first knot, freeing Fei's hands. Placing his hand on the rope that secured her feet and the chair to the railing, Leo meticulously and cautiously tugged at the knot. As he simultaneously unravelled both knots, the chair slid with astonishing speed, threatening to send the young woman hurtling downwards.

Li Li flinched, her eyes widening in alarm.

Leo caught her under the armpits and was slammed into the railing for his efforts. Hunched forwards, he strained against gravity to lift Fei's lethargic deadweight back onto the platform. They collapsed into a heap on the frigid metal surface. Fei let out a sigh, her eyes fluttering shut. Leo beamed triumphantly, inhaling deeply as he lifted his gaze to meet Li Li's. She let out a relieved laugh as she continued to swing in suspension.

Cradling Fei in his arms, Leo embarked towards the metallic stairs, determined to find a safe place for her.

But with a single breath, their attention shifted to Eddy.

Tiger delivered a forceful kick to Eddy's back. Dazed and unsteady, Eddy tumbled onto the cold platform, sliding beneath the railing and vanishing into the skeletal framework of the colossal structure. Tiger also flinched.

"Eddy!" Li Li shouted.

"Eddy!" Leo whispered, taking a shocked step forward on the metal stairs.

Fei held her breath while still in Leo's arms.

"Eddy…"

The sliding metal door below them glided open and Boss stormed into the vast hall.

He clutched his bleeding arm, his forehead covered with sweat and grazes. The door closed behind him, sealing the exit. With a fleeting glance at his weary young agents, he drew in a deep breath. His eyes were heavy with sorrow. He pressed forward, uncertain of his initial course of action.

"Boss!" Leo exclaimed in a hushed tone, taken aback by his presence, while Li Li released a relieved smile. Boss navigated towards the right side of the staircase where Leo and Fei stood. Leo cradled Fei and came closer.

"Boss, where's everybody else?"

"All of this is my fault. Nobody else should be here to take the hits but me." His eyes glazed over momentarily.

Eddy extended an arm and clutched the edge of the iron platform. He clenched his teeth as he struggled to haul himself up. Blood trickled down his forehead, falling from his chin. His palms turned slippery. Li Li watched, breath held, witnessing his precarious perch on the verge of a great fall.

The iron wall shifted aside once more.

KB strode into the colossal hall and the wall sealed shut behind him. Standing with his arms held behind his back, his eyes were cold and bloodshot. Boss fixed his gaze on KB for the first time in decades. Leo froze, tightly embracing Fei.

Witnessing KB's presence, Tiger stirred from his exhausted state. A distinct type of disgust and animosity filled his heart. Observing Eddy's trembling struggle to grasp the railing, he shook his head. Another surge of hatred tainted his mind.

Tiger dropped to his knees and grasped Eddy's hand. Taken aback, Eddy lifted his eyes, still harbouring scepticism. Tiger encouraged him with a smile. He narrowed his eyes in struggle as he pulled Eddy closer, rolling him onto the metal platform.

Boss was determined not to be swayed by the haunting memories plaguing his mind. Eddy leaned against the frigid metal, striving to regain composure. KB raised a hand in salute.

"It looks like we're back here again, old man."

Boss descended the metal stairs, his focus on KB.

"Ah, as you can see," KB added, his voice oozing with a calculated blend of confidence and malice. His arms swept wide, encompassing his surroundings with an air of self-assured dominance. "Indeed I have been thriving, my friend." A sardonic laugh danced on his lips as he remarked, "It appears you have managed to gather your own little flock." His tone turned darker, laced with venom and disdain. "Yet, let us not be deceived by appearances. These supposed 'disciples' of yours are nothing more than treacherous vermin, scurrying about in the shadows," he hissed, each syllable laced with a poisonous blend of resentment and ruthless determination. "Just like their leader."

"It looks like you've got some disciples of your own as well." Boss gracefully moved forward while stealing a quick glance at Tiger, who remained engrossed.

"Indeed, indeed! If that is the label we wish to attach to it. You see... every individual is bound by their own destiny. Yet more often than not, disciples obediently trail their masters."

"Let's set the kids aside. What happened is between us two."

KB's smile widened as he paused to contemplate.

"So be it then."

Leo gently guided Fei towards one of the metal walls, his eyes fixed on her face as he tried to bring her back to reality. Almost instinctively, she shook her head.

KB circled around Boss in a fluid motion, meticulously preparing his wrists and neck muscles. Boss carefully observed every move, flawlessly mirroring KB's steps. KB raised his hands, showing that he was unarmed.

Eddy's breath caught as he witnessed a new side of his chief. He'd never seen Boss so quietly angry before. A tingling sense of danger prickled his skin and brought him back to his own situation. In a blink, Eddy realised Tiger had vanished. But this wasn't his biggest priority right now. Locking eyes with Li Li, he gripped the railing and contemplated a safe way to free her.

Tension hung heavy as the long-lost enemies finally faced off after two decades of bitter separation. The scars of their past clashed with the present, stirring up a whirlwind of emotions and an unyielding thirst for revenge.

They fought with practised precision, their strikes deadly and calculated. The deep-seated hatred in their hearts fuelled every blow. Their power and finesse defied their older forms as if they had been transported back in time. Every collision carried the weight of their shared history through their bones.

The fight raged on, their mutual desire to emerge victorious overpowering any doubts. In this long-awaited reunion, Boss and KB proved that though appearances might change with time, the spirit of a warrior never truly fades.

In the midst of it all, Leo gently caressed Fei's head giving her a warm smile.

"I'll be back in a flash, I swear! You know, it's just that I got a whole world to save right now!" he said, rising up and staring at that big old iron structure above.

When he saw that Eddy was healthy and alive, he dashed up the stairs with urgent haste. When he reached his friend, he offered him an encouraging nudge as his eyes brimmed with tears.

"Time to roll," Eddy cut in before Leo could utter a word.

"I gotta tell you, my friend, I love you! Thank you for staying alive!"

Eddy responded with a gentle shake of his head as if to dismiss Leo's words.

"Nobody loves me?!" Li Li chimed in while kicking her feet. "Well, guess what? I love myself loads! But right now, I just can't show enough self-love to figure out how to get down from up here!"

Both of them looked up, their eyes fixed on the rope securely binding Li Li.

In the lower part of the hall, KB got back on his feet, wiping the blood from his nose. Boss leaned on his knees. Using both hands to support himself, he struggled to regain his composure.

KB lunged in with a spinning back kick. Grabbing onto KB's thick cloak, Boss forcefully pulled him closer. The fabric tore apart, revealing KB's abdomen, surprising them both.

KB instinctively held onto his clothes, trying to cover himself up. His body was marked with scars and burns stretching from his shoulders to his hips. Boss stepped back, once again troubled by haunting memories of the fire of the past.

Seizing the opportunity, KB unleashed a powerful kick to Boss' chest. The impact resonated through the room as Boss crumbled helplessly, his head smacking against the cold floor. KB's breath seethed with fury as he approached. Boss struggled against the mounting odds to get back up, his hair matted with the deep red of his own blood.

Meanwhile, as Eddy reached the topmost stair, he positioned himself against the railing. He reached up and grabbed the winch that controlled the connection to the rope hanging in suspension.

"Can you swing?" Leo asked.

Li Li met Leo's eyes and silently agreed. She started to sway like a pendulum in motion, longing to bridge the gap and get closer to the railing.

Eddy's nimble fingers manipulated the safety, unlocking the winch from its stationary state and allowing the rope to begin moving. The rope descended slowly, effortlessly aligning Li Li with the railing.

"Give it everything you've got! Kick harder!" Leo urged her as he firmly planted his feet and reached out with both hands. Li Li kept swinging until Leo grabbed hold of her foot.

"I've got her!" Leo shouted, his attention quickly shifting to Eddy. "Just a bit more power, and I'll bring her in."

Eddy manned the winch, his eyes locked on Li Li. As he focused back on the machine, a screw popped loose. It dropped in silence, vanishing into the abyss. The cable unravelled, escalating the situation with a shocking burst of speed. Eddy fastened his grip on the handle, but the mechanism wasn't listening any longer.

The rope rapidly descended in an exhilarating drop. Li Li's heart sunk as she felt her body free-falling. Leo leaned over the railing, his chest colliding with it as he desperately reached out and grabbed Li Li's other ankle. He wrapped his leg around one of the vertical posts to anchor himself, causing him to wince in agony as he teetered on the edge. Almost being dragged down along with her, he laughed out loud, surprised at the sheer luck in this ridiculous situation.

Eddy ran across the platform towards them. Leo clenched his teeth trying to keep hold of Li Li. She felt a dizzy spell creeping in as she hung upside-down. Eddy joined them, positioning himself beside Leo's body to lean over the railing and offer assistance. He firmly grasped Li Li, summoning his strength to lift her up. Together, they pulled her to safety.

Exhausted, all three collapsed in a heap.

Li Li sat upright, still trembling and staring in the distance. Leo reached out to untie the binding ropes from her wrists. Her eyes locked onto Eddy's as she delivered a solid slap across his cheek. Captivated by the intense exchange, Leo watched closely. Shifting her attention to him, Li Li stood up and kicked his shin, causing him to double over in immediate discomfort.

"You two took forever! Never, and I mean never, leave me hanging like that again. Understand?"

In that moment, all eyes turned to Boss. Both he and KB stood on the brink of fatigue, their energy nearly depleted. The scars etched across KB's back spoke volumes of the battles fought and the sacrifices made.

Eddy took the lead, descending the stairs.

"How charming it is to witness your daughter blossoming into a remarkable young woman. She bears a strong resemblance to her dear old father," KB sneered, savouring the sight of Fei lying motionless and helpless on the floor. "I must confess, at times I've pondered whether permitting this delicate soul to exist was the wisest of choices. She was, after all, merely a sinless child. Yet what set her apart in innocence from any other child?"

Leo and Li Li froze on the stairs, their attention captured by the weighty words that reached their ears. Approaching the final step, Eddy turned his head towards Boss. A nod of approval from Boss was met with a deep sigh.

"Release the kids, they bear no guilt."

KB's pupils dilated noticeably.

"Twenty-three years have passed since I made the choice to walk away!" KB shouted. "I revelled in every moment of this new life, fully ready to leave my past behind. But fate had other plans when you showed up before me." KB unveiled a concealed pistol and aimed it at Fei. She awakened with a start, her eyes now wide open in dreadful realisation.

Leo and Li Li jolted into alertness. Eddy stepped forward, positioning himself as a shield for Fei. Simultaneously, Boss stepped in front of the two, protectively extending his arms.

KB cocked his gun. Eddy lifted his head, tears shimmering in his eyes torn between confusion and determination.

KB's fingers itched to shoot as Boss pushed Eddy behind himself.

Just as KB's finger began to squeeze, a deep noise seized his attention.

High above on the iron structure, Tiger had returned. At his feet was a rusty barrel. He hoisted it and cascaded its contents downwards.

Leo and Li Li rushed down the stairs as KB's face twisted in a combination of confusion and growing anger. The smell of gasoline filled the cavernous space as the liquid spread across the floor. With the speed of a striking cobra, KB pointed his gun at Tiger.

"What do you think you're doing, you bastard?!"

Tiger shook his head, revealing the lighter in his hand:

"I am not your obedient slave. I am my own king!"

KB flinched, as if a lightning bolt had struck his senses. Boss mustered his strength, making a concerted effort to stay alert. Eddy enveloped Fei in a fierce embrace, her arms clinging tightly to his neck as he lifted her off the ground.

KB circled around Leo and Li Li, making a beeline for Tiger. With a confident smirk, Tiger hurled his blazing lighter over the railing. The floor was instantly set ablaze.

KB's eyes widened in terror as he involuntarily took two steps back, his heart pounding in dread as the fire grew before him. The flames seemed to have frozen him in his tracks. His will to exact revenge helped him forge a few steps ahead, his trembling hand clutching the pistol ready to unleash its deadly payload on Tiger. But memories blurred his vision as he moved up the stairs. As he reached the platform, his arm was barely holding the pistol up.

Tiger struck with a force that propelled the weakened KB backwards. His weapon slipped from his loose fingers and clattered along the platform. With a spinning kick, Tiger sent KB tumbling over the railing.

As KB hurtled towards the ground, memories of laughter and love filled his mind—playing with his daughters, his wife by his side, their happiness a beacon of light. But another scene intruded, a haunting tragedy—their lives taken, innocence shattered by a fateful gunshot. An unfathomable mistake committed by the very police force he had served. Discarding his badge, he ignited his uniform, symbolising his abandonment of justice's path, which had failed him and his family. Gripping a knife, he stepped into the abyss of the Triad's darkness, where his fate lay sealed beyond the grasp of the raging flames below.

The boundaries separating vengeance from justice had become indistinguishable. He had detached from a system that had failed him. Amidst the whirlwind of chaos and moral uncertainty, KB's determination had remained firm, propelling him forward in his pursuit of understanding and closure.

As the final descent commenced, the once-dancing flames below him lost their importance, their fiery glow fading into insignificance. All that mattered now was the impending collision with the callous earth. A blow devoid of mercy, sealing KB's fate beyond the realm of the inferno. In that fateful instant, the conclusive impact marked the culmination of his destiny. An irrevocable conclusion that permeated through the very fibres of his being.

As the team stood motionless, Boss closed his eyes.

Without wasting a single moment, Tiger descended the stairs, his movements filled with urgency. He arrived next to Eddy, who protectively cradled Fei in his arms.

The flames began to advance at an alarming speed, engulfing their surroundings. Tiger pointed towards a concealed exit, sprinting in that direction and flinging open the door for both the agents and Boss.

As the door to his office room concealed them inside, a deafening explosion echoed around them, sending shock waves pulsating through their bodies.

Tiger urged them to hasten their escape. As they entered another door, a harrowing sight greeted their eyes—the subsequent rooms were already consumed by raging infernos.

With no other option, Tiger fearlessly led the way through the smoke-filled corridors. Weakened by his injuries, Boss felt his strength waning, each step becoming an arduous struggle. Exhausted but resolute,

Eddy declined Leo's offer to carry Fei. Leo grasped Li Li's hand, motioning for her to hurry up.

The flames danced all around them, their heat intensifying while the exit seemed impossibly distant. Machinery, drugs, money, jewellery weapons and documents—all were reduced to ashes before their very eyes.

Tiger pressed on, his hand firmly covering his mouth to shield against the smoke. Boss surveyed the scene and memories of past losses intertwined with the present chaos. Tiger surged forward, considerably outpacing them and pausing only when he was certain the path ahead was secure. One by one, he guided them through the final threshold before the exit corridor. He himself, then remained behind. Haunted by the spectres of his fallen comrades, Boss stumbled as he cast a mournful look over his shoulder.

"Hurry up!" he shouted at Tiger.

But it was too late. As if the very fabric of fate had conspired against him, a colossal chunk of the ceiling broke free, hurtling down with a resounding crash. Tiger's eyes widened in shock as he leapt back. His retreat was futile against the fire that now towered before him.

Frozen in terror, the team turned their heads towards Tiger, their expressions etched with helplessness. Boss frantically scanned the room, his eyes darting from one possibility to another, desperately seeking a lifeline to snatch Tiger from the jaws of certain doom.

Tiger cast one final glance at his companions, etching their faces into his memory. His eyes locked with Eddy's and a bitter-sweet smile curved his lips.

“Tiger, no!”

Tiger shook his head in contentment.

"This is where I belong, my brother."

He lifted his hand, giving Eddy a salute that showed his strong loyalty and unspoken bond of friendship. It was a salute that transcended mere military tradition, a testament to the respect and admiration he held for his comrade.

Before anyone could muster the strength to intervene, Tiger retreated deeper into the blazing chamber and searched for a sliver of sanctuary to close his weary eyes. Eddy's heart sank as he shook his head in disbelief, unable to comprehend what was happening. Yet, even in the face of imminent peril, Tiger's smile remained, urging them to act swiftly.

Time stretched agonisingly as their eye contact was forcefully torn apart by the merciless blaze. The flames engulfed Tiger. They shrouded him in a cloak of swirling fire, severing their connection with a cruel finality. The deafening roar of the inferno filled the void left in their hearts.

Boss's steely gaze locked onto the smoke-filled hallway ahead. The team sprinted with a new-found ferocity. Boss silently vowed not to let them falter and be a burden to the mission.

At long last, they reached the end of the corridor. A vigilant agent from the force spotted their arrival, a beacon of hope amidst the turmoil. He rapidly rallied the others, his commanding gesture slicing through the suffocating haze.

Coughing and choking, the agents caught a glimpse of the ethereal glow that bathed the early summer evening. A symbol of their imminent liberation.

Leo and Li Li stumbled, their bodies hitting the cold asphalt. Leo held his ribcage as he groaned in pain. Their sense of freedom and relief was palpable. Boss glanced at his team to ensure their collective escape to safety.

Strained from carrying Fei, Eddy lost his footing and crumpled to his knees.

In the distance, the wailing sirens of approaching fire engines echoed through the chaotic scene. The bright beams of rescue lights streamed down, casting a soft glow on the tired and bruised faces of the injured. With urgency in their steps, a team of dedicated medics sprang into action, reaching out to provide solace and support.

As the medics tried to pry Fei from Eddy's grasp, he resisted. His fingers were tightly clenched around Fei's body, refusing to let go.

“Sir, we need you to cooperate.”

The medics brought a stretcher, cautioning Eddy to remain still. Fei extended her hand. Much to his relief, she showed some signs of vitality. A wave of gratitude washed over Eddy as he tenderly brushed her cheek.

"Thank you," she murmured, relinquishing herself to the capable hands of the response team.

The medical team wrapped Boss's wound and urged him to step into the ambulance. Boss waved them off and strode towards Eddy. They closed in for a big hug.

"Thank you," Boss's voice quivered with emotion, his ageing eyes gleaming with gratitude. "For keeping your word," he whispered, his voice carrying the weight of countless memories. “To each and every one of you—thank you, from the depths of my soul. Thank you for staying alive."

The medics commanded their silence, ushering them into the ambulance. Laughter erupted from both.

Strolling towards the cars, Eddy shot Leo a sharp military salute. Without missing a beat, Leo mirrored the gesture. Li Li grinned, extending a casual salute in a friendly manner.

In a seamless display of finesse, Leo spun on his heels and smoothly snatched Li Li's shoulders, sporting an exuberant smile.

"Look into my eyes and let me feel your vibes. It's all up in the air tonight! Can you smell it?" he said, his tone almost filled with seriousness.

"What, did you fart?"

His expression turned sour, his hands dropping down dejectedly.

"If you're gonna clown on me too, I'm done with both of you! You and Eddy ain't nothing but—"

She interrupted him with laughter, seizing him by the lapels of his blanket. Bravely pressing her lips against his, she expressed gratitude for all the moments shared, then clasped him from behind his neck. His palms tenderly caressed her cheeks, finally revelling in contentment. Just like in Hollywood.

Police car lights surrounded the crowded street. Ambulance sirens announced their imminent departure just as the fire-fighters arrived. The remaining Triad members who had managed to escape through the secret exits were arrested right away as the other young agents called for reinforcements.

Leo and Li Li joined their squad as the doctors sealed the ambulance door. At that moment, their gaze met a mysterious figure. Leo prompted a puzzled glance at Boss.

The tall, dark-haired individual politely extended his right hand towards Leo.

"Good day, my name is Jean-Luc Philippe Achille Yves René Bullion, secret agent from Paris."

Leo sat there, mouth hanging open in astonishment. Boss nodded in acknowledgement.

"*L'État, c'est moi!*" Jean-Luc then recited with a wise expression. "And justice! I am the justice!"

Leo rolled his eyes.

"Who said that, Hitler?"

Jean-Luc frowned as he held his breath. He shook his head to come back to his senses.

"Anyway, I'm pleased to brief you on our upcoming mission. My team has already been preparing the materials."

"Oh, piss off!" Leo waved his hand and leaned back against the ambulance wall.

Eddy rested his head, a tired smile on his face as exhaustion overwhelmed him, leaving him too drained to even laugh. With a tender motion, he securely held Fei's hand, her delicate fingers concealed under a cosy blanket on the stretcher.

Jean-Luc leaned in once again.

"Agent Leo, I am thoroughly impressed by your remarkable expertise. It is my utmost pleasure to be your partner in this forthcoming mission."

Silence fell all around them as they waited for Leo's reply.

"Stop the car, man! I'm getting off." Leo wiggled around, trying to climb over to the door. "I've had enough of this craziness. Ain't nobody got time for all this nonsense any more!"

The team burst into laughter as the ambulance embarked towards the hospital, its sirens resonating like a triumphant trumpet heralding liberation.

Chapter XVII

Three months later.

The soft grass in Boss's yard had turned into a lively green hue. The front door was wide open, allowing the refreshing air to circulate and fill every corner.

With a beaming smile, Boss carried more trays of food than he could hold and set them on the table next to the bright window. When he changed the tablecloth, Boss had made a solid choice to leave the past behind and embrace whatever the present and future held in store.

Eddy quickly got up and offered his assistance, but Boss declined with a smile, telling him to relax and not get in the way. Fei chuckled, thrilled to have her father back as the person she had longed for. As they all relished their day off, the room was filled with a large group of comrades. The agents grabbed plates, eager to dig in and help themselves.

Wearing a mischievous grin, Leo produced a small ring and a book from behind his back, presenting them both to Li Li. His gesture captured everyone's attention, resulting in some of the agents cheering. Blushing, Li Li peeked through her lashes.

"Are you asking me to marry you?"

"Jeez!" he frowned. "I'm asking you to be my girlfriend."

Li Li snatched the book from his hand, realising it was a cookbook.

"*How to Save with Jammes Olive*"? Are you joking?"

The rest of the agents erupted in laughter.

"Wait, hold up!" Li Li shouted, her voice dripping with anger. "So you're saying I'm wasteful? Nah, nah... That's not what I'm about. So you think I'm just in it for the cash?"

Leo shook his head, making Li Li even angrier. She balled her fist, ready to punch him. But instead she calmed down and forced a smile. Leo looked at her, completely puzzled by her sudden shift.

"Just hand over that damn ring already!" she exclaimed, her hand moving insistently.

Leo grinned as he placed the ring in her palm. She wasted no time and slipped it on her finger, her eyes gleaming with joy as she admired it. Leo revealed his own hand, proudly showing off a matching ring. The young agents applauded, their loud and excited voices filling the room with happiness.

"I'll love you until one of the actors on my phone goes through a divorce," she quipped, a mischievous glint in her eyes.

"What?"

Boss shot a quick look at Eddy, silently indicating the need for a private chat.

They stepped outside into the yard, casually walking along the path beneath the clear, wide-open sky. After a while, Boss stopped, facing Eddy with a friendly smile.

"Even to this day, I am filled with gratitude to have each and every one of you gathered here."

Boss rested his palm on Eddy's shoulder, a gesture of appreciation and reassurance.

The quest to locate the bodies of KB and Tiger proved utterly futile, given the circumstances at play. However, all the apprehended mobsters faced the full force of justice, resulting in their arrest and subsequent sentencing. Depending on the gravity of their participation, they had received either life imprisonment or indeterminate sentences ensuring they would pay for their actions for an extended period.

Not long after the incident, the Mobster-President and his security team were also apprehended by the authorities. Leo, being considerate, took the initiative to send the President a carefully selected CD containing Mozart's entire collection, along with other timeless classics. He also took the opportunity to advise the President about removing the imposing portraits that adorned his office walls.

The exact number of remaining Triad followers would always remain uncertain.

"You love her, don't you?" Boss asked with a smile.

Eddy winced.

"I'm sorry…?"

"Now now, don't play games with me. It's crystal clear. My seasoned eyes can spot it from any angle. You're quite fond of my daughter, aren't you?"

Eddy chuckled while intentionally avoiding making eye contact. Afterwards, he forcefully coughed attempting to compose himself with a serious and respectful demeanour.

"Yes, sir!" he responded, standing up tall and adopting a military-like posture.

Boss warmly patted Eddy on the shoulder before affectionately stroking his back.

"You're one lucky guy because I love you like my own. But let me tell you, should you ever cause her to shed a single tear, you'll find yourself six feet under."

Eddy stood there, momentarily speechless, his mouth hanging open. He attempted to laugh but could only muster a strained smile, clearly caught off guard by his boss's dark humour.

In the evening, Eddy, Fei, Leo and Li Li decided to separate from the rest of the group and take a break from the party.

Eddy took the driver's seat, with Leo joining him in his favourite spot. Fei and Li Li hurriedly joined them. Before they left, Eddy touched the photograph hanging from the rear-view mirror, which was a picture taken at the amusement park featuring Tiger.

They drove through the city until they turned onto a quieter path leading to a beautiful landscape. The night sky was filled with stars, the grass was lush and the sound of crickets covered the evening atmosphere.

Eddy parked the car and stepped out to admire the surroundings. Fei joined him, leaning against the car door.

Meanwhile, Li Li darted into the darkness hoping to catch an insect and play a prank on Leo. Leo on the other hand, ran in the opposite direction feeling the urgent call of nature.

Now alone, Fei took Eddy's hand and smiled while she watched the sky.

"A shooting star!" she then exclaimed, pointing with her index finger. "Isn't that classic?"

"Well, what did you wish for?"

Fei smiled and moved away from the car door, taking a step forward. As she approached Eddy, she squeezed his hand. With this gesture of approval, he gently kissed her.

Leo finished his business and walked through the thick grass, intending to return to the road. Lost in the tranquillity of the moment, his foot unexpectedly collided with a solid object, jolting him out of his reverie. Curiosity piqued as he halted and glanced down, his eyes locking onto an old, weathered vial half-buried in the earth. Its delicate glass seemed to hold countless untold stories within its confines, beckoning Leo to uncover its secrets.

His fingers trembled slightly as he reached down and carefully lifted the vial from the ground. The weight of history rested in his palm as he examined it, noting the detailed engravings and the faint remnants of what appeared to be an ancient inscription. It was a remarkable find, a relic from a past era.

He chucked it back into the grass.

"Counterfeit rubbish, man! People be throwing their shit everywhere they can."

He stepped back onto the road and sprinted towards his comrades.

Left behind, the vial rolled through the thick grass.

The clouds parted, revealing the gateway to the parallel world as the vial unfurled, forging a link between times.

The vial gracefully rolled again through the rain-kissed grass of past times.

General Lai Ji halted his search, wiping his damp face with the back of his hand. The black whirlwind materialised in front of his eyes. Within it emerged Princess Fei Yan, her eyes brimming with tears. Uncertain if she was a tangible presence or a figment of his longing, the young general remained motionless. However, as the princess approached with a radiant smile, she leapt into his waiting arms.

"Thank you for enduring such a long wait, my General!" she exclaimed, her voice barely reaching his ears amidst the unceasing downpour.

He pulled her into a tight embrace, a warm smile escaping his lips.

"My heart yearned for your presence, my dear Princess! The days without you stretched for eternity."

In the distant halls of the Imperial Court, a chilling silence hung heavy. As the emperor's lifeless body lay motionless, the rain continued its steady descent, incessantly cleansing the stains of his spilled blood.

Amidst the ominous tableau, a rebel appeared, his countenance bearing an uncanny resemblance to that of Tiger. A second rebel seized the moment and stepped forth. He cast aside his own disguise to unveil a heavily scarred face—the very individual consumed by an unquenchable thirst for the *king's blood.*

With sinister laughter that resounded through the empire, the scarred man mercilessly drove his sword into the abdomen of his loyal subordinate. The mirror image of Tiger crumbled to the ground, blood spilling from his lips.

With a gaze filled with unabated loathing, he fixed his eyes upon his leader for one final moment. His suspicions were validated and revealed the insatiable desire that burned within his leader for the imperial throne.

As the resonant echoes of approaching footsteps reached General Lai Ji's ears, he tightened his grip on Fei Yan's arm, embracing her with unshaken protectiveness.

Now surrounded on both fronts by the rebels, he cautiously retraced his steps. His vigilant gaze never faltered while ensuring the princess remained in close proximity.

Their adversaries composed an encircling formation, brandishing their menacing blades. Clinging to the general's arm, Princess Fei Yan struggled to catch her breath, her lungs weighed down by the heaviness of the torrential rain. Amidst the cascading downpour, Lai Ji meticulously surveyed his surroundings. A resolute vow silently forged within his heart to safeguard the princess. At any cost.

The veils of time gracefully descended, resuscitating the present era with renewed vitality and vibrancy.

Leo skipped joyfully towards the car and leapt onto the back seat, eager to enjoy the view from that spot. Meanwhile, Li Li came back with a sense of disappointment as she hadn't managed to catch any insects.

Sensing something amiss, Leo furrowed his brow when he touched the back seat. Eddy approached in a rush as he saw Leo dismantling his seat.

"What're you doing?"

Fei and Li Li rushed closer.

Leo pulled out a briefcase concealed beneath the seat. He opened it and astonishment spread across everyone's faces. The briefcase contained stacks of banknotes.

"Well, damn!" Leo exclaimed while giving the money a quick sniff.

Eddy discovered a hidden photo tucked away on the side of the briefcase. As he carefully lifted it, the image revealed itself to be the group photo captured by Tiger during their memorable visit to the amusement park on that particular day.

"Tiger…"

Li Li and Fei smiled in astonishment.

"Agent 00...?" Leo murmured, unable to look away from the briefcase.

"Yes, Agent 00," Eddy replied with a wide smile.

"What about a holiday for the four of us?" Leo asked, closing the briefcase with finesse and carefully stashing it under the seat.

"We're not keeping these."

"Oh yes, we are."

"We can't be holding onto these. I'm taking this straight to the department."

"Oh come on, my friend."

"Leo, no!"

"Half of it then."

"No."

Leo sulked and settled into his seat next to the driver. Fei gently patted the back-seat and both she and Li Li carefully sat down, diligently safeguarding the briefcase. Just before Eddy started the engine, Leo retrieved a pair of sunglasses. Eddy raised his eyebrows.

"What's going on?"

"You know what, my friend," Leo said with a thoughtful voice. "I've had an epiphany, my friend! It hit me like a truck! Truth is, not everyone can possess that unbeatable *swag* factor, you feel me? Little Kevin Lee knew what he knew."

Stretching his hand towards the radio, Leo instantly stumbled upon the perfect song.

"Call me Leo, call me Leo," Leo mimicked simultaneously with the music, mastering the moves as he nodded his head in rhythm. "Eddy, listen!"

Eddy shook his head.

The car effortlessly embarked on the open road, gliding with an air of undeniable coolness.

"Come on, half."

"No."

"A few banknotes?"

"No!"

As they ventured into the mystical night, streaks of shooting stars wove an enchanting tapestry.

Concealed among the towering blades of grass, the small vial trembled with a revived energy. A surge of anticipation filled the air as a profound and expansive dragon silhouette materialised, steadily emerging from the confines of its enclosure.

The ebony mist grew denser, seeping into the thick undergrowth. With an eerie vitality, the curse awoke in this unfamiliar realm, vowing to swiftly pursue its unsuspecting prey.

Ramona Lee Soo-Jun is a German-Romanian novelist and screenwriter currently based in London, United Kingdom. In 2012, at the age of 14, she wrote her debut novella "Destinul unei Flori de Primăvară" (The Destiny of a Spring Flower) within a 28-hour period. By the age of 19, she had published 11 books.

Lee adopted the pen name "Lee Soo-Jun" starting with her first publication to address issues of racism in the publishing industry, as Asian character names were frequently rejected by publishers. Upon turning 18, she legally changed her name.

In 2015, during the launch of her first "Agent 00" volume, Lee was recognised as Romania's first martial arts-action novelist.

In addition to her action novels, Lee has published works spanning romantic comedies, psychological dramas and fantasy genres.

Milton Keynes UK
Ingram Content Group UK Ltd.
UKHW012142040923
428018UK00004BA/289

9 781739 278632